Healed
by you

The Harbour Series

Book 2

I0598218

Christy Pastore

Copyright © 2017 by Christy Pastore
First Edition, 2017

Cover photographed and designed by Sara Eirew of Sara Eirew Photography, www.saraeirew.com

Editing provided by Missy Borucki, missyborucki.com

Book formatting provided by Stacey Blake of Champagne Book Design, champagnebookdesign.com

Publication Date: September 19th, 2017
ISBN: 978-0-9907099-9-2

Healed
by you

Some relationships go far beyond the Hollywood backdrop.

Fake romantic relationships have always been a thread woven into the fabric of Hollywood. In the old days, studios played the matchmaking game simply to promote their movies. Today the game remains the same, only now the stakes are higher and the players ever changing.

The two of us knew what rock bottom looked like and we needed a way out of the rubble before it destroyed our careers and our reputations.

From multiple staged paparazzi appearances and charity polo matches in the Hamptons to romps in the Caribbean and even being seen together at a high-profile celebrity wedding, the plan was simple—an agreement that would benefit all involved.

But, falling in love was never part of the plan.

And for two famous friends, one summer in the Hamptons could change everything.

Dedication

For my husband, Kevin—
Once upon a time there was a young woman who needed to be
loved. Your love healed me.

Author's Note

This book is the second in The Harbour Series—it absolutely can be read as a standalone.

For those who might be new to my writing or this series, I am so glad that you found me! And let me be the first to welcome you to East Harbour.

Earlier this year, I had the pleasure of reading Ava Gardner's biography as I was in the midst of writing HBY and something clicked. I fell in love with the glamour of the Golden Age of Hollywood all over again, if that was even possible. I started thinking about the studio fix-ups and what happens beyond the backdrop of Hollywood and thus, Healed by You transformed into something magical.

This story is perfect. It's better than I ever dreamed possible, and I'm really happy about that. Moreover I'm glad that I've given Grady and his lady the HEA they so richly deserve.

I hope that you enjoy "Healed by You." Grady and his lady are something special.

"I believe that everything happens for a reason. People change so that you can learn to let go, things go wrong so that you appreciate them when they're right, you believe lies so you eventually learn to trust no one but yourself, and sometimes good things fall apart so better things can fall together."

—Marilyn Monroe

Chapter
One

Grady

The bagpipes played that familiar tune. The choir joined in.

How sweet the sound.

Even amongst the sniffling, sobbing, and whimpering cries, the song was beautiful. I hoped it would provide peace to those who were in agony, like me.

She had mentioned this song to me before. I wondered if she could hear it.

My hands shook as I grasped the cool metal. We lifted her casket, and each note carried us out of the sanctuary and down the steps and towards the car that would take her to the cemetery. Her final place of rest.

The doors to the hearse closed.

The church bells rang out, as more people offered their condolences.

I climbed inside my limo. Just me alone.

I looked for a bottle of booze, but then I remembered that I'd asked them to dump every bottle. Every single one.

The car ride was short, and yet, I wished it were longer. I wasn't ready to say goodbye, I needed more time. We should have had more time. Tears cascaded down my cheeks, and my heart faltered. The pain in my chest was unbearable, as if I was being torn apart from the inside out.

At her gravesite, my hand rested against the top of the casket. "Baby, I will always love you. Thank you for giving me the greatest gift I could ever receive; your love was everything to me."

Ashes to ashes.

My hands shook, as I drew in a deep breath. "Your life was my life's best part. Rest in peace, my love."

Dust to dust.

My wife was dead, and so was my heart. Nothing could heal me now.

Except my wife wasn't dead, presently she was bent over the kitchen island with her personal trainer, Nate's dick pumping in and out of her. My marriage, on the other hand, was dead. *Time of Death, 6:39 p.m., November 7th.*

I'd just given the performance of a lifetime for my most recent film and I'd come home to find Heather giving Nate a performance of her own. Her black Lululemon leggings dangled from the leg she was standing on, while the other leg rested atop the silestone countertop. Nate's left hand fisted her blonde hair, the right planted firmly on her hip as he slammed into her.

"I'm going to come, baby," he growled and slapped her ass just as the crack of thunder boomed outside. Heather yelped and with a quick movement dropped to her knees.

That's when I involuntarily started a slow clap from the foyer.

"Wow, well done, Heather," I chided, before depositing the bouquet of calla lilies into the trash.

"Mr. James, it's not what you think, sir," Nate choked out, as Heather popped off his dick. How could this guy engage in formalities when my wife's mouth was wrapped around his dick? Definitely bleaching my eyes after this fucking experience.

"Things look crystal clear from my vantage point."

"Grady, oh my God," she shrieked stumbling to her feet.

I rolled my eyes watching Nate scramble to pick up his clothing that was scattered from the kitchen, to the dining room and outside onto the terrace. Heather struggled, unable to find her balance while attempting to slide her leggings up her slender legs. With her piss poor balance, I was definitely overpaying this guy for his yoga instruction. She wiggled her hips and finally got the material up over her ass. Not even going to lie, I would miss that ass.

Contemplating the situation at hand, I leaned against the wall. Heather attempted to pull herself together, while I kept an eye on Nate. I wasn't going to be "kicking his ass," the dude was stacked and I've learned that fighting with one's fists usually doesn't resolve matters of the heart. Case in point, my Indigo Row brawl with Ronan Connolly a few years ago that cost both of us some bad press.

On the other hand, the rage boiling inside me was probably all I needed to tackle the motherfucker and lay him out flat on his back, but I didn't need that kind of trouble and he could sell his tale to the tabloids. He strutted back into the kitchen like he owned the place—that set me off.

"Nate, I suggest that you leave *now*, get the fuck off my property. Consider me *not* paying for this session."

Nate hustled, scooping up his bag and mat and then making a beeline for the front door.

Heather took a deep breath. "I can explain Nate and me . . ."

Holding up my hands, I returned my gaze to my wife. "Save the explanation. Although I do have a question, how long have you been screwing him?"

"It was a onetime thing, I swear," she replied, wringing her hands together. Her blue eyes welled with tears, stabbing at the pain that radiated in my chest. She staggered towards me grasping my forearms. "Please, Grady, we can work this out."

"It's done, sweetheart, there is nothing to work out aside from the division of assets. Starting with this place, it's definitely going on the market."

Tears streamed down her face. "No, please don't do this," she pleaded as she stalked toward me.

I'd skipped post-production cocktails with the cast and crew to come home and celebrate with my wife. This film could potentially be the blockbuster that catapulted my acting career into the spotlight. I'd spent the last few years teetering between movies, television, and modeling. Modeling paid the bills, and I was very lucky that in my early thirties I was still able to book as many gigs as I did, but I wanted more—*more* translated into building a life with Heather, sharing our successes, and our setbacks. Over the years, I'd had my fair share of both, but *this* was a devastating blow. No pun intended.

Disgust sank into the pit of my stomach as I trekked up the stairs and down the hallway to our bedroom. Heather jogged behind me, trying to keep up with my rapid pace. My hands shook as I jerked the suitcase from the walk-in closet.

"Grady, what are you doing?" she asked, eyeing the suitcase.

Brushing past her, I tossed it onto the bench at the foot of the bed. Her eyes went wide with fear. "You can't leave!" she shouted, her voice was laced with panic.

"I'm not leaving, sweetheart, *you* are," I growled, turning back towards the closet.

Sobbing, she moved to stand in front of me, blocking my path. "I'm standing my ground. We have to talk about this."

"I can't look at you. The mere sight of you makes me nauseous."

She whimpered, running her hands through her hair. "You want to throw away our life? Our marriage? Over this?"

"I didn't throw it away, *you* did." I snapped my fingers and pointed at her, again, my involuntary reflexes taking over. I went into the closet and grabbed a stack of her shorts and tops.

Tears rolled down her face, and she wrapped her arms around her body. "It was a mistake, it was *one* time."

"And you think that makes it all right?" I asked, tossing her clothes into the suitcase. "I suppose I should be grateful that it wasn't an emotional affair of the heart."

"I don't know why this happened, I'm sorry. It meant nothing to me."

Heather slumped on the edge of the bed, burying her face in her hands, as her sobs turned to wails. It physically hurt to see her upset and crying, but none of that erased what happened, she'd been unfaithful. Not even therapy could heal the fact that she'd broken our marriage vows. I believed in second chances. I did. I just didn't believe that everyone deserved them.

"You have twenty minutes to pack your shit and leave. I don't care where you go, but you're not staying here."

She pushed to her feet, swiping away the tears. "So, this is really over."

I nodded and pointed to the closet. Despite the fact that my heart was crumbling under a hammer of pain, I wasn't faltering. Muffled sobs came from the closet, along with the sounds of drawers opening and slamming shut.

I scrubbed my hands down my face, counting to ten as I inhaled a deep breath. Walking to the window, I leaned against the glass, overlooking the canyon stretched before me. *Fuck.* I loved this house. It made California tolerable. At heart though, I was an East Coast guy.

East Coasters said what they meant, even if they could be rude at times. West Coasters, especially Hollywood types, they lie, they all told you what you wanted to hear.

"How . . . *when* would you like to announce our separation to the media?" she asked, smoothing her ponytail.

Turning to face Heather, my arms folded over my chest. "I think we should let our publicists decide."

"Fine. Can I ask a favor?"

"Not that you're in any fucking position to ask me for any favors, but let's hear it because I could use a good laugh."

"Can we agree to keep this incident out of it? I don't want the cheating leaked to the media."

"Do you think I want it broadcast to the world that you fucked your personal trainer? It's a fucking cliché, even for Hollywood." I shoved my hands into my pockets. "I swear to God, Heather, if you strike first on social media you will live to regret it. We have a prenup and it's ironclad," I reminded.

Expelling a deep sigh, she tugged a jacket over her shoulders. "I forgot about the prenup."

"Yeah," I huffed. "It seems that you did or the free porn show I viewed wouldn't have happened in our home."

"When I get settled, I'll send for the rest of my things."

I followed her through the study and the den as she gathered up her purse and a few miscellaneous items—her laptop and the chargers for all her electronics. Her fingers drifted over every piece of furniture, frame of artwork and surface as we made our way to the entry.

"For what it's worth,"—she pivoted to face me, her palms settling on my chest—"I'm sorry, and maybe we should sleep on this before making any rash decisions."

Oh, she was good. I wasn't totally blind to Heather and her ways of persuasion. I had opted to push through all that and just see Heather Young, the woman and now all I saw was Heather Young, actress—manipulative, ladder climbing, man-eater.

"Save the act for your next husband, sweetheart. You nearly ruined me once, and stupidly, I forgave you." I side-stepped her, clutching the door handle. "You fooled me twice, shame on me."

I gave her a loving nudge out the door and she rewarded me with a middle finger kiss off. As I watched her climb into her white Range Rover, I mentally cataloged a list of all the things I needed to get in order.

Pulling my cell from my pocket, my fingers hovered over the screen contemplating which call to make first. After grabbing the key from my hiding place, I walked to the bar in the den and then poured a glass of scotch. With Heather in and out of rehab, I decided to never keep booze in our home. Over time Heather got sober, and focused her energy on therapy, clean eating, and daily exercise. Those became her coping mechanisms, instead of booze or drugs.

One night she came home and presented me with a bottle of Johnnie Walker Blue Label and told me to drink up and then lock it up. Ten minutes later, a custom crafted bar cabinet was delivered. That was Heather, always full of surprises. Today was most certainly a surprise. I swiped the number and then pressed the speaker feature.

"Hello, Grady, what can I do for you?" My publicist's melodic southern accent sang out through the Bluetooth.

"Haven, I'm getting a divorce," I stated matter of fact.

"I'm sorry to hear that," she replied, her fingers flying over the keyboard. "Are you okay?"

"As okay as I can be after walking in on my wife fucking her fitness instructor at the kitchen island."

"Oh, ouch, so sorry, but if I may say. . ."

"I know how much you love being right, so is this the part where you say 'I told you so'?" I asked, before downing the final remnants of my drink.

"While, I do love being right, this is something I don't take any pleasure in," she replied, tapping against the keyboard. "Except for the fact that I won . . . fifteen hundred dollars."

I choked out a laugh. "You bet on my divorce with Heather? Who else was in the pool?"

"You don't really want to know that, do you?"

"Along with being correct, I know that you love being direct."

"That I do."

"Giving it to me straight, that *is* why I pay you the big bucks," I reminded, and poured another drink.

"We bet on how long the marriage would last. Your friend Ronan had ten months."

"That doesn't surprise me," I grumbled.

Ronan Connolly would be getting a call from me soon. It wouldn't be to harass him about the bet, I didn't care about that, I needed him put this place on the market.

"Okay, getting back to the matter at hand, my divorce. First, I want the best lawyer."

"You don't *need* the best," she interrupted. "You caught her cheating and you have a prenup, you'll get everything. But, since you are seeking my advice, go with Hersh, he's repped Denise Richards and Camille Grammer, or go with the DissoQueen. I'll schedule a lunch with Donna and the two of us will work out a joint statement for the press."

I dropped to the sofa in the den. "I'd like to leave the cheating out of this because the public doesn't need to know that, and I'm sure she'll agree to irreconcilable differences. However, because we are dealing with Heather, draft a few social media posts for me in the event that she decides to spin her story first. I need to be prepared. If she tries to imply that I was the one cheating, I have no qualms with resorting to petty tactics."

"You don't need to stoop to her level. You're the bigger star."

"Save the morality speech for another day."

"Consider it done."

I ended the call, and tossed my phone on the cushion beside me. This wasn't how I saw my day ending—alone and on my way to being good and drunk.

During filming earlier in the day, I channeled all my emotions; pulling from somewhere deep inside thinking about living in a world, existing in a space where my wife wasn't there. It sucked balls. Poor choice of phrasing given the situation at hand.

I'd felt the stress melt away once I'd showered and

changed after filming, because I had been on my way home to see my loving wife to celebrate. Now there was nothing to celebrate. Everything had changed, everything around me was cold, dark and hollow.

Chapter
Two

Harlow

S itting outside on the terrace of Caffè Torino, sipping a bicerin, the Turinese specialty drink made of espresso, bitter chocolate and whipped cream—*this* was my favorite part of the day. It was hard to believe that I had been living here almost a year.

My eyes scanned over the piazza, there were very few people on a laptop, a tablet or some kind of electronic device. Practically, everyone around me was talking, having real conversations. I adored the rhythmic tone of the Piemontese speech, the stressed consonants sounded like a commanding poem confirming one's affection for their true love. I've grasped a good portion of the Italian language, but I was no expert. Bringing the glass to my mouth, I blew across my drink. The outdoor heaters were on because this spring day was especially chilly. I didn't mind though; the city was bashfully beautiful hiding under the Alps with its misty grey skies.

Pulling my pashmina tighter around my neck, I concentrated on the article in front of me. I was weeks away from launching my new website—Cocktails and Couture dot com, a fashion, beauty and lifestyle website where I would be sharing my style secrets and favorite cocktail recipes. My agent told me that I'm a "global influencer."

By social media standards I was already popular being a lingerie model, and over the past few years I had been on Instagram sharing my street style and behind the scenes moments from my photo shoots.

When I started dating goalkeeper, Harry Brackman, my brand exploded overnight. Harry had been on loan from Chelsea to Juventus this past season. He was the first Englishman to play for an Italian team in thirty years and the team was hitting on all cylinders. A championship was a real possibility.

As much as I loved living here, I was chomping at the bit to get back to our home in London. I swiped over the most recent text message from my publicist confirming an upcoming photoshoot for Minx Bag in New York.

My phone pinged with a breaking news alert from Tinsel and Hollywood dot com.

It's the end for Grady James and Heather Young.

I swiped open the app and began reading though the story.

"We entered our relationship with love, and it's with love, respect, and kindness that we leave it."

Sadness filled my heart. Man, this was not the way to find out two of your friends had called it quits. Although, I used the term "friends" loosely, more like we ran in the same

Hollywood social circles. Heather introduced me to Grady backstage at the Nadia's Dream fashion show after they first started dating. Not to mention, Grady and I share the same publicist, Haven Cardwell.

Hollywood Vibes was the next outlet to report their split followed by *People* and then *TMZ*. Unusual, that they weren't the first media site to report any rumblings.

"Is this seat taken?" a deep voice asked. Not any voice, it was a voice that was quite familiar.

My breath hitched, when I looked up confirming the sight of his intense dark brown eyes staring back at me. They were the exact shade of the drink in my hand. After slipping my phone into my bag I gestured for him to take a seat. "Harry, what are you doing here? Did your training sessions go well?"

"Yes, so well that Brian gave me the rest of the afternoon off," he replied smoothly, signaling for a server. "We need to have a talk."

Dread filled me and my stomach sank. These are the last words I expected to hear.

"Un caffè corretto alla congnac, prega." The server acknowledged his order and Harry returned his gaze to me.

"I need to focus on my game—finish the season strong. And with the World Cup on the horizon, I think it's best if we cool things down a bit."

I stared blankly as his words swirled around me. Despite his rough, warm hand on top of mine rubbing softly, it didn't take the sting away from the words—*break-up . . . sorry . . . unbelievably sorry . . . distractions.* Each one sliced through my soul like a knife through soft butter.

"You did nothing wrong, please know that . . ."

The blood rushed to my ears, as my eyes darted from

table to table. My body shook and sweat climbed up the back of my neck, spreading over my skin like hot lava. He was dumping me and in public no less, knowing perfectly well that I wouldn't . . . *couldn't* make a scene.

"Harlow, I love you, I never wanted to hurt you."

I blinked up at the sound of his voice, numbness settled around me, gripping my heart and squeezing. Tears cascaded down my face and there was nothing I could do to stop them from falling.

Chapter
Three

Grady

I awoke to a splitting headache and swollen eyes. When I found more than the strength to just stare up at the ceiling fan, I managed to drink. Pain flooded my heart as it did every morning when I woke up remembering the image burned in my brain of my ex-wife being fucked like a porn star in our kitchen.

Pressing my palms into my eyes, I tried to scrub the memory from my mind. I stumbled over the rug, crashing into my dresser and sank to my knees. Groaning, I pressed my cheek to the floor, seeking the coolness of the hardwood.

Flashes of light and darkness mixed together. My temples throbbed with ache, and the memories from the last few weeks blurred together. After spending a month in my Manhattan loft, avoiding everyone and everything social except some unavoidable work commitments, somehow, I'd been persuaded to attend a party.

My agent scored me an invite to one of the hottest events of the year. The place was packed wall to wall with actors, models, athletes, and musicians. I wanted to avoid the stares, and the hushed whispers about the broken-hearted Grady James, so I tried to stay under the radar. Under the radar consisted of a shared bottle of tequila with a twenty-two-year-old Brazilian swimsuit model, neither a great choice for my health.

I think that chick broke my dick.

Enough time had passed since the divorce decree. Three months to be precise. I should be over Heather by now and enjoying being underneath a hot model riding my cock. I pushed up from the floor and managed to hobble down the stairs. Early light poured in from the windows, although it was still pretty dark. By my guess, it was probably five-thirty. The early morning surfers were undoubtedly gathered on the beach suiting up. I'd join them, but I was too tired.

I don't even remember how I ended up at my house in the Hamptons, but the one thing I did know was that I hadn't left this place since I'd arrived. In fact, I wasn't sure how long I'd been here, but it's been some time and my dick has healed so that's a plus. Days were long and slow, nights even longer. It had been weeks since I'd had a full six hours of sleep at night.

After downing half a bottle of water, I plodded to the couch, dropping like a bag of wet cement. Exhaustion hit me like a freight train, and the bottle of water slipped from my grip when I tried to place it on the coffee table. My eyes closed, but I managed to reach out tugging the blanket over my body.

"Mr. Grady, you need to pay me now."

Camped in front of my television wearing only a pair of old grey sweats, I looked up to see my housekeeper, Thora, standing with her arms folded, tapping her foot against the tile. She was annoyed about something. Bobbing her head like a clucking chicken, her lips were moving but I couldn't make out what she was saying. All I heard were the sounds of booing coming from the TV. Some bleached blonde, trailer park princess was yelling at her redneck boyfriend . . . husband . . . maybe it was her son. Clearly whacked out of her mind, this broad was the "rode hard and put away wet" kind.

"What is it, Thora?" I said, shoving a hand through my long hair.

"You need to pay me, Mr. Grady. It is Friday . . . *payday.*"

"Oh . . . okay."

Friday? Is she fucking serious?

A few years ago, Thora came highly recommended by Mrs. Carrigan, my nosy neighbor. Which for the most part, I appreciated her looking out for me.

Standing up from my couch, I then walked down the hallway to my study. Feeling a little light headed, I stumbled hitting the wall with force. My eyes lifted, I caught my reflection in the hallway mirror. *Jesus!* I looked pale as fuck. My skin was ash grey. Apparently, I'd been working on my lumberjack look with this scruffy beard. My eyes were glassy and that was when it hit me, the smell of sweat and old gym shoes. Images of the basketball locker room in high school came to mind. *Yep. That horrid smell is me.*

Scrubbing my hands down my face, I mumbled, "I need to get my shit together."

I opened my safe and pulled out a few hundred dollars. I preferred to pay Thora without the logistics of going through my accountant. Balancing my household expenses made me feel like a normal person with a grasp on reality, not the La La Land life.

Reality smacked me in the face, hard. I knew that I couldn't continue down this path. I needed to pull myself out of this funk and become a functioning member of society again.

"Here you go," I said with a grin.

She shook her head and walked away. I got the feeling Thora was as disappointed in me as much as I was with myself. The door closed behind her and I sighed with relief.

After a quick shower and shave, I pulled on a freshly washed pair of denim jeans and a grey zip-up hoodie. Grabbing my keys, I hit the road and parked my shiny black Mercedes at my favorite restaurant: an old-school diner that served the best cup of coffee you've ever had.

"Grady James, welcome back to The Harbour, sugar," Nancy, the owner called out to me over the ringing bells. Nancy's Diner was a local hot spot, and had been around for thirty years. Wiping her hands on her checkered apron she rounded the long counter and greeted me with a warm hug. Her thick, jet black hair smelled of syrup and bacon.

Minimal creases appeared around her eyes, when she smiled, it lit up the entire room. Pulling back from our embrace, her light brown eyes gave me a once over.

"Sugar, you are much too skinny these days. What kind of work they got you doin' out there in Tinsel Town?"

Her question was as charming as her southern drawl. Shaking my head, I gripped her shoulder and said, "Work is just fine."

Fine and just fine were the only emotions I could seem to admit openly to feeling. Angry, pissed off, distraught, helpless, overwhelmingly sad and gutted were my true feelings—the total cliché of a broken man. But, as long as my mental faculties were with me I would shove those way the fuck down, because showing them would only get me sent straight to the therapist's office.

The only healing I needed was the ocean. Surfing or sailing the waves, the ocean was truly the last free place on earth. I think Bogart said something like that.

The diner was barely packed mid-morning on a Friday, a few locals sat at high-top wooden tables and a group of fisherman huddled together in two small booths. The smell of fresh pancakes and apple-cinnamon from the baked goods case made my mouth water. I saddled up to the far end of the counter and Nancy poured me my usual cup of coffee: black with a pinch of sugar in the raw.

Placing the steaming mug in front of me, she said softly, "I was really sorry to hear about your divorce. How you holding up, sugar?"

I put my hand over hers and lied. "I'm doing okay, doll. Thank you for asking."

"What can I get you to eat?" she asked, pulling her notepad and pen from her apron pocket.

"A short stack with blueberries and a side of maple brown sausage." Before she turned to walk away I gave her my irresistible smile to further my case in the "I'm just fine, the same Grady James" façade.

"You got it."

I scanned the diner, sipping my coffee. The place was nearly the same as it was last time I was here, it was a comforting feeling. I practically grew up here.

My father was a writer, and over the years he penned dozens of books and screenplays during our summers spent in The Harbour. He took me to the Polo Club and bought me my first pair of riding boots. I learned to swim, surf and sail all on the waters that surrounded The Harbour. This town held an abundance of fond childhood memories. My parents were so vibrant here I was moved by the nostalgia of it all, giving me cause to buy a place.

"Here you go," Nancy announced placing the hot plate in front of me. "Can I get you anything else?"

Unwrapping my silverware, I shook my head. "No thanks, Nancy."

I ate my breakfast in comfortable silence, occasionally drumming my fingers to the music piping through the speakers. My phone pinged with a message from my agent.

Jennifer: Don't forget the casting call today. I'm sending you the information. .

Fuckity Fuck. Fuck. I forgot this was today.

Me: Do I really need this job?

Jennifer: I'm not your accountant but, if you'd like to purchase that damn sailboat you keep talking about, yeah, I suggest you attend this callout.

Me: Yes, Boss.

Chapter
Four

Harlow

"Rise and shine, sleeping beauty."

The voice belonged to Afton Buchanan, my former college roommate. I'd been staying at her place in The Hamptons since Harry decided to rip out my heart. Nothing like being told that you're a physical, mental and emotional distraction to your significant other's professional career.

Pushing my eye mask up onto my forehead, I let out a long groan. "Do I have to?"

"Yes, there is only so much sulking I can allow you to do," she said, plopping down on the edge of the bed. "You're coming into the office with me today. We have a casting call and I'd like you to take over our Instagram for some behind the scenes exclusives."

Afton was the President of Buchanan Beauty, her family's

cosmetics company. I had mad respect for her; she was a tough as balls business woman, not an entitled rich Daddy's girl who was handed the corner office. Instead of taking the summers off to party and travel the world during college, she spent her time at the company studying sales figures and listening to lectures on the latest remedies in skincare.

I rolled up to a sitting position. "I don't know, Afton."

"You're officially done moping, Lo," she ordered, rolling up to her feet. "You need to get out of bed, and back to the land of the living." She moved to stand in front of the mirror, fluffing the ends of her dark brown hair.

As much as I wanted to crawl back underneath the sheets and sleep my life away, she wasn't wrong. It was easier to hide away and not face reality that my perfect life had fallen apart. It was easier to ignore the fact that the man that I loved more than anything in the world had shattered my heart. Every morning when I woke, I hoped and prayed that it had all been a bad dream.

"Come on," she said, grasping my wrists and tugging me forward. "Take a shower and then put on something cute. I'll schedule you for hair and makeup when we get to the studio."

I laughed. "Okay, okay fine. I'll go with you."

"Excellent." Afton's smile grew wider, highlighting her dimples and the twinkle in her blue eyes. "Get moving. We're having breakfast on the patio in thirty minutes."

My head rested against the headboard and as I scrolled through the notifications reading the morning headlines and gossip. Nothing interesting.

For a moment, I allowed my thoughts to drift to Harry and my fingers itched to Google his name. I wondered if he was telling me the truth about our relationship being a distraction, or if he had fallen in love with someone else. My mind retreated to the darkest places. The only time his name appeared in the tabloids was in direct reference to soccer. Nothing personal.

We agreed to keep our break-up out of the media. It's not like we needed to release a statement to the press. We weren't married, but twenty months together felt like years—wonderfully happy years.

My publicist urged me to leak our break-up to the tabloids. She tried to convince me that it would be beneficial to the launch of my site. My moral compass had the better of me, and I absolutely refused.

Who knew that decision would turn out to be the biggest mistake of my life?

Chapter
Five

Grady

"**S**he did *what*?" My words screeched, vibrating back through the speakers in my car. I couldn't hear a fucking thing except for my own words ricocheting through the Bluetooth.

"This morning, Heather went on *Wake Up with Stacy* telling the whole world how you made her go to rehab." Haven's voice rang out once more enunciating the words with flair.

"I *did* make her go to rehab. This is not news."

"No, not like that Grady, she went on to say that you told her going to rehab would revitalize her career. Telling her that she wasn't a good actress and this was the only way to get her back in the media spotlight."

Shit. Fucking shit.

I slammed my hand against the steering wheel as I pulled onto the main drag in the middle of town. How anyone would believe a shred of truth to Heather's story was beyond my comprehension. *Heather and her goddamn publicity stunts.*

"It's all lies and total bullshit. No one is going to believe Heather. Her past is littered with fabrications. She's not exactly a stable source."

"There's more . . ."

"More? How can there be *more*?"

"Heather said outright that you were emotionally and mentally abusive."

"Oh fuck that shit!" Rage coursed through my veins.

Haven exhaled a long sigh. "I'm sorry, Grady, the press is having a field day with this one. She actually started crying on cue, I guess her acting skills were on point this morning."

I had loved Heather so much that I made her go to rehab for her wellbeing, because I wanted her to be around for a long time. At the time, she was spiraling out of control with pills and booze. The fucked-up part about all of it, is that Heather *was* a good actress. Not only that but she wrote poetry and had a lovely singing voice. Sometimes she would go down to the Jazz Bar in Los Angeles in disguise and sing during one of their open mic nights. When I could, I'd sit in the back, drinking a beer and just listening to her while she performed.

She has real talent.

"Do you have a plan, Haven?"

"If there is one thing I know about Heather Young it's that she loves the spotlight. I don't think you should say anything. We could refute her lies, but we all know that she is just looking for attention. Instead, I think this is a case where your actions speak louder than her words."

I let Haven's words roll around my brain, because everything inside me wanted to call Heather and give her a piece of my mind. No good would come from that conversation. Knowing Heather, she would record the call and then leak it to TMZ, giving the public her version of my "angry" side.

I needed to pour my emotions into something positive.

"Send me a list of events happening with my favorite charities. I'd like to do some volunteer work."

"I'm on it, boss," she replied. "And don't sweat this situation. You're going to nail that call out today and then we can turn our focus to something positive."

"Thanks, Haven." I killed the call and Rebel Desire's latest single blasted through the speakers. If I didn't have this call out, I'd keep driving. If I had my way, I'd be on a boat or my board surfing those waves.

Okay, time to put the Heather situation on the backburner and focus on the task at hand. I didn't need the money, but this campaign would set me up for a lot of good things, especially financially. Plus, I could essentially take the entire summer off if I landed this job.

Chapter
Six

Harlow

"Call outs are my favorite," Afton squealed, before taking a drink of her iced tea. "I can't wait to see these hotties in person."

I rolled my eyes. "Hey, President Pervy, here's an idea, how about not treating the models like pieces of meat?"

She pursed her lips together. "You're no fun."

"I'm about to bring some of my super awesome 'bursting with fruit flavor' fun to this Instagram account of yours so send in the models."

"We've got about fifteen minutes," Afton replied, shuffling through the folders splayed in front of her. "Today, I am looking for someone who will capture the confidence of a refined but rebellious spirit. A man with a natural, alluring masculinity, and an effortless sense of style."

"Aren't we all," I chided, pushing up from the chair. "I'm

going to get a bottle of water. You need anything?"

Afton leaned across the table to tap the intercom. "I can have Kayla bring you anything you need."

"No, no," I said, standing. "I'll go to the executive break room and grab one. Besides, I need to stretch my legs."

It was a short walk to the executive breakroom. The lobby outside the conference room where they were holding the call out was starting to fill up with pretty faces. I recognized a few faces, a lot of *new* faces. I remembered my first casting call like it was yesterday. It was hard not to stress over what to wear to the audition. My biggest fear was that I'd forget the photographer's names that shot the pictures in my book if the casting director asked.

I pulled a bottle of San Pellegrino from the refrigerator and then grabbed a bag of almonds from the pantry. Sagging against the hallway wall, I swiped my phone and glanced through my messages, I had about ten from Haven.

"Excuse me, are you here for the model call?" I heard a deep voice ask from behind me.

I turned around to see a face that I was all too familiar with thanks to magazine covers, television and billboards.

Grady James had a picture-perfect face—luscious lips, a strong jaw with just the right amount of stubble. Let's not discount his dreamy blue eyes and his long brown hair that fell perfectly over his brow. A human God chiseled from marble and sculpted masterfully, standing in front of me wearing a grey t-shirt and dark denim oozing James Dean cool attitude.

Dayum. So much for taking my own advice, I just objectified him seven ways to Sunday.

"I can't find the receptionist," he said glancing up from his phone. "*Hey* . . . Harlow, it's good to see you."

Shaking the lustful thoughts from my mind, I refocused.

"No, I'm not here for the model call. Do you use that line on every woman you meet?"

With a laugh, he stepped forward giving me a warm embrace. "No, I'm genuinely lost," he admitted, releasing me from his hold. "Plus, I think Haven gave me the wrong room number."

When he pinned his blue eyes on me, and I could see he looked as if he hadn't slept in days. His complexion was pale and his skin was visibly ashy. Despite looking a little out of sorts, he still managed to take my breath away, but this simply wouldn't do.

He cocked a brow, drawing my focus back to his eyes. "Why are you looking at me like that?"

Pivoting on my heel, I tossed over my shoulder, "Come with me."

He strode up beside me. "Thanks."

"Are you sure that you're a model?"

"Been in the business since I was twenty-two, I'm sure."

"Why didn't you bring your A-game today, then?" I challenged.

Sighing he scrubbed a hand over his jaw. "I know, I know. I think I drank too much last night."

"That's a big no-no, and I suppose that you had a ton of caffeine this morning and not enough water. If I was betting woman, and I am, I bet you also had a greasy breakfast."

He held up his hands. "Guilty as charged."

We turned the corner and walked into one of Buchanan's spa treatment rooms. Glancing at my watch I knew that I had at least twelve minutes to get Grady ready for his audition.

"What are we doing in here?" he asked, shoving his phone into his pocket.

"I'm saving your ass, park it in that chair." I pointed to

the makeup chair and then handed him my bottle of mineral water. "Drink up, all of it."

"I never knew that you were *this* bossy," he said as he twisted off the cap.

"You call it bossy, I call it being assertive," I replied, sifting through the stash of samples. I needed a brightening serum and eye-cream.

"Touché," he said, before tossing back a drink. "So, if you're not here for the call out, what are you doing?"

Would Grady like the short version or the long version that included my heartbreak and homeless situation? He didn't need to hear my drama. I guessed that he had enough of his own problems from the way he looked walking in here today.

"Afton, she's the President of the company . . . we were college roommates, anyway, she asked me to take over their Instagram account today for behind the scenes exclusives."

I found a sample of brightening cleanser, and the directions said that it could be left on up to ten minutes. As much as I wished I could put a redefining mask on his skin, this would have to suffice. "Step over to the sink, I need you to use this cleanser and leave it on your face for at least five minutes."

His fingers laced over mine when he reached for the bottle. Grady's hand was warm and his fingertips were rougher than I expected. What I didn't expect was a zap of electricity shooting over my skin.

My eyes met his, the man had intense blue eyes and his brow game was strong. He held my gaze, and nodded to the bottle that I was still holding onto. "Oh . . . sorry," I stammered, shaking my head. Sidestepping him, I turned on the faucet and pulled a towel from the bin.

What the fuck was that? It's been a few weeks since I've

had the touch of a man and this was my reaction? He must have picked up on my needy desperation.

"This stuff smells awesome," he said, pumping the cleanser into his hand.

"Yeah, it's one of my favorite products," I admitted, picking up the bottle and then twisting the cap. "It's going to clear out your pores and extract those dead skin cells. You won't believe how this stuff brightens up your skin."

"Thank you for your help, I don't want to fuck this up." He blew out a deep breath and dropped into the chair. "Honestly, I forgot I had this call out today. My agent sent me a text while I was having breakfast. I'm afraid I've been off my A-game for a while, far too long."

My fingers ached to reach out and touch him. Anything to feel the rush of tingles again, I'd love to run the back of my hand down his cheek to that sexy five o'clock shadow. That jawline could have its fucking way with me.

Wow. Okay, enough, Harlow.

"We all have our off days," I offered, giving nothing more. My belief was that silence was better than bullshit. However, this was a special case, and all of us do have off days, so not total bullshit. I didn't want to pry into his personal business, but I had a feeling that Grady was referring to his very public divorce. There were accusations of cheating on both sides that was about as much as I knew thanks to a copy of *US Weekly* in the gym. Not *entirely* credible journalism.

Pivot. Subtle topic shift needed now. Otherwise I would feel compelled to commiserate with him.

"What did you have for breakfast?"

He furrowed his brow. "Huh?"

"You said your agent reminded you about today over breakfast. What did you have?"

He smiled that slow heart stopping smile again. "Pancakes . . . a short stack with blueberries and a little bit of whipped cream and a side of maple brown sausage over at Nancy's Diner."

"Best French toast on the coast," I said, grabbing a bag of cotton balls. "Man, I love that place, I'm afraid I haven't had a chance to go there since I've been back."

I busied myself with the self-appointed task of restocking the makeup stations with sponges, cotton balls and mascara wands.

"Oh yeah, you've been living in England, but now you're back?"

I exhaled a sharp breath. "Yeah, I've got a new website to launch and some other projects going on, so moving back to the States made sense."

Little white lies.

"Can I take this stuff off yet?" he asked, running his thumb along his jawline.

"Yeah, rinse and then pat your skin dry."

I'd be lying if I said that I didn't want this moment to last a little while longer. Besides the fact that Grady James was easy on the eyes, the conversation was easy. It was always nice talking to someone who was in the business. In a way, it made me feel normal. If being famous could be considered normal.

Looking at me in the mirror, he smiled. "Do you have any inside tips on what they're looking for today?"

Resting my hip against the counter, I watched as Grady washed his face. "You don't need my help for that. I know for a fact that you've been to thousands of these things."

I was certain there were very few things that Grady needed help with, and I could only assume that he excelled naturally at everything.

"Next, I'm going to have you apply a vitamin C serum and then an all-day moisturizer." I popped the cap off the bottle placing it beside the sink. Then I had him apply the moisturizer. Once he finished, I tidied up the vanity area wiping down the faucet and the counter top.

"Why haven't you and I ever worked together before?" he asked giving me that famous pretty boy smile of his. "I mean we have the same publicist, so you'd think Haven would have tried to get us together at one point."

The meaning of his words, they were laced with innuendo, but I knew better than to make that assumption.

I lifted a shoulder. "Maybe there hasn't been a project she thought that suited us both."

"Hmm." He cocked a brow, and sidestepped to stand in the doorway. "I'm not convinced."

"The Sage Conference Room is where you need to be for the call," I replied, switching off the lights.

"Thanks again, Harlow," he called over his shoulder. "You saved my ass."

Chapter Seven

Grady

As I sat in the hallway outside the conference room my fingers itched to swipe open my phone and read what the tabloids were saying about me and Heather. It was driving me crazy and I don't know why I should care, I never allowed these things to bother me before, not even after our divorce.

Two of the models sitting across from me kept whispering and pointing to their phones. I rubbed my palms over my thighs. The urge to ask them what they found so interesting was strong. I needed a distraction like a book or a magazine to read.

The door to the conference room opened and a young brunette appeared. "Grady and India, they're ready for you both."

As India and I strolled through the doors, I saw Harlow

standing off to the side near the photographer.

"Hey there, good to see you again, India," the woman with brunette hair called from behind the table. "I'm Afton Buchanan, so nice to meet you in person, Grady."

From the corner of my eye, I caught Harlow's head lift in my direction. At the sound of my name, she smiled giving me a subtle thumbs up. Somehow having her in here made me feel less on edge.

"Likewise, Ms. Buchanan."

After a round of rapid fire questions from the panel, the casting director ushered India and me over to the photographer. The photographer introduced herself as Alice and then instructed us on what she was looking to capture. We took a few test shots. Something was off between the two of us. It was probably on my part.

"I think I'm going to be sick," India whispered in my ear.

I pulled back from our embrace. "What?"

"Are you hot?"

I shook my head. "Do you need water?"

"I feel dizzy. . . I can't tell if it's just nerves or something more." India's hands trembled as she gripped my forearm for support.

"Can we take a break? India isn't feeling . . ." She went limp in my arms before I got the last word out. *Shit.*

India was still conscious, mumbling broken syllables. I lowered the two of us to the floor, dragging her back against my chest. Harlow and the photographer rushed towards us. My bet was that she didn't eat breakfast or worse that she had been starving herself for this audition.

"Here's a bottle of water," Kayla offered.

"It's okay, India, everything will be just fine," I reassured. My hands gripped her shoulders as she struggled to lift the bottle to her lips. After a few minutes, India was focused, but still hazy. The director asked her if she thought she could continue with the session and she politely declined. I helped India to her feet, and Kayla escorted her out the door to the seating area.

"That was scary," I admitted to Harlow.

She nodded in agreement. "All the color drained from her face, she looked like a ghost."

"I'd like to get a few more shots with Grady," Afton announced. "Harlow, do me a favor and stand in with Grady."

"What?" she asked.

"I need a female figure. You're a model and the same height as India. It will be painless, I promise."

We took our marks, and I wrapped my arm around Harlow's waist pulling her against me. A warm, sweet fragrance curled around me, I inhaled deeply getting my fill of honey and peach. Taking direction from Alice like a pro, Harlow's hazel eyes landed on mine.

Fuck. She was insanely gorgeous. Surely, I'd noticed this before. As we changed up our positions, I thought back to all times I'd had encounters with Harlow.

"Great job, you two. I'm getting some great stuff here. Have you ever worked together before?"

"No," Harlow spoke up as her eyes met mine.

"Well, you should because you two have sensational chemistry," Alice said, placing the camera onto the table.

A dark blush spread across Harlow's cheeks as she stepped back from our embrace. "It's probably because we've known each other for a few years."

I nodded in agreement. But, in truth, what did I really know about Harlow Trembley? One thing was certain, I was overcome with the fascination of finding out much more.

Chapter
Eight

Harlow

"Saturdays were made for spa days," Afton said, tipping her champagne glass in my direction. After refilling our glasses, I sat back feeling totally relaxed. The Hawaiian sugar scrub treatment was doing wonders for my feet.

"And in celebrity news, Actress Heather Young dropped a bombshell on daytime television. In an interview with Stacy Carlton, the Common Place star alleged that her ex-husband, actor/model Grady James, made her seek treatment for drugs and alcohol. The Emmy nominee revealed that he was both emotionally and mentally abusive."

My champagne glass hit the edge of the end table when I jolted upright in my chair at the news coming from the television. I stared at the screen as the video clip rolled showing Heather with tears carving two mascara stained paths down her cheek and Stacy grasping her hand in comfort. Her words were vile and tasteless.

"Whoa," Afton murmured. "She *can't* be serious."

I shook my head in disbelief. "No, *no way*. This is a total fabrication. Heather spiraled out of control days before Fashion Week. I know for a fact that she went to rehab voluntarily."

I knew because she called me from the rehab facility "spa" telling me how much sympathy she would get from the media and her fans. She just knew that she would be back on television or the catwalk in no time. My fingers flew over the screen of my phone as I scanned the comments section on Tinsel and Hollywood dot com. I'd turned off all my notifications for all the gossip sites right after Henry ended things with me.

"What are they saying? Do they believe Heather?"

"Heather is getting a lot of sympathy, but Grady has more celebrities speaking out for him."

"If this goes bad for Grady, I don't think I can hire him for the campaign. I can't take the negative publicity."

"Oh, come on," I scoffed. "When have you ever cared what the public thinks?"

"I've always cared a little. More so since my sales figures took a hit last quarter," she staged whispered across the space between our chairs.

"I blame Cynthia," I shot back. "That bitch was nothing but trouble for you."

"At least she had the good sense to publish after my father passed away."

Cynthia Manson, Afton's ex-stepmother, wrote a nasty tell all book about the Buchanan family. The book was mostly fabrications, however the stuff about Afton's father was true, rumors of womanizing, philandering, gambling, and a hefty dose of political scandal. It hit the bestsellers list and Buchanan Beauty took a sizable financial hit through the holiday season.

"Luckily her time in the spotlight quickly burned out. I have no doubt that the company will bounce back, especially with this new campaign. I just cannot take any more negative press."

"I understand," I said, before taking sip of my drink. "I'd hate to see Grady lose this opportunity because of Heather."

"Since when do you care so much about Grady James and his career?" Afton asked, eyeing me over the rim of her glass.

I shrugged, leaning back into my seat. "I don't know. I kind of felt bad for him yesterday. We talked a bit before the call out, I got the feeling that he had been going through a rough time ever since the divorce."

That was the biggest reason I believed what Heather was saying was nothing but a pack of lies. Grady looked as if he had been the one put through the emotional ringer. It made me wonder what exactly happened that ended their marriage. And I know that it is none of my concern or business, but for some reason my heart ached for Grady.

"And now we turn to sports. All eyes will be on Russia with the World Cup only days away and Team USA is gearing up to play England in the first round."

My heart slammed into my chest at the words tumbling from speakers. Before I could stick my fingers in my ears and hum aloud, Afton had the manager switching channels.

Afton dragged me out to The Hutton Summer House for a lobster boil and cornhole tournament. The sky was streaked a magnificent shade of lemony yellow and tangerine as we pulled up to a historic sprawling whitewashed estate. Stylish couples walked hand in hand up the gravel driveway in their staple East-Coast, preppy attire, bright Lilly Pulitzer and striped J. Crew dress shirts. It was all very matchy-matchy, like they planned to have photos taken for their annual Christmas card. So, the two us fit right in—Afton in her billowy, white Issa dress and me in my Isabel Marant silk-crepe dress. I loved yoga pants just as much as the next girl, but it's always fun to get dressed up.

Gazing around the property, I sighed taking in the perfect scene right out of a Ralph Lauren catalog. Couples sat in Adirondack chairs facing the ocean watching the classic Chris Crafts, wooden Rivas, and catamarans rock back and forth. Umbrellas and blankets as colorful as the men's coral and lime green shorts dotted the croquet course.

We stepped up to the bar—the Belle de Brillet Champagne Cocktail, Cherry Blossom Martini and classic gin and tonic were the specials for the evening. Cooling stations sat at either end of the bar, adorable pitchers of water infused with strawberries and mint. If staying hydrated wasn't your thing there were handheld oriental fans and parasols.

Strands of lights hung overhead illuminating the way, as we took our champagne cocktails over to the comfy seating area near the fire pit and cornhole boards.

"Here's to a night to remember," Afton professed, clinking her glass to mine. "Let's get you laid tonight."

I nearly choked on my drink. "Um, if this is your plan for the evening. I'd never have come out with you."

We all have that friend, the one who thinks we need to

get laid, like our lives are in turmoil if we're not regularly getting dick. Actually, I should be worried about Afton. I had zero knowledge of her current, dating situation. The last guy I remembered her telling me about was the investment banker from Boston.

"Tell me about your sex life, Afton," I mused, smiling at the guy sitting with his significant other one seat over.

"No, this is not a topic for discussion." Her voice trailed off as she pretended to fumble with her phone.

"Look, I'm not going to force you to talk to me about your dating life, and I know that your mom taking off for parts unknown is weighing heavily on you. On top of that, online dating sucks balls . . ."

She waved me off, eyes still focused on her phone. "Yeah, yes . . . online dating is full of weirdos. Much like carbs, I've cut dating out of my routine."

I sipped my drink, realizing Afton wasn't going to open up about her love life. For all I knew she was texting a booty call. "So, why are we here, exactly?"

Afton hummed and held up a finger, still committing to the role of pretending to be on her phone, checking messages or emails. "We're here because you need to be seen and meet people." She rocked back and forth, bopping her head up and down. "Meet people and party. *Party* and *meet people.*"

I rolled my eyes. "I *so* don't need to meet people and party."

"Speaking of meeting people," she said, while jutting her chin towards the far end of the lawn. "Do I spy with my little eye . . . some eye candy named Grady James?"

The answer was, yes. Yes, she did. I hid my smile behind my martini glass. "What did I tell you about ogling the models?"

She shoved her phone back into her clutch. "It's part of my job," she replied, running a hand through her newly sun-kissed highlights or babylights as she referred to them. "It's not wrong to appreciate the male figure in all it's delicious glory. It's polite."

"Polite, ah yes." Crossing my ankles, I sipped my beverage. Moments of my time in Europe flashed back through my mind including my last day in the piazza. Polite society, much like there, tonight everyone was engaged in conversation. They weren't snapping a hundred selfies trying to get the right angle or make sure they had photographic evidence of each little moment. No, they were enjoying those little moments, being present. That's what I loved so much about The Harbour.

"What are you thinking so hard about over there," Afton asked.

"The decline of polite society."

She shifted, placing her elbows on her knees. As much as Afton loved clichéd girl talk, she enjoyed obscure topics of discussion more.

"Are manners, politeness, and courtesy simply dead rituals or are we as a society destroying them?"

No sooner had I asked the question than two people walked past us, saying hello to Afton, and then nodding in my direction. I smiled and said hello.

"Good question, if I'm being honest I think people are destroying them—manners exist for a reason."

A shadow passed over us, and I looked up to see Grady James standing in front us. Being this close to him, nearly took my breath away.

"Harlow, Afton, nice to see you both again," Grady said with his eyes trained on me as if Afton and the guy standing next to him didn't exist.

His blue eyes, those damn blue eyes of his, they were beautiful. The kind of eyes you get lost in and I guess I did because they rendered me speechless.

"Harlow? Are you okay?" Grady asked waving his hand inches from my face.

"Oh sorry," I said, shaking the cobwebs. "I thought I heard . . . *fireworks* across the sound."

"Ridge Stephens," he said, lobbing his drink between Afton and me. "I'd like you to meet Harlow Trembley and Afton Buchanan."

During the brief exchange of pleasantries, I learned that Ridge played polo with Grady. He was good-looking, tall with broad shoulders, dark brown eyes and dirty blond hair. When Afton invited the two of them to sit with us, I took that as a good sign that maybe tonight was a cheat day where her dating life was concerned.

"What were the two of you talking about when we came up?" Grady asked, setting back onto the cushy chair.

"We were discussing the fall of polite society."

Ridge nodded, tossing back a swig of his beer. "Look around, this is the last of polite society."

I nodded in agreement. "Manners and politeness are designed to ease an awkward or uncomfortable situation. Even if someone bumped into me, I say I'm sorry. It's not that I'm admitting fault, I'm acknowledging that it happened and that there was no malice intent behind it."

The three of them nodded in unison.

"The other day I was at the grocery and a woman," Ridge began, setting his beer bottle on the table. "Certain societal norms will say that I'm not allowed to address her age or her height as a probable issue, however she couldn't reach the item that she needed on the shelf. As a man, do I insert my manners and offer help or do I walk away and allow her to work it out on her own?"

"I say insert your charm and be gentlemanly," I replied, and tipped my glass to him. "I have no problem with it at all."

"And just because I can't reach a can of tomato soup off the top shelf, for me, that doesn't translate that a man is trying to fuck me or assert his male dominance," Afton added.

"I think it's nice to offer help," Grady spoke up. "Manners are designed to acknowledge others. There's no need to complicate the matter of opening a door with feminism or being a gentleman. It's simply a door that needs to be opened and it's flat out rude to slam it in a person's face."

"Here, here," Ridge announced, tipping his beer bottle in our direction. "To reviving manners and basic politeness."

"To chivalry," Afton added.

I chimed in, with the final anecdote. "And common respect for your fellow person."

The four of us clicked our glasses and engaged in idle chit chat until refreshers were needed.

Ridge pushed to his feet. "Afton, would you care to join me for a round of croquet?"

"I'd love too," she replied.

They walked away leaving Grady and me alone. I didn't expect to be face to face with Grady again, well, at least not this soon. My eyes shifted to his hands, the same hands that held me close to his body hours ago.

He scratched at the skin under his watch. "Hey, there's a row boat over there," he said, pointing towards the beach. "Let's get some drinks and take it out."

I shrugged. "Can we do that?"

"I don't see why not, I think it belongs to Hutton House."

A sunset boat ride with Grady James, this should be interesting. Grady distracted the bartender with a conversation about New Zealand wines while I grabbed a bottle of champagne. The warm breeze drifted over my skin as I hopped down the steps, taking in the smell of fresh cut grass.

Grady appeared beside me, just as I kicked off my heels. I wasn't about to get sand on these new strappy Jimmy Choo's. Once he took his own shoes off, he helped me to climb into the tiny turquoise colored boat, and then pushed us into the water.

As I took a deep breath, a familiar scent filled my senses: salt and seaweed. As much as I loved city life, there was nothing more heavenly that the vast ocean. During the school year when Afton was missing home, we'd drive out to Rockaway Beach so she could feel closer to the sea. She missed beach hair and the gusts of salty wind on her skin. At one point, I wondered if Afton was a real-life mermaid.

The light passed over Grady's face and I recognized that same sullen look he had before the photoshoot. He stopped rowing and we drifted along as the sun sank lower over the horizon. The sounds of waves lapping against the boat drowned out the music coming from the shore.

"I just wanted to tell you that it was really great working with you yesterday," he said, pulling the oars from the water.

"Oh, no, you were the star that day. I was just filler."

His brows rose as he tapped finger along the edge of the boat. "That's not true, the camera loves you. We had plenty of great shots together that prove it."

No, the camera loves you.

"Well, thanks." I handed him the bottle. "I hope you get the job."

"So do I, I could use some good . . ." He cut himself off,

and lifted the bottle to his beautiful perfect lips.

"Good press, because of ex-wife drama," I offered, tucking my hair over my ear.

"Oh, you heard about that?" His voice cracked with laughter.

"Yeah," I admitted, dragging my gaze to meet his.

He passed the bottle back to me. "I never thought loving someone would hurt so much. I made her go to rehab because I loved her enough to see her well."

I paused to take a gulp of champagne. I understood what Grady was saying, Nicholas and I tried a few times to get our mother to rehab, but she refused help. She was convinced she could quit anytime, and she would—for a while.

"Well, I've sufficiently killed the mood," he said, dipping the oars back into the water.

I smoothed my palm up my arm, trying to relieve the sudden chill from the breeze coming off the water. "No need to apologize, the mood is perfect for eating lobster and playing lawn games. Wouldn't you agree?"

"I would definitely agree,"

Chapter
Nine

Grady

The week crawled by at an agonizing pace. The paparazzi were all over me after Heather's publicity stunt on *Wake Up with Stacy* was reported by every media outlet and somehow even the *NBC Nightly News* decided our former marriage was an interesting story for the evening broadcast. My concentration was off a bit during polo practice and Ridge wasn't shy to let me know I sucked.

The only moments of peace I had were early mornings when I'd hit the waves on my board. The ocean air wrapped around me, reminding me of another peaceful moment—my time with Harlow at the Hutton Summer House shindig.

"You haven't touched any of your food, Grady. What's the matter? Does the quiche not taste good?"

I looked over to see Ella Connolly frowning. "It's not a new recipe. I've made it at least a dozen times. Did I forget an ingredient?" she asked out loud to no one in particular.

"Babe, it's delicious. Stop stressing out," Alex said.

"It's all great," I said, digging my fork into the home fries. We were sitting on the patio at the home she shared with her fiancé, Alex Robertsen. Ella's brother, Ronan and his fiancée, Holliday Prescott, sat across from me sipping Bloody Marys. Three years ago, I would have laughed my ass off at the mere thought of sharing a meal with Ronan Connolly, but the two of us had become friends. All thanks to a night out in Park City that involved a bottle of Irish whiskey and three stolen snowmobiles.

Holliday was one of my favorite people in the world. My relationship with her had been complicated—*previously*. We'd gone from lovers to frenemies, finally settling into a comfortable relationship as friends. If I was being honest, Holliday had become one of my closest friends. Having Alex's and Ella's friendships were an added bonus. Despite giving me shit about Heather, all four of them offered me unconditional support during the divorce.

"What's up, Grady?" Holliday asked.

"He's miserable because men do not brunch. It's not in our DNA," Alex offered, rocking his son to sleep. "Saturdays are for sports and beer, *not* brunch."

"How could you not like brunch—tons of food, booze and conversation. What's not to love?" Ella's English accent was light with laughter. "Although I hate you lucky bastards who get to carbo load."

"Seriously, Ella, everything tastes great," I reassured, pouring more coffee into my mug.

"That's the second time he's used the word, *great*," Ronan pointed out. "Okay, James, out with it—what did Heather do now?"

How was it possible to be sitting at this table and not a soul here had heard about Heather's little "cry me a river" stunt.

Holliday punched his arm. "That is a name we do *not* mention, I thought we agreed henceforth she will be addressed as Lulalamoan—like a *whore.*"

I'll never live this embarrassment down. Ella and Alex exchanged glances and nearly woke their son, Will, with the laughter. Holliday had a smug look on her face, fully satisfied with the clever nickname she'd given my ex-wife. It *was* clever, I'd give her that.

Neither Ella, nor Holliday were fans of my ex-wife for reasons that involved Ronan. He held little regard for her and I couldn't say that I blamed him. There were times—multiple times—when Heather had been selfish and manipulating. What she did to Ronan and me was almost unforgiveable, but I believed in her and that she was capable of change. When she begged me to help her get clean and sober, I did. I loved Heather in her darkest hours and it hadn't been enough. *I* wasn't enough for her.

I shook my head. "There's not enough bleach in the world to scrub that memory from my mind."

"We could try hypnotizing you," Ella offered. "Or there's always electroshock therapy."

"I thought electroshock therapy was used to regain lost memories," Holliday said, stabbing a strawberry with her fork.

"I believe it's more commonly used to treat depression, and I remember Carrie Fisher saying that it causes memory loss."

Four pairs of eyes locked on mine, two sets narrowed the others wide-eyed.

"Yeah, I know stuff," I replied, cocking a brow. "Not just a pretty face. I do have a degree from Brown, you know."

Alex stood and then carried Will inside, placing him in his bassinet. He returned with the baby monitor or at least I think it was a baby monitor, it looked like a high-tech gadget from the MacGyver collection.

"You know what you need,"—Alex pointed to me with this fork—"You need to get back in the game."

"I agree, our wedding is coming up in a few weeks." Ella nudged Alex, and then plucked one of her famous home-made, raspberry-lemon, gluten-free muffins from the basket. "I can set you up. Honestly, it can't be that hard getting over Lululamoan."

I groaned pressing my palms to my eyes. "Please don't set me up, Ella."

"How about we give the man some time to heal before we pile on the hate for Heather and start compiling a list of eligible bachelorettes to be the next Mrs. James," Ronan said.

"Per *Page Six* and Hollywood and Tinsel dot com, Grady *is* back in the game," Holliday interjected.

"Yeah, I think I read something about you hooking up with a model," Ella added, sliding her blonde hair over her shoulder. "You were photographed outside Vacancy in LA a month ago, with a certain dark haired L'Oréal model."

"A model, huh?" Ronan asked, draping his arm around Holliday's shoulders.

"Maybe you should date someone not so famous," Holliday offered, before popping a grape into her mouth.

I laughed, jutting my chin in their direction. "That's rich, says the woman who is going to marry a movie star this summer."

"All right," Alex said, scooping some fruit onto this plate.

"So, are you dating the model . . . or just sleeping with her?"

"I'm not sleeping with her . . . *anymore*." I decided to give them a morsel and put them out of their misery. I returned my focus to the quiche and my *great* mood, tuning out the chatter around me. When I married Heather, I was ready for everything including serial monogamy. I had convinced myself, I wanted it all—the house, the two point five kids and the dog *or* cat, maybe both. Did I still want those things? It was hard to say that love and marriage was for suckers when I was sitting at table surrounded by happy in love soon to be married couples.

"Well, I guess we know what has Grady in a mood," Holliday announced, tapping at her phone screen. "The headline on *Gossip Cop* reads: Heather Young spotted leaving dinner with friends in Malibu after *Wake Up with Stacy* appearance."

"What happened on *Wake Up with Stacy*?" Ella asked, pushing her plate towards the center of the table.

Normally this was Ella's bread and butter, being clued in on all the celebrity gossip. "Read the article, I'm sure all the sordid details are there."

Their hands flew to their phones, as I scooped some red pepper, feta and spinach scramble onto my plate.

Ella jumped up from her chair. "That cow!"

"I'm disappointed, Ella, I thought you'd be right on top of my drama." I smirked.

With her head still focused on her phone, she flipped me the bird. "I've been a little busy, plus everything in the tabloids has been so boring lately. I've just been focused on Will, the wedding, and the shop."

Holliday huffed out a humorless laugh. "Emotionally abusive? That's a joke—a total lie."

"What a twat. That woman is a lying *twat.*" Ella began gathering up the plates, but Alex stopped her by pulling her onto his lap.

"Wow, man," Ronan said. "So, what are you going to do?"

I shrugged. "Haven advised that I not say anything, she seems to think that Heather is just seeking attention."

"No shit," Holliday scoffed. "There is one thing for certain—she loves the spotlight."

"I told Haven to set up some appearances with a few of my favorite charities over the next few weeks," I said, reaching for the Bloody Mary pitcher.

"Don't forget Pour Fest is next weekend," Ella added, pointing at me. "It's no Glastonbury, but I guess we'll have to make due."

"I don't want to encourage the paparazzi to follow me around while I'm out with you guys."

Ella shook her head. "No, I didn't mean it like that—we can post a few pictures of you on Instagram and twitter of you having fun with your friends."

"It's not a bad idea," Ronan said. "And you know I don't normally get on board with this shit."

"Your fans will love seeing you surrounded by your support system," Holliday added. "Fuck Lululamoan, gobble up all the positive press."

Yeah, and I wouldn't mind getting some sense of satisfaction that it would drive Heather crazy with jealousy that despite her underhanded tactics I was out having the time of my life.

Chapter
Ten

Harlow

The kickoff to summer transformed this once sleepy destination for creative types and very old money into the likeness of party hopping Miami Beach. Afton surprised me with tickets to The Harbour Pour Fest and I somehow managed to pry my brother, Nicholas, away from Chicago for the weekend.

Craft beers and couture cocktails from some of the best bars in the Hamptons were all nestled beneath three white tents. We knocked back our shots, and Nicholas continued flirting with our server.

"I get off in thirty minutes," she purred. "Maybe you'd like to get off with me? You can bring your friend too." She eyed me up and down. "I'd be into that."

Nicholas nearly spit out his drink.

Staring at her name tag, I waved my empty glass in the

air. "I'm going to clue you in, Tara. He's my brother and I don't play for your team. He needs another beer, and I'd like a Cucumber Vodka, please."

"Sorry, sweetie, I didn't mean to imply anything incestuous. I'll be right back with your drinks."

I tucked my hair behind my ear, and counted to five suppressing the urge to roll my eyes. "Nicholas, how in the world you manage to find all the . . . *sexually adventurous* ladies boggles the mind."

He smirked, and waggled his fingers in front of me. "It's because I'm a doctor, if shit goes awry they know that they're in good hands, and the kinkier the better."

I narrowed my eyes. "That's the stupidest thing I've ever heard."

"Dr. Trembley enjoys house calls, and I'm always ready to play."

This time I rolled my eyes. "Correction, *that* might be the stupidest thing I've ever heard."

Before Nicholas could respond, Tara dropped off our drinks along with two more shots of tequila.

Nicholas handed me a shot glass, and I picked up a lime wedge. I downed the liquid, relishing the burn as it slid down my throat. "Why do you think Monty disowned us?"

His brow crinkled. "Interesting topic shift, Debbie Downer."

"Yeah, well, years of therapy still have me questioning my own self-worth."

"Do you really care?"

"Call it a general wondering of why people are wired a certain way."

Nicholas tossed back his shot. "I often wondered why Mom loved him so much, in spite of the fact that he's a first-class asshole. If she knew what he'd done to us before her death . . ."

"No, it was better that we didn't tell her—that fucking disease, in that capacity spared her from ever knowing what he did to us." I laughed a humorless laugh, as my finger traced the rim of my glass. "When I was ten and he missed the choir performance, the one where I scored my first solo, Mom told me that he loved me in his own way and to give him more time."

"You can't be serious," he huffed, swirling the contents of his glass.

Blowing out a harsh breath, I shook my head. "I hate that I think about him, and spend energy on him. Hating your children . . . I've read many articles over the years on reasons why this happens."

"Personally, I think he was jealous of all of our accomplishments."

"I read a few cases regarding parents having jealous or envious tendencies towards their children. Like Mrs. Robinson in *The Graduate*. She had to drop out of school, and get married because she was pregnant. That's why she did all that hateful shit to her daughter."

"Are you saying I should keep any future girlfriends away from Monty?"

"I think that you're safe."

"Where is the old man these days?"

"Last I heard he was drinking, gambling and golfing his way up the coast—somewhere in between West Palm Beach and Charleston."

Time has healed most of my childhood wounds or at least I wanted to believe that I was healed. I hadn't seen or talked to my father since my senior year at NYU. He'd invited me to lunch at Ai Fiori in Midtown and I stupidly went. At a quiet out of the way table, I sat there and listened to him tell me that he was done being my father.

"I've done all I was obligated to do for you, Harlow. You are not my financial, legal or emotional responsibility any longer. I've deposited the remainder of your inheritance into your account. I'm cutting all ties."

His eyes were cold, vacant and he spoke in a clipped tone with no emotion. At the end of the meal, he actually asked the waiter to split the bill. No other words were spoken, he walked out of the restaurant and out of my life. No goodbye, just a fuck you—I don't want to be your father anymore. Monty wasn't much of a father anyway, but it still stung. That was the day I decided that I actually *hated* my father.

Monty delivered the same news to Nicholas with a voicemail. I didn't even have time to warn Nicholas, our father called him immediately following our lunch that day.

"How's Harry doing?" Nicholas asked, dragging a hand through his dark hair. "He must be pumped for the World Cup."

"I am sure that he is, but I wouldn't know."

"Did you two split? Is that why you're hiding out in The Harbour instead of over in Europe with him?"

I swallowed past the lump in my throat. "We did break-up, but I am not hiding out. I'm giving Harry his space so he can concentrate on his game."

The expression on my brother's face told me that my story lacked a convincing measure. I didn't want to share my "oh poor me" story—I was becoming a cliché. First my father left me, then my boyfriend. I missed Harry, but if he didn't want to be in a relationship with me, I had to pull up the big girl panties and move the fuck on.

"Are you planning to stay here permanently?" he asked, concern filled his eyes.

I lifted a shoulder. "I don't know. I could always move back to Mom's place in the city. It's sitting there empty."

Nicholas tossed back his drink. "I think that we should put it on the market."

I didn't want to think about selling Mom's place. It held too many memories, plus it was like I still had a piece of her with me.

Smiling, Tara approached our table. "Can I get you two anything else?"

"Yeah, before you go, could I get another?" I asked.

"Of course," she said, and bumped her hip against Nicholas' arm.

She leaned in close and he whispered in her ear, unfortunately I could still hear the words. "What I want isn't on the menu."

God, those lines actually worked on women. Nicholas was smooth, I'd give him that. My brother apparently dealt with his issues by having casual sex. To my knowledge, he'd never had a steady girlfriend. It seems that med school left little room for serious dating. I could only imagine that working at the hospital was exactly like *Grey's Anatomy*. The two of them made their plans and I busied myself by playing *Candy Crush*.

"Are you sure it's okay that I take off?"

"Absolutely, go have fun."

Nodding, he slid some cash in front of me. "For the cab *or* you can have a few drinks on me."

I shoved the cash into my wristlet. "I really like the bar where Tara works, and I'd like to continue to be a patron of the establishment. So, if you could maybe not be a dick to her when you cut and run later, I'd appreciate it."

He chuckled, and hugged me tightly. "She knows what this is all about, but I'll be sure to reiterate."

Once they left, I sidled up to The Harbour Brew Company's bar in the VIP tent and ordered sparkling water and a pint of their summer ale. The combination of tequila and vodka left my brain feeling muddy. My eyes drifted to the other side of the bar. Out of the corner of my eye, I saw Grady James sitting in a chair holding a glass of scotch. Possibly whiskey. Damn. He looked good wearing a grey t-shirt and dark denim jeans.

Speaking of moving the fuck on.

I hadn't seen him since the evening at Hutton House. Now, he was here at the festival and talking to a tall blonde. I couldn't see her face. Were they on date? I've barely stopped thinking about him since that day and I've had a reoccurring fantasy that involved the two of us on a secluded beach. Not very original, I know.

Armed with my beer in one hand, I made my way to the other side of the tent to Grady. If he wasn't on a date, perhaps he could help me with the sex part, *literally* my "to do" list.

I pushed through the crowd and the gawking gazes from a group of "fitness is my life" fuckboys, only to be halted by Afton's tequila induced state.

"Hey, girl." She shimmied up to me, and grasped my arm. "Having fun?"

"Um, yes, and it looks like you are too." I nodded in the

direction of the yummy Paloma she was holding in her left hand.

We were the same age, born exactly one month apart. The two of us met at freshman orientation at NYU. After an epic conversation that spanned our love for all things Murray's Cheese, gel manicures, and cab-to-curb heels, we were instant besties.

"I thought maybe you'd picked up a hottie and jetted out, but here you are."

"You're funny. Not me, but Nicholas left with a sexy red-head, Tara from Castle Hill Beach House."

"Hmm, I don't think I know her," she replied, before licking the salt from her glass.

My eyes darted towards where Grady was sitting. Just my luck, he was gone.

"You want to go check out the band?" she asked, lifting her glass towards the south lawn.

"Yeah, let's go."

I followed Afton through the throngs of people crowded around the stage. She swayed to the beat of the music, the afternoon sun bounced off her shimmering gold shorts. Afton was insanely beautiful with her sun-kissed skin and long legs. By my count there were at least ten guys with their eyes on her.

"I love this song," Afton yelled. "I want to go to Glastonbury this year. You want to go with me? We can make it a whole 'traveling through Europe' thing."

"I'll think about it," I yelled over the music, and looked up the festival dates on my phone. What I wanted to tell her was that traveling through Europe from one music festival to another wasn't really my thing. Public toilets, drunken people sloshing their drinks on me, and listening to loud music that

I couldn't decipher the words to gave me anxiety. This festival was okay because it wasn't too crowded, the weather was perfect, and the portable toilets were private trailers. These units looked better than some of the hotel bathrooms I'd been in while on spring break.

Closing my eyes, I sipped the beer in my hand and lost myself in the rhythmic melody of the music. I didn't usually sign up for outdoorsy events. My preferred outdoor enjoyment consisted of cocktails on the East Terrace of the Salon de Ning at the Peninsula in Manhattan or Le Bain in the Meatpacking District. Now, I was compiling a mental list of the ten best rooftop bars in New York City.

The DJ announced a quick break as the low hum of drum beats came over the speakers. Glancing in Afton's direction, she was wrapped up in a conversation. A guy with wavy blond hair, wearing a pair of dark grey pants and a white and grey button down shirt listened intently as she discussed why cities should stop building concrete buildings and focus on music festivals. When the words "cheaper more equitable path toward creating culturally vibrant cities" came out of her mouth that was my cue to exit stage left.

Upon my exit, I came face to face with Grady James. His blue eyes landed on mine and that boyish smile tugged at something deep inside of me.

"Harlow, hey."

"Hey, Grady, I didn't take you for the beer festival type."

"Oh." He arched brow. "And what type do you take me for?"

A nervous laugh bubbled in my throat as I formulated my answer. "I picture you as more of the club type, the kind of guy who listens to techno or the latest mixes from the hottest DJ's in Europe. I bet you have an Idris Elba playlist."

My reasoning was solely based on what I read in the tabloids. Grady always made the headlines. Years ago, his feud with movie star Ronan Connolly was a hot topic. As a couple, Grady and Heather managed to keep a relatively low profile, but when they were spotted outside Vacancy or Indigo Row the paparazzi were never far behind. Before *and* after Heather, *Page Six* had photographs of Grady with some leggy brunette, a swimsuit model or European socialite nearly every weekend.

He smiled. "Interesting analysis, but you'd be wrong, although now that I think about it, I should check out some of Idris' tunes."

Suppressing the urge to ask him about the blonde he'd been talking to earlier, I settled on a different question. "Did you come here by yourself?"

He shook his head. "I met up with friends, but they had to leave. What about you?"

I hooked my thumb over my shoulder. "Afton, she loves these events. This really isn't my scene, good people watching though and the churro bar was a nice touch."

"Fried food is always a good idea. I haven't indulged in a while, at least not since I was scolded by a certain lingerie model."

I smiled over the rim of my cup.

"Although if people watching and all things fried is your thing, the Clam Bar is a must."

"Oh, now that's a blast from the past. I haven't been there in years."

"You don't say. First Nancy's now you say you haven't been to the Clam Bar," he said shaking his head. "Put those places on your good eats list."

Before I even realized it, Grady and I were walking

around sampling craft cocktails and talking about our favorite Hamptons' hangouts. I'd spent plenty of time here in college, being Afton's roommate and friend had its advantages. My first encounter with The Harbour was her parent's annual Labor Day weekend party. When the two of us were bored with Manhattan life, we'd drive or fly out here just to escape. I'd fallen in love with everything about The Harbour—the people, the charming shops, and the posh restaurants.

"Drink this, do it right now." Grady handed me a beverage—a cloudy peach concoction with a rosemary sprig as garnish.

"What is this?" I asked, using my long hair as a shield to subtly sniff the drink.

"A Dalmatian, made with gin, grapefruit juice and black pepper syrup."

I took a sip, the bite of grapefruit and pepper making their presence known in the back of my cheeks. "Ooohhh, that's a spicy meatball," I choked out.

"Are you okay?" he asked, handing me a cocktail napkin.

I nodded, and took another sip feeling the effects of the booze swirling in my system.

Grady laughed. "Yeah, that black pepper and gin will do that to you."

His deep voice wound its way through my body, reminding me that Grady was a very sexy man. I ordered a Paloma, but still hung onto the drink Grady bought for me. Darting in and out of the crowd, he managed to find a table for two and motioned for me to take a seat.

Try as I might, my eyes refused to avert from his gaze. He leaned closer, so close and smelling perfectly divine. I inhaled deeply getting my fill of his clean soap and water scent. It was like he was everywhere. No one else existed in this space but the two of us.

"Would you like to grab dinner?"

"Tonight?"

He gave me a warm smile. "If you're free—*yeah.*"

"It's not that I don't want to, but we . . ."

"Don't say no, just say yes."

I could say yes. I *wanted* to say yes. It felt wrong to have these scandalous thoughts—wasn't I supposed to be on step three of the break-up phase? Bargaining? Instead I was sliding into frat boy therapy: *The best way to get over someone is to get under someone else.*

Very bad decisions were creeping into my head and most of those involved me and Grady naked.

Chapter
Eleven

Grady

At present, I was teetering on the precipice of insanity. To say that Harlow Trembley had been on my mind was an understatement. When she wasn't consuming my thoughts during the day, she was creeping into my dreams. Waking up every morning with a massive hard-on and using my hand for relief as I pictured Harlow on her knees in front of me taking my cock deep into her mouth.

I was consumed with thoughts of the woman—a beautiful woman who was a friend of my ex-wife's. But, how close were they? All I recalled were casual dinners and the two of them hanging out during after parties. Perhaps they were friendly acquaintances.

What would be the harm in having a few drinks and dinner? I wasn't an animal, I could control my urges.

Cheers erupted outside the tent when the last band of the

evening took the stage. Harlow swayed her hips to the beat of the music and I wondered what it would be like to have her wrapped around my body. Her hands digging into my shoulders as I fucked her into my mattress.

"Hey, Harlow!" Afton waved as she strode up to our table. "Can I borrow her for a minute, Grady?"

"She's all yours."

Earlier, I'd stood across the tent, admiring Harlow from a safe distance. She'd been sitting at a table with a guy that I'd originally thought could be a date, but then he took off with a red head laying my curiosity to rest. I watched as she plucked off tiny pieces of her churro, dipping them into honey and chocolate and then licking her fingers. I was entranced, and that led me to compile a list in my head of sauces I'd want to taste on her skin.

Scrubbing my hand over my jaw, I had to figure out a way to not think about fucking her in every position imaginable. Making it through this event without laying hands on her was going to be a greater accomplishment than becoming a ten-goaler in polo rankings.

I stood catching a glimpse of Harlow as she walked towards the bar.

She is gorgeous.

Her head was tilted to one side, those loose waves of auburn sliding over her shoulders. For a moment, I wondered what it would be like to wake up to all that hair wild and unruly in my bed. Then my thoughts shifted to wrapping her hair around my fist as I fucked her from behind.

I'm acting like a savage animal.

Why couldn't I think of normal shit like having a nice evening with Harlow? We'd had an awesome afternoon together. She was easy to talk to and incredibly funny.

"Excuse me, Grady?" I heard a feminine voice say from behind me. "Will you take a photo with us?"

"Sure thing," I replied, smiling at the young woman and her friend. After posing for a dozen photos, my eyes drifted back to Harlow who was engaged in a deep conversation with Afton.

I turned my attention away from her and back to the band. They started playing a song that reminded me of Heather. She would play the hell out of "Closer" by the Chainsmokers.

Fuck. Was this a sign that I shouldn't have asked Harlow to dinner? *Fuck that—Heather is the past.*

A young woman with blonde hair streaked with blue tips bounced towards where I was standing. "Hi, you're Grady James, aren't you?"

"I am."

She asked for a photo and then handed me her phone. Outstretching my arms, I leaned into her and snapped the pic. The young woman introduced herself to me and talked for a minute about how all her friends would be jealous. Her fingers flew over her phone, as she mumbled something about uploading to Instagram.

My gaze swept back to Harlow, her sweater had fallen off her left shoulder exposing her skin. A black bra strap revealed itself under the grey tank top she was wearing beneath the sweater. This led me back to picturing her hair draped across my pillows and her naked skin on my sheets, which further led me to wonder if her panties were black.

Harlow caught my stare and arched an eyebrow. A smile tugged at the corners of her lips as she lifted her sweater back up over her shoulder.

I needed to stop thinking about Harlow. More importantly, I needed to stop thinking about her naked.

"So, if . . . *when* I get the campaign with Buchanan, I'm finally going to buy a sailboat."

"Buying a sailboat is on my bucket list or maybe it's more of a wish list."

My brows rose. "Is that so?" I asked, scooping more of the rice and chicken onto my fork. Harlow was working on her second pork taco topped with fried plantains. This was very dangerous territory, sharing a meal with Harlow only drew my attention to her lips. Her sexy pink lips that I pictured wrapped around my dick instead of that taco. I'm blaming my perverted thoughts on the heat. *Yeah, that's it, the summer heat.*

"Hmm, yep." She nodded, bringing her napkin to her mouth. "Side note, this food is delicious. You weren't kidding about this place."

"What else is on this bucket slash wish list of yours?" My eyes fell to the necklaces draped around her neck. One of the chains had a pineapple charm.

"Finding somewhere to live is my top priority. I also need to find a decent coffee shop."

I laughed. "Will you be buying a place here? And, how have you not found a decent cup of coffee yet?"

"I could always move back to my mom's place in Manhattan, but I kind of like the idea of having a home here, I fell in love with The Harbour years ago. True fact, Starbucks over roasts their beans," she said, pointing her finger at me. "I'm working my way through a few around town."

"The coffee shop on Harbour Drive is excellent, great

coffee and pastries. You should try Nancy's too."

"What's the housewife in yoga pants scene like?"

I shrugged. "Never noticed before."

Harlow leaned in closer, her hazel eyes twinkling. "Grady James, notorious playboy and charming flirt, somehow I don't believe you."

There were an infinite number of ways to decipher her comment, but there was only one fact that remained just below the surface—my *former* reputation for being a player. Not even a marriage could erase all the years I spent with my name attached to an endless list of models and actresses.

Or perhaps I was transparent and Harlow could see right through me, knowing that I have spent half of this dinner picturing her naked. How could I tell her I've been cured of my player ways when I'd spent a considerable amount of time conjuring up various fantasies all starring her? Would she believe me or would she think it was some line I tell every other woman I wanted to sleep with?

"Would you believe me if I told you that I never lie?"

Leaning forward she tilted her head, and her dark hair spilled over her shoulder. "I think I could."

"In that case," I whispered, leaning in closer. "You should know that you are the most beautiful woman in this room tonight."

Her eyes met mine, and her lips parted slightly. "Is that so?"

I nodded. "It is. And you're going to believe me. Case in point, I told you this was the best place in The Harbour for Cuban food and you agreed."

She lifted a brow, rubbing her necklace between her thumb and forefinger. "You're pretty smooth, Grady James."

"That's just it I'm not trying to be smooth. I mean I am,

but I thought . . . I just wanted to give you a compliment."

Smiling she stared at me for a moment. I felt the tip of her sandal sweep across my leg.

"Sorry," she said, shifting in her chair. "I didn't mean to kick you."

She didn't completely hate the compliment. If she had she would have laughed or rolled her eyes, instead she took the compliment. However, I chickened out on taking it any further. The signs, I thought they'd been there and I was wrong. I saw the ways her eyes lit up at the mention of having dinner together. That was all this had been, it was just dinner and nothing more.

"Did you want dessert?"

"No, I can't even finish this last taco. I am stuffed. Another thing on my list, finding a place that serves New York cheesecake."

"Noted," I said, before downing the remains of my water. "Shall we leave?"

She nodded, and wiped her mouth. I signaled for the bill. On the upside, I liked hanging out with Harlow—a lot actually. It was clear that she was very busy, and I needed to respect that fact.

We both reached for the check, and my fingers grazed the back of her hand. I held her gaze, taking note of the faint smile tugging the corners of her mouth. Her beautiful, kissable mouth. Why did Harlow have to feel so good against me? Home would consist of a cold shower for one and slipping into my bed alone.

"This one is on me," I said, placing my card inside the cover.

"Okay," she murmured. "But, I owe you a meal now."

"I'll be looking forward to the next time."

Chapter
Twelve

Harlow

Morning came way too early, I slipped out of bed to find the light from Afton's kitchen cascading waves of bright light across the pool. Restless was the way I'd slept last night with Grady James on my mind. I stared at the ceiling for hours, replaying our dinner conversation over and over in my head.

I reached for my cellphone and checked my text messages. Nicholas had made it back to his hotel suite around two in the morning. I shot him a quick message and then sent one to Afton.

Harlow: Can't sleep either?

Afton: No, I'm making coffee. You need?

I needed a lot of things. Then there was my list of wants. Surprisingly, at the top of that list was Grady James. In the span of a few short days he'd managed to push to the top, ousting the cheesecake, coffee shop and sailboat. He'd become the leading man in my dirty fantasies. The shower head and my vibrator were the understudies. Last night's conversation over Cuban food and mojitos, I realized I wanted him more than I previously anticipated.

Harlow: Yes, please. Be right over.

But first, coffee.

"Are you going to tell me about your dinner with Grady or are you going to make me beg for the details?" Afton asked as she poured me another cup of coffee.

"It was uneventful, really." I ran my finger along the tabletop. "But, I did learn what Grady plans to do when he lands the fragrance campaign."

She arched a brow. "Tell me more."

"He's going to buy a sailboat. I guess it's a dream of his."

"So, he's sharing his hopes and dreams with you already, huh?"

I sucked down a swig of my coffee. "Hardly, it was just a conversation. We talked about a variety of topics."

"I saw the way he was looking at you last night, and he is smitten with you, kitten." Her phone buzzed against the top of the counter, she glanced at it and then swiped the screen.

"No, I think he was just being nice, he said he wanted to thank me for helping him out at the shoot."

She rolled her eyes. "Oh please, that man wanted an opening to take you out. Did he talk about Heather and her grotesque accusations?"

I shook my head. "No, neither one of us mentioned our exes."

"Good," Afton said as she rinsed her mug out into the sink. "Forget Harry. And I can tell you that I'm probably going to hire Grady for the campaign."

"Really? I thought you were all worried about his negative press."

"No, I'm interested in so much more." Afton held up her phone and my eyes popped wide at the leading story on Tinsel and Hollywood dot com.

Grady James Spotted with Mystery Woman at Harbour Pour Fest.

My hair had hidden my face, but it wouldn't be long before the rest of world figured out that I was the woman in the photo.

Chapter
Thirteen

Grady

My usual Sunday routine consisted of a five mile run on the beach or a long swim followed by brunch with friends, but this morning I found myself sitting aboard a private yacht. Instead of my circle of friends, my agent, Jennifer March, and Haven were my brunch companions.

"Whose brilliant idea was it to have a brunch meeting after a night of heavy drinking *and* at sea no less?" Haven asked, sliding her sunglasses up the slim slope of her nose.

"That would be yours," I reminded her.

Jennifer popped two pills into her mouth washing them down with sparkling water. "This wasn't our best idea," she agreed. "This might be the mother of all hangovers."

"A swim will cure your hangover faster than anything," I advised. "Jump into the water."

"Maybe later I'll have a swim at the club, but with these little beauties," Haven replied, shaking the bottle. "I'll be feeling better in no time."

"Look alive, sweeties, hair of the dog," Jennifer said, as the server delivered our drinks to the table.

"Isn't that Ella Connolly standing over there?" Haven asked, pointing towards the docks.

"This town is all a buzz with their upcoming wedding," Jennifer said. "Ella is incredibly sweet, and I love everything La Vienne Rose. It's a good day when I go in there and spend less than seven-hundred dollars."

"Same here," Haven chimed in, raising her champagne glass. "Grady, are you going to their wedding?"

"You know that I am, but I'm not giving either of you any details because I signed an NDA." I flipped over the menu card, debating between Nutella stuffed pancakes and the Eggs Benedict.

"It could be Ella, the guy standing at her right resembles her fiancé, Alex," Jennifer replied, refilling her glass. "All of Hollywood is curious about Ronan Connolly's little sister's upcoming nuptials."

"Well, the *world* is interested in Ronan Connolly's wedding." Haven leaned across the table, eying me suspiciously. "Rumor has it that he and Holliday Prescott are also tying the knot this summer."

I scrubbed my hands down my face. "Can we get to the point of this impromptu meeting?"

"Yes," Haven replied, folding her hands in her lap. "You are making headlines and not in a negative way."

Haven slid her iPad in front of me. I read post after post. They all said the same thing; it was about me and a mystery woman. I knew with one glance who the woman was in photos—Harlow.

"And this is the reason that you both flew in from Manhattan?" I asked, eyeing them both. "We could have discussed this over the phone."

"Who is she? Are you in a new relationship?" Jennifer asked, before taking a drink of her martini.

"She's a friend, and I am not disclosing any information to the two of you."

I chuckled to myself that Haven didn't recognize her own client. In all fairness, the pictures were blurry and Harlow's auburn hair covered her face.

Jennifer leaned forward. "If you tell us, we can kill the story or drive the narrative."

"It's up to you, Grady," Haven added.

Honestly, this thing with Harlow took me by complete surprise. At this point, I didn't even know or understand if there was a narrative. All I knew was that I couldn't stop thinking about her, and where that was going I had no idea, but I'd like to find out.

Chapter
Fourteen

Harlow

"Ah, there is nothing like rooftop cycling!" Afton yelled, pumping her fist into the air.

Sweat poured down my back as I peddled my stationary bike faster. Afton's personal trainer, Mandy, was kicking our butts today.

"Come on, ladies, gimme that extra little push right here," Mandy challenged. "Visualize that goal, focus on your breathing."

Pushing myself hard the last two miles, I relished the burn in my legs. I focused on my breathing while I watched the sailboats rock back and forth on the water. The cinematic view of The Harbour from the rooftop of the Buchanan Building made the pain substantially less.

"And done. Good job, ladies!"

"Whoop! Thanks, Mandy!" Afton shouted.

I slowed my pace on the bike, cooling my legs from the workout. "Shit, that was intense."

She hopped off her bike and grabbed a mineral water from the bar. "I know all I want is a big cheeseburger and some fries now."

I huffed out a laugh. "Was that what you were visualizing?"

Afton picked up her phone and a huge smile spread across her face.

"What are you so smiley about?" My legs shook as I climbed off the bike. "Is that a guy?"

"What guy?"

I toweled off my neck and chest. "Play it that way if you want, but I think you've got yourself a guy."

Ignoring my comment, she tucked her phone into her bag. "Let's go to Rum Bar, we totally deserve it."

"Okay, and if I get enough booze in you, perhaps you'll tell me about this mystery guy."

"You're not going to drop this are you, Lo?"

"Not a chance."

Apparently, everyone else had the same idea because the bar was packed. I needed another drink, and our server had disappeared. Walking towards the bar, I glanced back at our table where Afton and Nicholas were engrossed in a deep discussion.

"Could I get another beer?" I asked, sagging against the railing of the bar.

As I waited for my drink, I stared at the sky-blue accents that popped against the all-white walls. My eyes closed and I allowed myself a quick daydream that included Grady and an afternoon on the water. Instead of lusting after Grady, I should be focusing on launching my website. I couldn't push it off too much longer. Haven, my publicist, had been sending me multiple emails each week urging me to settle on a new launch date.

"One blonde ale," the bartender said with a full smile.

"Thanks, put it on our tab."

"So far, the Zika virus outbreak is considerably narrow," Nicholas mentioned, as I passed by the table on my way to the patio. Afton was obsessed with the latest Zika virus news. You'd think she was preparing for the end of days with the amount of bug spray she's stocked up on.

Feeling sober-ish, I leaned against the pale-yellow, wooden railing watching two boats crawl across the water. Sipping my beer, I lost myself in my earlier daydream. My thoughts focused on Grady's scruffy jaw, and tousled hair blowing in the breeze. I wanted to run my fingers through his hair and feel his mouth on mine. I wondered if he'd seen the tabloid headlines from Pour Fest.

"Twice in one weekend, is this fate or what?" Grady rasped in my ear.

I glanced over my shoulder for confirmation that he was really here and that the slight effects from the beer and the smell of salt water weren't toying with my senses.

"Possibly," I said. "What brings you out for drinks on a Sunday afternoon?" I turned around to face him, biting my lip to stifle a moan at the sight of him in a pair of grey shorts and a dark blue t-shirt. His baby blues were hidden behind a pair of aviators and his dark hair was mussed and swept over his brow.

"Would you believe that I happened to be in the neigh-borhood and wanted to see what the party was all about?"

"I might believe that," I said before taking a sip of my beer.

"Actually, I am glad that I bumped into you." He pried the glass from my hand, and then took a drink. My eyes dropped to his lips, and then to his Adam's apple as he swallowed.

"Oh, and why is that?"

Inching closer, he passed the beer back to me. "It seems that you and I are being talked about online."

I smiled. "It seems that *you* sent tongues wagging. I'm just the mystery woman."

"Mystery woman," he repeated, tossing his head back slightly. "I met with my agent and Haven this morning, it seems they are very interested in knowing about this mystery woman."

"Well, it won't take long for Haven to figure out that it's me in the photo. She will probably want to spin it to the press that we're dating when I launch my website."

"What website?" he asked, flashing me a charming smile.

"What? Didn't you know that I'm a 'global influencer'?" I pretended to feign shock. "Cocktails and couture dot com. It's a fashion, beauty and lifestyle website where I'm sharing my style secrets and my favorite cocktail recipes."

"Congratulations, that's very cool. See you are full of mystery, I guess the press was right."

I tried desperately not to blush. Words escaped me at the moment. Harry had been my biggest supporter when I'd told him about the website. I wasn't totally sold on the idea, but it was Harry who convinced me to go for it.

His gaze shifted to my cleavage and then his finger was

trailing over my clavicle. My nipples, the jealous attention whores they were, decided this was the moment to show up to the party. With a subtle movement, my hands gripped the Kimono style cardigan I was wearing closing it over my chest.

"What's this all about?" he asked, sliding his finger under the chain of my necklace.

Electricity raced through my blood. My eyes dropped to where he was touching my skin. Rays of afternoon sun glinted off the tiny gold pineapple charm.

"It's a pineapple."

"I can see that," he mused, his eyes trained on the delicate piece of metal fruit.

His finger skimmed over the rise of my breast and a rush of tingles skittered down my spine. "I like pineapples."

Grady's attention turned to my lips. "That's the entire story?"

I twirled the charm between my fingers. "I hadn't realized that we were playing twenty questions."

He pinned me against the railing with his hips. "Oh, I can go all night."

Swallowing harshly, I couldn't seem to find my words. All I could manage was a nod. The strands of lights above us flickered and the bartender rang the bell. "Blue light special! You know what that means!"

The announcement jolted me and he stepped back. Grady's blue eyes remained fixed on me. There was no mistaking the heat between us. After spending a vast majority of my days dreaming about him, I had solid evidence that he wanted me as much as I wanted him. The fact that his erection connected with my stomach told me everything I needed to know.

"Hey, Harlow," Afton called out. "Oh, *hey*, Grady."

"Hi, Afton, Harlow was filling me in on the details of her new website."

"It is very exciting, I see big things happening this summer for Harlow," she replied, before pinning her brown eyes on me. "I paid the tab, and Nicholas needs to get to the airport."

"Okay, I'll be right there." I looked at Grady, a wry smile playing on his lips. "I guess I need to be going."

"Me too," he said, dragging a hand through his hair. "I have an early practice tomorrow, there's a match coming up soon."

The breeze kicked up, whipping my hair across my face. "Oh, are you playing in the Stars and Stripes match? I heard that was a big deal around here."

"I am. Would you like to be my guest?" he asked, tucking my hair behind my ear.

"Maybe."

Chapter
Fifteen

Grady

My entire drive home was consumed with thoughts of Harlow. Her lips were too damn tempting. Those pink lips of hers, I ached to kiss them. Just one taste.

I maneuvered my car up the driveway, and then pulled into the garage. Closing the door, I was alone again. The world shut out while I stayed tucked away in my beach hideaway.

Once inside, I tossed my keys on the counter. This place was set off the main road hidden by trees, but light from the large glass windows poured over every exposed beam and piece of wood.

Wood. Exposed.

Raking a hand through my hair, I blew out a harsh breath. Harlow Trembley. I'd spent at most fifteen maybe twenty hours with her and now I was having filthy fantasies about her. What the actual fuck?

In a short span of hours, she seemed to have seeped into my every thought and I couldn't flush her out. All that hair, those gorgeous auburn waves. When I'd been within inches of her, the scent of her hair crashed into my senses exploding every receptor in my body.

It didn't help matters that I was staring at every flat surface around me, wondering how her copper colored hair would look fanned out over the counter as I ate her. Then there were her eyes to consider. There was smolder in those green eyes whispering "come fuck me."

As I led Elsa, my horse, into the stables, Chelsea Hodges approached. Chelsea and her family owned the polo grounds and the East Harbour Athletic club.

"Mr. James, there's an urgent message from Haven Cardwell, she needs you to call her as soon as possible."

"Thank you, Chelsea."

I kicked up and jogged towards the clubhouse. The worst thoughts entered my mind that someone had died. When I reached my locker, I could have taken the door off the hinges, instead I punched in my code. I grabbed my cell and swiped Haven's number.

I didn't wait for her to speak. "Is my mother okay? My sister?"

"Your family is fine, this is another matter."

Relief flooded my body. "Out with it, Haven." I sagged against the lockers, wiping the sweat from my brow.

"It's your ex-wife—she claims that the mystery woman you were with is the woman you left her for."

"Fuck!" My fist collided with my locker. "Fucking Heather—you know that she is a goddamn liar."

"Yeah, I know, but if you'd let me I'd like to control the story. Give me the greenlight, Grady, and tell me who the mystery woman is and I will smooth everything over."

I dragged a hand through my hair. "That's just it, if we tell the whole world, it won't be smooth. Heather *will* flip out."

"Fuck, Grady, what have you done? Who is she?"

"It's nothing, I swear, we're not even dating, but . . ."

"But? What?" Haven asked dragging out the words.

"Well," I began, dropping a hand to my hip. "She's also a client of yours, and I'm not sure if that is a good thing or bad thing."

Haven gasped, which is a sound I've never heard from her lips. "Who? Who is she?" The sound of ice clanking against glass told me that Haven was about to pour some of her Grandfather's bourbon into a glass. Her family owned one of the oldest bourbon distilleries in Kentucky.

"It's Harlow Trembley."

Silence hung on the line for a few moments. "Don't worry, Grady, this will be handled."

The call went dead and I had no doubt that Haven was working some of her Hollywood Fixer magic. In that regard, she was like Olivia Pope, except Haven didn't wear a white hat—no hers was black and I was pretty sure it had red devil horns.

All I knew is that I needed to talk to Harlow and fast.

Chapter
Sixteen

Harlow

It was highly unusual for my phone to start blowing up at two-thirty in the afternoon on a Monday. I left the device sitting on the credenza across the room as to not be distracted while I hammered out the finishing touches on the website.

The constant buzzing was driving me insane. I should have used DND. I stalked across the room and scrolled through the notifications. Haven had called me twice. My friend, Zanita Van Haren, had called me about fifteen minutes ago, and now there was a demanding text ordering me to answer my fucking phone.

"Where's the fire, Zanita?"

"Fucking finally, you answer." Her Dutch accent delivered each syllable with sharpness. "The fire is online. The UK papers are claiming that your recent break-up with Harry is the reason for his terrible cockup against Team USA. The gossips are saying you ripped his heart out."

I looked at the date on my laptop, sure enough the World Cup had started and I was oblivious.

"None of that is true! He broke up with me, for the love of God." My fingers flew over my keyboard as I did a Google search for my name.

"Gossip columnists don't care about that and the UK tabloids are especially vicious."

Fuck. Fuck. Fuckity Fuck.

There it was in bold letters:

Model Harlow Trembley dumped England goalkeeper Harry Brackman before World Cup gaffe.

"The British tabloids are saying you're the reason he's playing so poorly and missed that block that led to the tie game."

Headline after headline and all of them painted me as the villain. These Brits are serious about their soccer. They're looking for any excuse to give their star player a break.

"Yeah, I can see that."

"So, what are you going to do?"

"I don't know if there is anything I can do, they're going to believe everything they read anyway."

I ended the call with Zanita and returned my focus to the computer screen. Secretly, I was hoping that either Harry or his agent would clear up the confusion. Every article included a single quote from Harry, saying that he was sorry to the fans and his teammates for the error. No mention of me, and the fact that we broke-up weeks ago.

Why, Harry? Why would you allow this to happen?

Chapter
Seventeen

Grady

Normally, I loved the sound of silence but today, not so much. I tried to call Harlow's cell three times and each time it went to voicemail. I only hoped she didn't think I was a psycho. I needed to get out of my house—it felt too small. Too quiet.

Just as I opened the door to my garage, my phone rang. It was a number I didn't recognize.

"Hello, this is Grady."

"Grady, this is Kayla from Buchanan Beauty. I have Afton Buchanan on the line."

What good luck, maybe she could put me in touch with Harlow.

"Great, thanks, Kayla."

"Grady James, I know this is highly irregular, but I wanted to let you know that we'd love to offer you the campaign.

I've already shipped the contract over to your agent, Jennifer March, so act a little bit surprised when she gives you the good news."

"Thanks, Afton. I'm happy to accept. And I can't wait to work on the campaign. Um, by chance do you happen to know where Harlow is today?"

"Well, I assume that she is still at my beach house working on her website. Why?"

"I was trying to get in contact with her about a personal matter." I opened the door to my Range Rover and climbed inside.

I heard Afton tapping on her keyboard. "I'm going to give you my address. You can drive over and talk to Harlow in person. She might have her phone on do not disturb since she's working."

Afton rattled off her address and I logged it into my GPS. "Thanks, I really appreciate this and the opportunity to be the face of the new campaign."

"Not a problem, Grady. I'm elated to have you on Team Buchanan."

Fifteen minutes later, I found myself maneuvering my vehicle around a circular gravel driveway, in front of a classic Hampton's shingle clad home surrounded by lush landscaping.

Once I parked, I walked around the back of the main house, past the pool and then trudged up the back stairs of the guest house. I knocked on the sliding glass door, and Harlow appeared from the hallway. She gave me a small smile and a quick wave.

"Grady, what are you doing here?"

The smell of fresh cut flowers hit me when she opened the sliding glass door. Harlow wasn't wearing any makeup, and her auburn hair was piled high on top of her head in a messy bun. Her eyes were red and puffy, which told me that she'd been crying.

"Hey, are you okay?"

"I'm not sure what I am." Harlow motioned for me to come inside. "Would you like something to drink? I'm thinking of pouring a glass of wine, maybe the whole bottle."

"Sure, I'll take a glass."

On bare feet, she sauntered towards the wine rack. As she reached up for a bottle, the white tank top she was wearing rose, exposing her flat stomach.

"Make yourself at home," she called over her shoulder. "I assume Malbec is okay?"

I nodded and made myself comfortable on the couch. Everything in the living room was grey and white with splashes of pinks. My gaze followed her as she went into the kitchen, popped the cork and then poured two glasses. With the bottle and two filled glasses in hand, Harlow joined me on the couch.

"What's got you feeling down?"

After handing me a glass she took a large gulp. "Well, it seems that I'm the reason that my ex is playing so horribly in the World Cup."

I narrowed my eyes. "I'm going to need a bit more information."

"Harry Brackman, my ex, I assume you know who he is, apparently, the UK tabloids are blaming me for his poor performance. We broke up last month . . . actually, I should say that he broke up with me—to focus on his game." She handed me her iPad. "Knock yourself out. I'm the evil bitch who stomped on his heart."

I read headline after headline, each one more hurtful than the previous. And I thought I was having a bad day with the tabloids.

"So, what brings you out here, Grady?"

Leaning forward I set the glass on coffee table. "I'm having some issues with the tabloids as well." Scrubbing my hands down my face, I looked over to the window and stared out at the pool.

"More Heather drama?"

I turned back to face Harlow. "Yeah, I guess that today's headlines are packed full of lies."

"More than usual, anyway." She rolled her eyes. "What's Heather done now?"

I blew out a deep breath. "She claims that the mystery woman in the photo is the woman I left her for and that is why our marriage ended. What kills me is that Heather begged me to keep the cheating out of the tabloids."

Her eyes went wide. "Wait, she cheated on you?"

"Yeah, with her personal trainer."

"Oh my God, with Nate?"

I nodded. "Yeah, I walked in on the two of them going at in our kitchen."

"Real classy, Heather," she said, before polishing off the rest of her drink.

"Anyway, I ended up having to tell Haven that you were the one in the photo."

Harlow curled one leg underneath her, and poured another glass. "Well, I'm sure that Haven had a good chuckle over that bit of news."

I sagged against wall. "Actually, she said it would be handled, but now with your tabloid woes and mine, it's got me thinking that we could use this to our advantage. What would you say if we pulled a publicity stunt of our own?"

She cocked her head. "How so?"

"Instead of denying the relationship, let's admit it."

Chapter
Eighteen

Harlow

*D*id I hear him correctly? A million negative thoughts ran through my mind and I couldn't stop the obnoxiously loud laugh that shot out of my mouth.

"Have you gone crazy?"

He flashed me that irresistible boyish grin. "No, far from it . . . hear me out. Why not let people think that we're in a relationship?"

I shook my head. "Right, and confirm that I've 'already moved on'? The UK tabloids will crucify me. I'll be the most hated woman in all of England."

"No, we share *our* stories—the real stories. We let Haven work her PR magic and then we tell the world the truth. Heather cheated on me and that's why we divorced. Harry stomped on *your* heart. You can choose to say as much or as little as you want."

"I don't know, Grady," I said, twisting the ring on my finger. "This could go either way."

"It's a risk, but we're the good guys here." He crossed the room, and dropped beside me on the couch. "And in Hollywood, the good guys are supposed to win and get the happily ever after."

"I've never pulled a publicity stunt before. Something about the concept has always felt . . . *dirty* to me."

I never thought I'd be the kind of celebrity that would use the paparazzi for staged publicity. Even when my mother passed away, I wouldn't let Haven leak the story. My mother died just before the Nadia's Dream fashion show was scheduled to air on television. The special had already been taped, but Haven suggested that I allow the press to ask me about it during the red carpet. Haven was coming from a good place, she thought it might be an opportunity to start a dialogue about Alzheimer's, but I had no interest in becoming a spokesperson for the disease.

Grady finished his glass. "Yeah, I get that." He fell back against the pillows, and blew out a sharp breath. "Now I feel terrible for suggesting the idea. I'm sorry. I need another drink."

His fingers laced in between mine as he grasped the bottle. My eyes landed on his—Grady's brow game was strong. Those gorgeous blue eyes looking deep into mine, pulling me right in.

"No, don't feel bad. Seriously. It's my own issue. At some point, I should play the Hollywood game."

Grady raked his hands through his dark hair and crossed them behind his head. My gaze darted to his arms and away from his mouth, giving me a moment to admire the honeyed bronze color of his skin. His forearms were beautifully toned and muscular. Playing polo does a body good.

I wondered what Grady James looked like on horseback, controlling a thoroughbred with one hand gripped on the reigns and the other wrapped around a mallet. Delicious was the only word I could come up with in my head. Tingles curled around my core, imagining the feel of his hands on every inch of my body—stroking, gripping and pleasuring me in ways I could only dream hands could.

"I can't date someone prettier than me." The words tumbled from my mouth, and I hiccupped. "People would never believe that you'd actually choose to date *me*."

Regret hit me immediately, as I twirled the stem of the wine glass between my fingers. I wanted to grab the words that hung in the space between us and shove them back down my throat. Grady turned his head to look at me.

He cocked a brow. "What? Are you kidding me—*you* are gorgeous."

The blush crept up my neck, heating my cheeks. His body was so close to mine that I could feel the warmth rolling off his skin. This man was making it difficult to keep my salacious thoughts at bay.

"Remember how I told you that I never lie?" he asked, tucking his fingers under my chin. Grady was touching me, those same electric feelings elicited once more.

"Yes."

"You are gorgeous. That is not a lie or a line."

I couldn't help but smile. "You're easy on the eyes too."

Leaning up from the back of the couch, he twisted his body towards me. Breathing in his scent was intoxicating. My eyes dropped to his lips. I wanted to reach out and brush the tips of my fingers to his skin. I studied his five o'clock shadow and allowed my mind to explore the possibility of what it would feel like scratching against my thighs, my stomach, and my neck—everywhere.

The buzzing of Grady's phone pulled my mind out of the proverbial gutter.

"It's Haven. I should take this call."

"I hope it's not a Heather related matter."

He stepped outside and I watched him as he leaned against the railing. I took another sip of wine, and contemplated his offer. Movie studios used to arrange relationships all the time for the sake of selling their pictures. During the Golden Age, Hollywood produced dreamy images of adventure, glamour, and most of all, romance. If an actor or an actress was rumored to be gay, the Hollywood fixers would leak rumors to the press of a budding romance.

I picked up my phone and swiped the screen, scrolling through the stories again. Whatever possessed me to read the comments was beyond me, my agent warned me time and time again to never Google myself.

"Luckily no Heather drama, there's a charity event that I've been invited to attend," Grady said, stepping in from the patio. "There's an organization in South Carolina that rescues and finds homes for retired polo horses."

"Oh wow, that's wonderful."

"Yeah, I've donated my time to a few organizations like this one," he said, shoving his hands into his pockets. "Guess I should be going and get my things in order for the trip."

"Okay, I'll walk you out." I stood up from the couch. "Where in South Carolina is the event?"

"Palmetto Bluff. Have you ever been?" he asked, holding the door open for me.

"The low country, not to Palmetto Bluff, but I have been to Hilton Head."

He laughed. "Who hasn't been there?"

"I know, right?"

We stopped just short of his Range Rover. "I don't suppose you'd like to come with me to this event?" He avoided eye contact when the words rolled off his tongue. It was cute the way he shuffled his feet against the gravel. Shyness wasn't a word I'd use to describe Grady.

It was a bit frightening how much I *wanted* him to invite me to join him on the trip. I found it even more frightening when I said yes.

Chapter
Nineteen

Grady

I'd had my hands on her for a few seconds and I wanted more, I was greedy. Another restless night—tossing and turning and thinking about Harlow's body bowing beneath mine as I kissed across her abs, tasting the salt and sun on her skin.

Thinking about her led to something I'd never done, I spent an undisclosed amount of time stalking her social media accounts. She rarely updated her Facebook page, the last status update was from a month ago: *Any good recommendations for cheesecake in The Harbour?*

Her Instagram was filled with snapshots of her looking beautiful in various "outfits of the day" type posts. Stumbling across pictures of her and her ex, Harry, was a bit of a surprise. I'd scrubbed my accounts of all things Heather the day our split hit the media. Harlow's Twitter account was nothing but business, mixed in with her Instagram posts. *Did Harry take those "look of the day" pictures?* Jealousy hit me hard.

So, I did the next logical thing, I Googled her name.

Jackpot.

Avoiding the posts about her ex, I skimmed over the current news. Dozens of articles that she'd written for *One Park Avenue* and *Bella Magazine* appeared. Harlow's name was attached to featured articles, guest interviews, and photoshoots along with a ton of fashion and beauty edits. I read her words, devouring everything from juice cleanse routines to brow shaping. I didn't care if it was feminine, girly stuff. It was all Harlow and she had a way with words. No wonder she was starting her own website. Everything she wrote oozed culture, intelligence and refinement.

Most people thought that I was incapable of having a discussion on complex issues. Even though I had a degree from Brown, it was hard to get people to take me seriously. I knew people made fun of male models—after all I'd seen *Zoolander.* Through the years, I heard the opinions regarding my gender in the fashion industry. When you typed, "are male models . . ." into the Google search bar, the suggestions included tall, stupid, insecure, rich, and photoshopped.

I think most people would be surprised to learn that my reading material included subjects pertaining to the destruction of marine ecosystems, particularly coral bleaching, and the benefits of offshore wind farms. I wanted to save the reefs, but the Earth was losing that battle far too rapidly.

Glancing at my clock I noted the time. *Fuck.* I needed sleep. In a few short hours, I would have to be up and at The Harbour Polo Club for my final practice before leaving for Palmetto Bluff. I tossed my phone onto the nightstand, flipped onto my side and blew out a breath hoping my mind would stop working overtime thinking about Harlow Trembley. I don't know why I bothered though, since we were going to be together for the next several days in close quarters and if I was being honest I wasn't sad about that— not one bit.

Chapter
Twenty

Harlow

"**A**s your friend and your consultant for 'Operation Bone Grady James,' I am giving you this advice, first you need to get your nails done, then your hair and you must stop by La Vienne Rose for some sexy French lingerie pieces," Afton instructed over the phone. "And make sure you've waxed."

"Oh my God, I am *not* sleeping with him. But, for your information, I've already been buffed and waxed."

Sure, I'd fantasized about Grady, but over more than his body, I wanted his mind. It's a different kind of intimacy to have someone who understands your mind. Things with Grady were interesting, he offered more than just a pretty boy smile and an ass that wouldn't quit.

"He's taking you to Palmetto Bluff. It's beautiful, secluded and romantic—that place oozes sex. Grady will have no problem charming the panties right off you."

"So, you're saying that I'm easy," I joked.

"No, but he did ask you to be his fake girlfriend. And in my opinion, he absolutely wants to sleep with you."

Rolling my eyes, I pivoted on my heel and slid right into the display case of lemons and limes at the market. My shopping basket managed to hook the edge causing an avalanche of citrus fruit, nearly taking out a family of four.

Shit. I didn't even say goodbye I just killed the call and dropped my phone into my bag. Mortified didn't even begin to describe how I felt.

A little boy traipsed up to me and handed me a lemon. "Mommy likes these in her adult beverages too."

The mom gave me a nod and mouthed, "Aisle twelve."

Booze, here I come.

I'd seen better days. In under an hour, the morning went from bad to worse. I managed to break the heel of my favorite pair of shoes. The cherry on top was dumping a large iced coffee all over the side of my new car. As much as I hated to admit it, agreeing to go away with Grady might have set a series of unfortunate events in motion.

Perhaps this was the universe's way of telling me I'd made a mistake. After a ten minute freak out session, and downing a glass of champagne, I searched the internet in desperation to replace my shoes. I hoped that I could order them and have them delivered to the hotel where we were staying.

Sold out.

Not the color I needed.

Had the color, but not in my size.

Instead of throwing my laptop into Afton's pool, I decided to walk away slowly. A stroll along the beach would take my mind off my crappy day. The one thing about being near the water is that it calms the soul. Wading into the water, I watched as my feet sank deeper into the sand.

Thunder rumbled in the distance, as the clouds swirled and chased away the sun. I walked so long I hadn't noticed the mass number of beachgoers had dissipated. Looking up at the sky, a droplet of water hit my cheek. My eyes redirected to the ocean, to see the storm approaching.

I darted back down the beach to Afton's place. My lungs burned and my quads ached as I pushed myself further. I needed to take up running again apparently. Thunder boomed, doing its best to unleash the rain.

I made it back to Afton's place just before the sky ripped open and unleashed a downpour.

Was it too early to just go to bed?

I had to finish packing because Grady was picking me up in twenty minutes. *Fuck.* I had some major outfit changes to make in a little amount of time.

Our car pulled up to the front of a beautiful white house that oozed classic Southern style. It reminded me of something out of a movie with its white columns and old street lamps. Once the driver unloaded the luggage, our butler took them to our rooms—separate accommodations.

After dumping my handbag onto the bench at the end of the bed, I flopped forward. I landed on the cozy comforter and grasped all the icy white softness I could. This king bed was like a dream, and I didn't want to move. As I rolled onto my side I couldn't focus on anything other than Grady. Staring out the window, I drank in the sight of the lagoon and the grounds.

Afton was right, this place is romantic. The first day of summer did not disappoint.

"Mr. James," I heard our butler, Vernon, call out from the hallway. "The car will arrive in forty minutes to take you and Miss Trembley to the polo grounds."

"Thank you, Vernon."

"My pleasure. May I get you a drink, sir?"

I couldn't make out Grady's response, but I knew that I needed to freshen up. Haven had emailed our itinerary, and first up was the charity polo scrimmage match, followed by a cocktail reception. I'd purchased the perfect dress to wear to the polo event: a navy and cream striped dress with a belt at the waist. La Vienne Rose.

Knock. Knock.

At the sound of rapping against the door, I looked up from the bed to see Grady leaning against the doorjamb—shirtless. It took everything inside me to not let my eyes bug out of my head.

"I see that you are making yourself comfortable," he smirked.

Propping myself up on my elbow, I smiled. "This bed is something else, and the view of lagoon is breathtaking."

"It is." He glanced at his watch. "Well, you better hustle, we have to leave soon."

As I eased up off the bed, Vernon appeared in the

doorway carrying a tray which held champagne and sparkling water. Grady smiled at me, and I shook my head.

After the glasses were poured, and Grady offered Vernon
a glass of sparkling water, the three of us raised our glasses in
a toast. Grady James was full of surprises. I really liked that
about him.

I had a front row seat under a white canopy to admire my
sexy roommate for the next few days. Gazing around the are-
na, my fingers traced over the neatly pressed linen. I spotted
him right away in his navy and white jersey with the number
four emblazed on the back. He looked regal, and handsome
on horseback. *Just as I imagined.*

The smack of the mallet lashed out like a thunderbolt,
sending my heartbeat drumming in my ears. The horses gal-
loped up and down the field in an exuberant fashion. Expertly
hooking his stick around the opposing player, Grady swung
in defense. The ball was knocked away, and they raced back
up the field. Grady's arm swung back in perfect forehand shot
form. The ball flew to player number three allowing him to
score with ease. Whistles and cheers of appreciation erupted
from the crowd. After six chukkas, the match came to an end.

The players dismounted, and handed over their equip-
ment. I sipped my drink, the specialty cocktail was an
Elderflower Spanish Gin and Tonic. In the distance, the
bright blue sky began to dim to a light grey.

"Well, well, if it isn't my little Harlot."

Fuckity fuck, fuck, fuck it all. I knew that goddamn

voice—a voice that was attached to bad memories and laced with venom.

My father would have the ability to turn blue skies grey. "I'm not *your* anything. My name is Harlow, and in your old age you've probably forgotten the correct pronunciation. Shouldn't you be jerking off somewhere else?"

He took a seat in the empty chair to my left and I scanned the crowd looking for Grady. "Sitting all alone are you?"

"Actually, this table was reserved for me, *privately*," I said, gesturing to the card with my name on it that sat in front of a vase filled with an artful arrangement of delphiniums, roses, hydrangeas and hyacinths.

"Spreading your legs for a few polo players, are you?" he asked jutting his chin towards the field. Embarrassment flooded through me at my father's words. My eyes landed on Grady, he was chatting with the player wearing the number three jersey.

"God, you are a piece of work. Do you think that it's okay to speak to me that way?" I asked, feeling my cheeks heat.

Monty got to his feet, and leaned close. "Are you a lesbian or slut like that whore mother of yours was? I can't imagine any man with any decency that would come sniffing around your worthless fat ass." My father should take a good long look in the fucking mirror at his portly physique.

The fat ass comment stopped bothering me long ago. I wasn't fat. Worthless, now that was another story. It was hard to feel self-worth when the man who was supposed to be your father didn't even care about you as a human being. I had the desire to scream and shout that he was wrong. That there *was* a man interested in me and he was standing across the field, but I suppressed my urge. The man didn't earn any right to the details about my life. He lost that a long time ago.

He strode off laughing and that's when I caught a glimpse of his latest gold digger. I watched as the two of them rubbed elbows and sipped champagne with some of the most elite members of the polo society, a mass of power players—politicians, entrepreneurs, and celebrities. Couldn't these affluent people see what a terrible person Montgomery Sinclair was? I wondered if they would care about the fact that he'd disowned his children. All the money in the world and my father was the least classy person that I knew.

Seething with aggravation, I downed my drink and then motioned for another. Perhaps my mother had it right when she started drinking before noon. Staying aloof was probably the only way she could tolerate my father when they were married.

Forget the drink. I needed to get out of here. Pushing to my feet, I grabbed my purse and walked briskly to the main tent. The people all blurred together and my mind wandered to Grady. How would I even begin to explain my father to him?

I hated telling Harry about my father and what he'd done to me. The thought of telling someone else I was estranged from my father, and the fact that he disowned us, was an awful feeling. Sickness swirled in the pit of my stomach. Tears welled in my eyes, as much as I tried to push them down.

"Harlow, hey," Grady called out to me.

I stopped near the bar of the main tent, and held the tears at bay. Turning around I plastered a smile onto my face. "Hi, nice match. Congratulations on the win."

"Thanks, are you leaving?" His brow furrowed. "You should stick around for the trophy ceremony." He hooked his thumb back towards the field.

"Um," I paused, feeling blush spread across my neck. "I

would but I'm not feeling all that well. I think I'll just go back to the house."

"Oh, I'm sorry to hear that. In that case, let me grab my gear and I'll go with you."

God, why are you so damn sweet.

"No, you stay. You played well, you deserve to celebrate," I replied. "Thanks again for inviting me, Grady, and congratulations."

I slipped through the crowd, and made my way towards the valet to call for our driver. It was better this way. I'd spare him the agony of my sour mood that would lead to a conversation wherein I spent all evening complaining about my father and revealing dirty family secrets.

It's better this way.

Chapter
Twenty-One

Grady

It was eight o'clock and Harlow was nowhere to be found. The good news was that Vernon said that she had returned and changed clothes after the match. I guess she wanted to go for a walk.

So here I sat on the couch, catching up on the day's baseball games. Sports Center and a cold beer, this was not at all how I pictured this day ending. I wanted it to end with Harlow. If I was being totally honest, I wanted my day to begin with her as well. Perhaps I was turning into the lonely divorcé after all this time. My bed had seen better days. It had been a long time since I'd woken up next to woman.

Blowing out a harsh breath, I walked to the kitchen to discard my empty beer bottle. Reaching into the fridge, I grabbed another beer and then plodded back to the couch.

I thought Harlow wasn't feeling well earlier, but now

thinking back the expression on her face and the way her hands gripped her purse told me that she was upset. It was as if she couldn't get away from me fast enough.

Lightning lit up the muggy sky, thunder shaking the house. I popped off the top of my beer when my phone chimed, probably a severe weather alert.

Where are you, Harlow?

Instead, of the weather it was a message from one of my longtime polo friends, Ridge Stephens.

Ridge: Hanging out at The Inn. Wet t-shirt contest happening thanks to the rain. You in?

My thumb hovered over the screen as I formulated my response. I just wasn't up for it, plus I wanted to be here in case Harlow returned. Thunder roared out unleashing buckets of rain.

Grady: Sorry, buddy, thanks for the offer. I'm exhausted from the match. Raincheck?

A sharp knock at the front door, and I glanced to my phone. Fuck, Ridge was impatient. I pulled the handle to find Harlow standing on the porch. Her clothes soaked from the rain, and her auburn hair perfectly slicked back as if she'd styled it that way on purpose.

"Harlow . . ."

"I'm sorry about running off earlier. Today has been a really shitty day." Blowing out a deep breath, she ran her palms over her wet hair. "This morning I broke the heel off my favorite pair of Jimmy Choo's. I managed to dump coffee down the side of my car, and I caused an avalanche of citrus fruits at the market that almost took out four people."

"And now you're here—with *me.*"

She crossed the threshold, and her hands framed my face. "You have a crazy ex-wife and I have Daddy issues. I'm thinking that we can fuck ourselves into some pretty amazing orgasms."

My brows lifted. "Daddy issues, huh?" I asked, as my hands landed on her waist.

Her teeth grazed over her bottom lip as she nodded.

I kicked the door closed. "I can work with that." I hoisted her up and she roped her arms and legs around me. I slammed her back against the wooden door, and crushed my lips to hers. She moaned, as I grazed my tongue against hers.

She pulled back breathless, her palms smoothing over my shoulders. "By the way, I'm sorry I said your ex-wife was crazy. I wasn't trying to be insensitive."

I kissed down her throat and across her collarbone. "Well, she *is*, so . . ."

My eyes met hers. Harlow's mouth pulled into a tiny smile, and her hands wrapped around the nape of my neck drawing me to her lips once more. "I'm sorry sometimes I forget not everyone on Earth is a sensitive pussy who needs a trigger warning." The words came out a little broken, as her teeth chattered.

"You're freezing. Let's get you out of those wet clothes and into a hot bath."

"You know," she said, her body shaking as I set her feet to the ground. "There are other ways to warm me up."

"You've got a dirty mind, and I *like* what you're suggesting, but we'll get to that." I grasped her hand, leading her through the living room and up the stairs to the master bath. As she stripped out of her clothes, I turned on the shower.

"I thought you wanted me to take a hot bath?

"I want to warm you up slowly. First, you rinse off in the shower. I'm going to draw a bath, light some candles and pour the wine."

"Grady James, you really know how to treat a girl on a first date."

"Fourth."

"What?"

"This is our fourth date *technically*," I pointed out. "We shared drinks and conversation at Pour Fest. Then we ate dinner at the Cuban restaurant. I'm totally counting the pint we shared at Rum Bar as a date. And you've come here on this little trip with me—that's four. I'm thinking about including the polo match as a date as well. A date within the date."

She raised a brow, seeming unconvinced. *I'm sweetening the argument.*

"I think you could use a nice meal and a bottle of wine." I slid my fingers under the straps of her pink lace bra, needing to touch her skin.

"I'll accept the Cuban Restaurant as a date, because you paid, and I'm willing to accept Pour Fest even though you didn't ask me out," she said, her hands grasping at the hem of my shirt. "Rum Bar is a stretch, but this weekend totally counts."

This girl. We *were* going to see each other naked and she wanted to debate specifics on the number of dates we've had.

"Good, I'm glad that we agree." My knuckles grazed down her arms. "We should discuss my earlier proposal. I think we can give them something to talk about."

She tilted her head, staring up at me with those gorgeous eyes. "Possibly, but what if I told you that I was just in it for the sex?"

It took everything inside me not to haul her up on my shoulder and carry her caveman style into my bedroom, but this needed to be on her terms. I wouldn't push.

"You strip, and get into that shower." My fingers tugged under her chin.

Stepping away, I opened the door to the linen closet. She stood gazing at me, as I hung a towel on the hook outside the shower for her. I turned on the bath, and then added in foaming lavender bath salts.

"Do you take baths frequently?" she asked, waggling her eyebrows. "You seem like an expert."

"Hardly, but I've read somewhere that women love taking them. I'll come back shortly, once you're in the shower." As much as I didn't want to, I left her alone in the bathroom.

I raced downstairs. I wondered about her earlier comment regarding "Daddy issues." Was it something she wanted to talk about?

The wine selection was incredible, and I hadn't even visited the wine cellar in the house. Ultimately, I selected a bottle of Sancerre from the wine fridge, and then a glass from the cabinet. There was a freshly prepared margherita pizza in the fridge or Vernon said we could order anything from the Inn's kitchen. *Fuck the food, for now.*

My attention slipped back to Harlow, who was in my bathroom and very naked right now. As I walked down the hallway I heard her voice. She went back and forth between humming and singing. Leaning against the wall, I listened as she whipped through the chorus of "Needed Me" by Rihanna.

"Are you just going to stand outside the door all night or come inside?"

Her voice was low and husky—relaxed. I gripped the handle and slowly pushed the door open. As I stepped farther into the space, I saw that she was in the bath, with her eyes closed and her arms resting on the sides. The water hit just above the rise of her breasts.

God, I wanted her.

"Wine?" I asked, splashing liquid into the glass.

"Yes, please."

I handed her the glass, and she smiled. "Did you plan on joining me?"

"I could, if that is what you'd like?"

She sipped the wine. "I don't plan on being in here that much longer."

I cocked a brow. "Oh no?"

She passed me the glass and then I took a long drink, finishing the contents. I poured another glass as I pondered over ten possible scenarios. Incredible restraint on my part, it took all I had not to jump into the tub with all my clothes on. Instead, I pulled the wooden stool up beside the tub, and sat facing her. Handing her the glass, I stared into her eyes.

"No," she shook her head, and sipped from the glass. "I plan to be in your bed, writhing beneath you while you give me the best orgasm I've ever had."

I smirked. "Such a dirty girl, I could have sworn that you were an angel."

She winked, and handed the wine back to me. "Guess you were wrong."

For once, I was so very glad to be wrong. I set the wine glass aside, and then dipped my hands into the water. Harlow's tongued darted over her bottom lip, and she glanced up at me through her dark lashes. My fingers trailed up the inside of her thigh, her breath hitched at the caress of my hand sliding higher. She held my gaze, her hazel eyes brimming with lust.

Harlow was gorgeous. She was raw and open to me—absolutely stunning. My fingers stroked higher, and she parted her legs. She wanted this, she wanted me.

The foam from the bath salts dissipated revealing her breasts. Teasing her, I glided my fingertips along her ribcage up to the underside of her breast and I couldn't resist cupping the soft flesh in my hand. Harlow arched into my touch, as the scent of lavender permeated my senses. A soft moan was my reward when my fingers carefully rolled her nipple.

That sound, it was beautiful, and I wanted to hear it again. Her hands gripped the sides of the tub, as my fingers skated down her stomach. Another wave of lavender washed over me, as her legs stirred beneath the water.

I was inches away from thrusting inside her and finger fucking her into the first of many orgasms I intended to give her. Weeks of fantasizing about Harlow did nothing to prepare me for this moment of having my hands all over her naked body.

"Grady," she moaned.

"Yes."

"You should kiss me now, or I'm going lose my damn mind."

"Dirty and demanding, what a treat for me."

Harlow shifted, dragging her wet hands through my hair pulling me closer. Water splashed everywhere, but I didn't care. She crushed her lips to mine, for a hurried and impatient kiss. I drove my tongue against hers with the same hungry need.

Before I knew it, I had hauled Harlow out of the tub dragging her body against mine. Her hands grasped the hem of my t-shirt pulling it up as far she could and then I took over the task. Her hands went to my shorts, pushing them along with my boxers to the floor. After getting a good look at my cock, she looked up at me, those beautiful eyes wide gazing into mine.

"Grady," she whispered. "I need you to take me to bed, *now.*"

The heat in her eyes brightened, and I wasted no time carrying her off to my bed where I couldn't wait to see how many times I could make her call out my name.

Chapter
Twenty-Two

Harlow

Grady's hands dug into my ass, alternating between kneading and caressing my bare flesh. I was in his bedroom, naked and kissing him. This was way better than my paradise sex fantasy.

Naked *and* kissing him. Yes, it was worth repeating.

He kissed me hard, slipping his tongue deep inside my mouth. My fingers brushed down his chest and over his abs. The scent of clean soap mixed with an incredible spice tantalized my senses. I was mindless. Lust swamped my veins, frying any rational thought my brain was processing.

His hands tangled in my hair, and his erection pushed into my stomach. "Just the one orgasm, then?"

"Two, *three*," I moaned, while his lips trailed up my neck, nipping at the skin beneath my earlobe.

"Multiples, those are my specialty," he murmured, lifting

me up and then dragging me to the middle of the bed.

I was certain that everything was this man's specialty. For the love of God, he was one of the sexiest men on the planet. Not that looks were an automatic guarantee for being a sensational kisser, a phenomenal lover or even a gifted—*what was I saying?* Grady's lips swept across my collarbone as his fingers drifted to my breast. My entire body felt jellied and all we'd done was kiss.

"What happened earlier today?"

The question, it was too heavy, and answers even heavier. I couldn't talk about my bastard of a father, especially not while I was in bed with Grady. These aren't the sort of pillow talk moments you want on the . . . *fourth* . . . *third* . . . date.

Redirection needed now.

"Why did you ask me on this trip?"

He kissed down my throat and across my chest, licking the valley between my breasts.

His eyes met mine, as his fingers danced just above my center. I rubbed against him, silently begging for the friction I so badly wanted. "I wanted to spend time with you," he murmured, dropping his lips to my breast sucking my nipple into his mouth. "I'd be lying if I said, I haven't thought about you once or twice in the last few weeks—usually it involves you being naked."

My hands tugged in this hair. "Oh, Grady, *fuck.*"

"You are so beautiful."

He eased a finger inside me and I heard myself moan. My hips came up off the bed, when he added a second finger sending bursts of electricity to every cell in my body. He crushed his lips to mine, his fingers working a delicious friction.

"Grady, please, *more.*"

"I want to hear that sound," he growled against my breast. "You breathless and calling my name, begging me to fuck you."

Oh God, *yes*. Grady James was a dirty talker. The scruff on his sharp jawline, every scratch sent my blood rushing through my veins. A shiver vibrated through me, and I couldn't stop my orgasm sending me soaring over the edge at warp speed.

"That's one," he whispered in my ear.

His fingers continued massaging me, stoking the fire that burned deep inside. It was too much. Too intense.

"Grady, you gotta give me a minute."

He twisted his wrist and gently slowed his rhythm. "Anything you want, sweetheart," he rasped.

His fingers left my body, and I groaned at the loss. "I'll be right back." He pressed a kiss to my lips and then jumped out of bed. I felt a wide lazy grin tug at the corners of my mouth. I rolled up and then slipped between the soft fabric of his sheets.

That just happened. Grady James had given me a wonderfully mind-blowing orgasm, and that was with just his fingers. Holy shit. The sex would have to be incredible.

The last few weeks had been stressful, but right now I was anything but stressed. All the tension and worry liquefied and drained out of my body.

For the first time in weeks I finally had a full night's sleep. It was the first time I didn't wake up every hour on the hour.

Or even at my usual five a.m.—waking up at that ungodly hour had been my ritual since my days at NYU. The wonderful thing about rising before the break of dawn in Manhattan was that you could hear yourself think—actually *think*.

The reasons for not hitting the snooze button were simple, the hours between four and seven a.m. were the city's most poetic hours. On any given day, it was a roulette wheel of chance from spotting naked taxi-cab hailers, to a possible Cardinal Dolan sighting and according to an ex hookup of mine, it was the perfect time to get a haircut.

On this morning, the smell of fresh coffee beckoned me from dreamland. When I peeled my eyes open, the realization that I was in Grady's bed hit me like a tidal wave. I thought it had all been a dream. If this was a dream, don't bother waking me up because I wanted to see how it would end.

Chapter
Twenty-Three

Grady

When I came back upstairs to the bedroom, Harlow was nowhere to be found. I walked towards the bathroom stopping short of the door realizing she might be on the other side. Instead, I went back downstairs to the kitchen and was caught off guard at the sight of Harlow standing there wearing only a pair of black cotton panties and nothing else. Her back was to me, and her hair was piled up into a knot. Although I loved seeing the slope of her neck, I preferred when she wore her hair down, something about her long copper colored strands begged to be pulled and wrapped around my fist.

My eyes travelled down her back, pausing a moment at her perfectly sculpted ass. She rolled up to the balls of her feet and that drew my attention to her legs and those shapely calves. All those weeks, I'd waited much too long to have my hands on her body. Last night hadn't been enough, it wasn't near enough.

Patience flew out the window. Taking hurried steps across the wood floor to reach her, I needed to taste her, wanting to feel her skin in my hands.

My hand slipped between the fabric and her skin easing her panties down over the swell of her ass. She sucked in a breath, as a shiver raced over her body. Harlow gripped the edge of the counter when I pushed my fingers inside her, moving them in and out.

My hand wrapped around the base of her throat, pulling her mouth towards mine. I kissed her as hard as I fucked her with my fingers. Our tongues thrashed together, and she arched further into my touch.

"Oh my God, Grady," she moaned.

I wanted to hear my name on her lips, just like that for the rest of my days. Curling my fingers inside her, I felt her walls begin to surge and contract.

"Yes, *yes*, don't stop." Her palms slapped against the counter when her final release arrived. Moans and curses bounced off the walls as Harlow rode my hand clinging to her orgasm.

"I'm not even close to stopping with you."

She turned to face me, and I gripped her panties sliding them back up and over her ass. A lazy smile crossed her lips, as she leaned against the counter.

"Take your hair down."

She reached up pulling the holder from her hair. Her silky strands fell in a sexy tangle around her shoulders. Harlow roped her arms around my neck, pulling me closer for a kiss. With our bodies pressed tightly together, I lifted her off the ground and she coiled her legs around my waist.

Palming her ass, she flexed against my erection.

Harlow groaned at the contact, the sensation sparking between us was palpable, but I wasn't about to have a quick fuck in the kitchen. Wasting no time, I carried her back up the stairs and down the hallway.

With her hands sliding into my hair and her tongue gliding against mine, it was a miracle I'd made it up the flight of stairs to the bedroom. Setting her feet to the ground, her nails scraped down my back sending a fine tremor of pleasure winding through me, touching every nerve in my body. I lifted my hands to her face, and kissed her, pouring into it everything I had—weeks' worth of emotion.

"Grady," she sighed, her fingers digging into my shoulders.

"Do you always walk around topless?" I asked, palming her tits in my hands.

Her lips pulled into a tiny smile. "Every other Sunday, sometimes on Thursdays, and definitely on holidays."

"Damn, guess I just caught you on a rare occasion."

I kissed across her chest licking the valley between her breasts. She moaned, and her nails scraped across my scalp.

"It was a special occasion, to seduce you."

Laughing, I tipped my face to meet hers. "Your plan worked. I'm under your spell."

Her palms smoothed over my shoulders and down my chest. "I've had this fantasy . . ." Her hazel eyes twinkling deviously.

I cocked a brow. "A fantasy, tell me more."

Harlow gripped the hem of my t-shirt pulling it up over my stomach.

"Well," she whispered. "It's you, and then there's me and we're on a beach."

I tugged my shirt up over my head and tossed it onto the floor. The two of us on a beach—outside. In public. This was a woman after my own filthy desires. If this fantasy was half as dirty as the ones I'd been conjuring in my head . . . *fuck*, the thought of her thinking of me and thinking naughty was enough.

"I had this fantasy that you and I were on a location shoot in the Caribbean . . ."

The words rolled off her tongue with a heated rasp. I nipped and kissed her skin, breathing in the lavender scent that lingered. I kissed her everywhere I could reach without dropping to my knees. At my height of six foot she was two inches shorter than me.

"During the shoot, we remained completely professional but when the cameras stopped rolling. That's when you and I would, well, you get the gist."

"I don't want the gist, woman, I want every dirty detail or I can just make up some stuff and you can tell me if I'm making your fantasy come true. I'm up for the challenge either way."

"I like the sound of that, surprise me."

I pulled her panties to the side probing my fingers against her, dragging the slickness up and over her ass and then slipping my finger inside her. "I want you to come all over my cock, beautiful."

In a blur of movements, I had us stripped out of what little clothing we were both wearing and dragged her up the middle of my bed. Possessiveness took hold, and I pinned her beneath me. My tongue traced her nipple as her nails scraped up my back. Her flavor filled my senses while my teeth nipped over her skin.

I pushed up and stared down at her for a moment. "You

are so beautiful." And it was the moment I'd been fantasizing about—all those auburn waves fanned out over pillows and it was better than I fucking imagined.

My fingers thrust deep inside her, pumping in and out. "Oh God, Grady. Oh God. Oh God."

I twisted my fingers, hitting all the right spots. On a cry of my name, her hips shot up off the bed. I wanted all her screams. I wanted all her moans. I wanted to fuck her until neither of us could see straight. My hand flew to the nightstand where I grabbed the condoms I put there last night. Yeah, I was a man with a plan.

"Fucking you now, beautiful," I said as I rolled the condom down my shaft.

I spread her legs wide, nudging her wet center, teasing her with the tip of my cock before slamming into her, giving her the fucking of her life. I'd taken my time with her last night but now I couldn't wait any longer. I needed to be inside Harlow.

"Fuck, *yes*. Yes!"

Her nails dug into my biceps as I pounded into her. "Grady. Oh my God. Grady!"

Harlow chanted my name over and over making me feel like a king, a god even. I kissed her neck, nibbling that soft spot under her ear.

"Please, oh, don't stop."

My hands gripped her hips as I drove into her unleashing everything I had, giving her exactly what she needed. Fuck. She felt so fucking good. An orgasm stirred at the base of my spine. Her walls tightened around my cock and I knew that she was close too.

"Harlow, let go, sweetheart."

My name spilled from her lips on a long moan. I tilted

my hips towards her clit going deeper. The spasms of her orgasm rippled around my cock.

"Grady, *yes*," she whimpered, her body jerking beneath me. My hips rolled against her, and she rocked against me in response. My orgasm erupted taking us both over edge—her *again*.

"Holy fuck, you're amazing," she said, trying to regain her breathing.

I leaned down pressing my chest to hers, my cock still pulsing inside her body. She pulled my face to hers for a long slow kiss.

"Yeah, we're definitely doing *that* again."

A warm lazy smile appeared on her lips. She was perfect—undeniably sexy. I disentangled our bodies, and rolled out of the bed to discard the condom.

"Yeah, I think I'd like to do that again," she said, rolling onto her stomach. I watched as she shoved a hand through her hair sliding it all to one side.

I eyed her, trying to get a read on what *she* wanted. Just sex? We had chemistry, that was clear, but I wasn't going to push her into anything she didn't want.

Leaning down, I pressed my fists to the bed. "You want to go again right now, sweetheart? I'm game."

Harlow rolled up to her knees, dragging the sheet across her body. My eyes met hers, when her fingers slid through my chest hair. "Maybe, but first let's chat about this arrangement you mentioned before."

"You're considering being my fake girlfriend. The sex sealed the deal, huh?"

Ignoring my question, she asked one of her own. "What should the rules . . . *terms* be?"

Rule one, you only fuck me.

"I think the terms should be simple. Attend events together. A few date nights or days, causal encounters like coffee shop dates, trips to the farmers' market or working out. Trips like this, I think the Caribbean is a must. And you're definitely going to be my date for Ronan Connolly's wedding in August."

That sated smile returned to her lips. "Do you really think we could convince people that we're in a relationship?"

"After what we just did, I don't see how it's *not* possible. We have chemistry, Harlow."

"And you're a good actor."

"Just good?" I joked, climbing back onto the bed, and dragging Harlow down with me. "I don't believe I'll have to do any acting with you."

Where Harlow was concerned, this wasn't an act. Although, I wasn't completely sure what I was doing, but for now I didn't need to have the entire plan rolled out. My fingers mapped along the curve of her hip. What I did know, is that I didn't want to move from this spot—maybe for the rest of the summer.

Chapter
Twenty-Four

Harlow

The early evening sky was a glowing mixture of gold and pink. The warm breeze whipped over my skin as Grady wrapped his arm around my waist pulling me closer. Heat spread everywhere, sliding through my veins igniting my deep need for him. He looked incredibly sexy wearing a black tuxedo with a white bowtie.

We smiled for the cameras, and the two of us waved to the crowd as we posed for photos on the red carpet before the charity dinner. We talked and laughed all the way down the press line. Nothing about this felt staged, forced, or the slightest bit awkward. Nervous, *sure*.

"Harlow, who are you wearing?"

I smiled at the reporter. "This is a custom Charlotte Ricchetti design and the strappy heels are Sergio Rossi. The jewels are my own."

She gazed at my diamond earrings. "A gift from your date?"

I laughed. "Nope, these belonged to my mother."

"Have I told you how beautiful you look this evening?" Grady whispered into my hair, sweeping me down the line. "This sheer gown is inspiring illicit thoughts."

Keeping my eyes forward, I answered, "A few times, but you can tell me again."

"Grady, are you and Harlow dating?" someone from the crowd shouted.

"Yes, do you want to confirm the rumors that Harlow is the mystery woman?" another voice called out.

Grady chuckled. "You mean the rumors that you guys started?"

That earned him a generous laugh from the crowd. When Grady looked at me, I couldn't contain my smile. He owned the red carpet, and commanded the attention of every single woman here.

"That's a perfect answer," he said. "We don't need to say anything, y*et*."

I nodded in agreement, as we walked into the ballroom. Large wooden poles adorned with a flowing assortment of greenery and white flowers were anchored all around the room. White candles in tiny vases hung off the branches. It reminded me of an outdoor restaurant in the French Riviera.

My gaze stopped on a woman in a silver gown, she looked exactly like the woman I'd seen on my father's arm at the polo match. As I scanned the crowd, dread wound its way through me at the thought of my father being here in the same room as Grady and me.

A tall man with jet black hair and green eyes approached us with a curvaceous blonde in a single-shoulder red gown on his arm. "What are you doing all the way over here, James?" he asked, jutting his broad chin. "The roulette tables are way over there."

"No worries, I plan to drop a sizeable donation later," Grady assured as he slapped the man's shoulder.

"Are we going to raise a ton of money tonight or what?"

"I have a good feeling that we will exceed last year's total." Grady grasped my hand. "Ridge, you remember Harlow.

We exchanged hellos, and then Ridge smiled gesturing towards the blonde sipping champagne. "This is Marcy."

She rolled her eyes. "It's actually Marni," she corrected. "Ridge and I met the other evening. It's a pleasure to meet you both."

Ridge whispered something into her ear and a slow smiled appeared on her glossy pink lips. "Catch you later, James, the roulette table awaits."

As we walked through the enormous space, Grady's arm left my waist for a moment to shake someone's hand then returned. He leaned in kissing me on the lips. Cheers erupted from the black jack table, effectively breaking our moment.

He smiled at me in the dim light. "Walk with me."

Grady led me through a darkened hallway and up a grand staircase. When my foot hit the last step, he pushed my back up against a wall. It was much darker up here, only tea lights atop a few cocktail tables lit up the space. Slipping his hand underneath the slit at the side of my gown, his fingers drew circles on my thighs. "I want to fuck you here." His fingers dipped lower, pushing my thong aside, and finding me completely wet.

"But, what about dinner?"

"Personally, I don't give a fuck about food." He glanced at his watch. "However, we have twenty-three minutes."

"You can fuck me in twenty-three minutes?"

He cocked a brow. "That's plenty of time to give you a mind-blowing orgasm, cleanup, and then grab a drink."

His finger eased into my pussy, teasing me with a tantalizing rhythm. "Show me what you got Mr. James."

"Your pussy is so wet. Is this all for me?"

I heard myself moan, a little too loudly, but with the way he was stroking me I could care less. It was too good. "*Yes*, all for you, Grady."

"Good answer. Fuck me, sweetheart. I want you to come all over my cock again," he rasped, fisting his hand into my hair.

"Take my cock out, *now*, Harlow. I need to fuck you. Condom is in the left pocket inside my jacket."

I reached inside his jacket and took out the condom. Lost in a haze of lust, my hands fumbled with his zipper. His hands cupped my face, as I ripped open the foil packet with my teeth.

"*Now*, Harlow, put me inside you."

This display confirmed that the rumors about Grady loving public sex were in fact true. His hands palmed my ass, as he kissed his way up my neck. I pushed to my tiptoes, positioning him at my center. He was thick, and hard—perfect. I nearly lost my mind when my thumb brushed against my clit as I sank onto his cock.

"You feel incredible," he said, his words were deep and seductive. "Do you feel that?"

As he fucked me slowly, lighting up every cell in my body, I kissed him deeply, our tongues finding one another over and over. My hands gripped his shoulders when he picked up the pace, our movements hurried and unapologetic.

"Oh yes, fuck me."

Grady had awakened my senses and stirred my soul. It was crazy how much I enjoyed that. My hips jerked, seeking more contact. More. Deeper. Harder.

"Please, I need . . . need . . ."

"I know exactly what you need," he said, picking up the pace.

Everything tightened and coiled and I knew that I was close. It didn't take much because his fingers were right there sending me soaring off into oblivion. I wanted to scream, but all could do was moan into his shoulder, muffling the sounds of my orgasm as Grady pounded into me unleashing his own orgasm.

"Did you enjoy that, Harlow?" His lips found mine once more kissing me, his fingertips whispered up and down my back. "I know you loved that, and I want to hear that dirty little mouth admit it."

"Yes," I murmured against his lips.

"And you wanted me to fuck you here like this, didn't you?" he asked, his teeth scraped across my neck sending hot trails of fire pricking over my skin.

"Yes," I hissed. "I wanted you to fuck me."

"Good."

The evening faded and the room had thinned from triple digits to doubles. Dinner was full of conversations about to-night's cause and the dozens more that filled the calendars of our philanthropic table companions.

I'd talked to a few women about my website and they all

seemed pretty excited to check it out. There were one or two eye rolls at the mention of my career as a Lifestyle Blogger. One woman even offered to write a few guest posts if I ever needed content.

"What's on your mind, sweetheart?" he asked, his voice thick and quiet. Our feet moved in a small circle, our bodies swaying in time with the beat of the country song playing. The words, "hit me like a hurricane" piped through the sound system and I couldn't help but think how true those words reflected our situation.

"Just wondering what will happen when our photos are splashed online later."

Pulling back, his blue eyes searched my face. "Are you having second thoughts? If you are, that's okay."

"No, not at all. Call it a general wondering."

He smiled. "What else do you wonder about?"

"Do you have a sex tape?"

"Not to my knowledge." He shook his head. "Why do you ask?"

My hands smoothed down the front of his jacket over his muscular chest. "Just wanted to know if there was any downside to being your fake girlfriend. Assessing any potential scandals."

"That's fair. So, what dark secrets are you keeping, Harlow?" His thumbs stroked lazy circles against my back. "Do *you* have a sex tape?"

"No, the thought of someone hacking into my phone creeps me out, not that it matters anyway the whole world has seen most of my body."

"I get it. It's one thing when you're on the runway or at an editorial shoot. You've consented to the job. It's another thing altogether when someone invades your privacy."

"Speaking of privacy, I should tell you that I have an IUD and I'm clean."

"I'm clean too," he whispered in my ear.

"We really know how to kill a mood, don't we?"

"My mood is perfectly pleasant," he said, shaking his head. "We're working out the logistics. It's good to know that if I wanted to fuck you bare, I could."

Wetness pooled between my thighs, at the thought of having him inside me with nothing between us. Apparently, the mood was not dead. Not at all. My hands drifted up Grady's arms, bringing them to the back of his neck.

"I think we should kiss a little more and think a lot less," he murmured, before pressing his lips below my earlobe.

"Is that so?"

He stared at me for a moment and then leaned in brushing his lips to mine. Our kiss deepened, his tongued licked mine, teasing me until my body was drowning in need. A thousand emotions flickered through me when his hands came up to frame the sides of my face. Everything about tonight had been perfect. I was almost sad we were leaving to go back to The Harbour tomorrow morning. This wasn't an ending, it was a beginning.

Chapter
Twenty-Five

Harlow

G rady James and Harlow Trembley PDA at Palmetto
Polo Pony Rescue Charity Event—Heather Young
Disgusted with Both of Them

*Can photographs tell an entire story? Grady James and
Harlow Trembley spent a hefty part of last week together.
Heather Young is furious. We're a little unsure as to why, because she had nothing but negative things to say about her
ex-husband on Wake Up with Stacy. Why would she care?*

*Whether James and lingerie model, Trembley, just hap-
pened to be at the same event respectively or if they attended
together is unclear. Sources say the pair looked quite cozy on
the red carpet together.*

*It's no secret that James, an avid polo player, loves ani-
mals. Over the years, he's helped rescue countless retired polo
ponies and been a large supporter to the Adopt Don't Shop*

Movement. Trembley isn't particularly known for her philan-
thropy as much as she is for stripping down for the runway.

A close friend of James said, "Grady and Harlow have
been friends for a long time. They were just laughing and hav-
ing a good time supporting an important cause."

But, they were holding hands. That must be a total shot
to the heart for Heather, who happens to be great friends with
Harlow as they often appeared on each other's Instagram ac-
counts. The two ladies came up in the modeling scene togeth-
er about the same time and formed a friendship because of it.
Perhaps Heather being upset has less to do about Grady and
more about her friendship with Harlow.

Dating your friend's ex—doesn't that go against the girl
code? This story is shaping up to be one filled with jealousy,
cheating and wild accusations of abuse. Are you excited about
this possible new couple alert? Tell us your thoughts in the
comments below.

And so, it begins.

"Well that didn't go as well as we planned, did it?" I
asked, rising from my seated position on the couch. The
paparazzi were waiting for us outside the airport. We
managed to ditch them and decided to hideout at Afton's
guest house.

"I love the 'great friends' mention. That's a stretch.
Heather and I, we're more like, well acquainted people who
sometimes attend the same events together out of obligation
for work. I applaud them for their stellar journalism."

"Son of bitch," Grady cursed, scrubbing a hand over the
curve of his jaw. "*Fuck,* there's nothing the world loves more
than building up celebrities only to tear them down."

I walked to the kitchen to discard my yogurt cup into
the recycling bin. Lightning flashed in the morning sky as

warm rain began to coat the deck of Afton's pool. *An omen perhaps?*

"Yeah, but *America* loves a comeback," I said, pointing my spoon in Grady's direction before tossing it into the dishwasher. "Despite the negative tone of the article, they did mention the charities—that's your silver lining."

He tilted his head, rubbing the back of his neck. "Yeah, that is a good thing. I hate the shade they're throwing your way. I need to get my name cleared of the abuse allegations."

I rested my hip against the counter. "You will and when the world finds out Heather cheated on you, oh, the shit will hit the fan."

He tugged his earlobe and then swept the pad of his thumb over his jaw. "You're right. I'm telling Haven to leak the story and then you and I are going back to my house. I want you to stay with me. Pack a bag."

Grady wanted me to stay with him, but he didn't exactly specify for how long. I didn't want to be presumptuous so I tossed in a few casual outfits and two bathing suits. It was just after one in the afternoon by the time I had my things packed. The sun started to peek through the clouds, chasing away the grey gloomy skies. We pulled onto the road that led to Grady's place to find a crowd of people outside—taking photos, shouting obscenities and shaking their fists in the air. Scowls painted their faces, and the roars of disdain became more audible.

A woman with red hair wearing a white floral dress

jogged beside us. "Grady, how could you do this to Heather?"

Another woman wearing black capris, and a pink tank top appeared on Grady's side. "You are the most deplorable kind of man!"

"You should be ashamed of yourself, you slut!" a feminine voice called out from the crowd.

This was the side of celebrity I'd never experienced. These must be those super fans I keep hearing so much about. Luckily no one did anything remotely violent, like pound on the windows or step in front of him while he was driving.

"Do you have security?" I asked, as he maneuvered his Range Rover up the driveway. Once trees cleared, my eyes took in a stunning grey, cedar shingled home with large expansive windows and white painted wood.

"I've never needed it here," he said, pulling his car into the garage. "But, I guess I should call someone now."

Once we're inside the house, Grady pulled his phone from his pocket swiping it to life. "Hey, man, I guess it's time that we have that chat about my security needs. Yeah, that sounds good."

That was all he said, before ending the call and then tossing his phone onto the kitchen counter.

"Are you okay?"

Tension rolled off him as he expelled a deep sigh. "I will be." Grasping my hand, he pulled me into his frame. "I'm just glad that you're here."

"I wouldn't be anywhere else." My fingers dug into the muscles of his back.

He kissed the top of my head, breathing me in and then his muscles relaxed. "So, this is my place—sans the horde of people outside, it's normally quiet."

It was certainly peaceful. He led me towards the living room. Everything was white accented with warm woods. There wasn't a space left untouched by natural light from the large windows that surround the two sides of his house.

"Wait, is that yours?" I asked pointing towards the large boat anchored at his dock.

"Yep, I've had my eye on her for a while." He wrapped his arms around me from behind. "And she's finally all mine."

I smiled. It was clear that he's talking about the boat, but a small part of me allowed the words to take on a different meaning.

"Have you taken *her* out yet?"

"Nope, but you'll come with me. We'll christen the boat properly."

He grasped my shoulders turning me so that I faced him. His lips captured mine in a slow kiss. It was warm, and wonderful.

The doorbell rang as we uncurled from our embrace. "That's my security appointment. You're welcome to stay or you can take your things upstairs to my bedroom."

We walked hand in hand across the room and I scooped up my bags. "I think I'll settle in and maybe get some work done while you're in your meeting."

His hands cupped my face. "There's a fully stocked bar upstairs, unwind with a glass of wine if you like."

Our lips met for a long, slow, torturous kiss that turned me into a big ball of need. If his doorbell wasn't ringing out, I'd have him upstairs and naked. The kiss ended, leaving me feeling an odd sense of loss.

Sunlight splashed over the grey-painted pine floors, as I crept up the staircase. When I landed in the master suite, the view of the ocean appeared—spectacular waves of blue spread out before me. My palms smoothed over the white comforter on his bed. Everything was white or soft beige, minimalism at its finest.

I hauled my laptop bag up onto the writing desk in the corner and began organizing a makeshift workspace. My phone buzzed against the tabletop. It was a text from Zanita. I swiped open the message, a link from one of the UK tabloids appeared:

Has Grady James netted a former WAG? Actor steps out with Harry Brackman's model ex.

A week after his blunder against Team USA, English footballer Harry Brackman has been dealt another emotional blow. The goalkeeper's ex, model Harlow Trembley was spotted on the red carpet at the Palmetto Polo Charity Event with the handsome model/actor. Rumors are circulating that the pair are dating.

Sources allege that Brackman's split from Trembley left him heartbroken and has contributed to his poor performance during England's opening match with USA.

James' ex-wife, actress Heather Young recently told US talk show host, Stacy Carlton that her ex-husband was abusive and said that he made her enter rehab to revive her career. The actress later admitted that she was devastated that Grady had moved on so quickly.

Quickly? The pair ended their marriage months ago. As for Brackman and Trembley, no one seems to know when the pair exactly called it quits. Although some sources claim she dumped him only a few weeks ago. Ouch.

I finished reading the link and sent Zanita a quick text back, thanking her for sending along the article. My fingers itched to shoot off a text to Haven asking if she had leaked the cheating story yet. Harry had yet to deny that our breakup was the cause of his terrible play. Fuck. It was starting to irritate me, but I know he doesn't read the papers when he's playing. Maybe he doesn't know what's being said. I'd give him a little more time.

But, Grady, he's not an abuser and why Heather would lie and trash his reputation was beyond me.

Chapter
Twenty-Six

Grady

Alex Robertsen crossed through my foyer, hooking his thumb over his shoulder. "What did you do, James, become an overnight celebrity?"

"Sorry about that mess outside."

"It's not your fault, my fiancée keeps me well informed where celebrity gossip is concerned. This is about what I expected."

I nodded. "You want a drink?"

"Nah, I'm good." Alex swiped the screen of his iPad. "With security, I will set you up with this system. It's the same one I have for our house, and Ella's store—top of the line. No one is getting in here. I'll have this place sealed tighter than the White House."

I wouldn't expect anything less from Robertsen Security. Alex's company was the best and I trusted his expertise.

"You have a system that includes rooftop snipers? I'm impressed, Robertsen."

His mouth twisted up, as if he'd actually entertained the idea once. "I can have one or two guys stationed on your property, whatever you like—do you want around the clock security or just a guy to have your back when you go out?"

Staring up at the beams in my living room, I shoved a hand through my hair. "What do you recommend?"

"I always recommend that celebrities, such as yourself, have security, but I understand that it can cramp your life-style. It's an adjustment. I can promise you this—any one of my guys will be as visible or invisible as you need them to be."

Weighing my options, I poured a drink. I'd never need-ed a fulltime security detail. Usually the studios would have someone who escorted me for appearances and movie pre-mieres, but I never felt the need to employ security—until today. Earlier, outside my driveway, *that* was a wakeup call. What was most important to me was Harlow's safety. I'd dragged her into this arrangement, now it was up to me to make sure both of us came out of it physically and mentally unscathed.

"I can see this is overwhelming, James. How about we do a trial run?"

I took a drink as I let his suggestion turn over in my mind. "Yeah, that sounds good."

After we squared away the details, he snapped his iPad closed. "I won't let you down, buddy. I've scheduled your in-stallation for this week and I'll be here to personally oversee it."

I blew out a sharp breath. "I appreciate that, but you're getting married in a few days. Don't you have better things to do than babysit an installation crew?"

He lifted a shoulder. "I'm the groom, all I have to do is show up."

I smirked. "Sure, buddy, keep telling yourself that."

I stepped into my bedroom, just as Harlow appeared in nothing but a towel. "Well, it looks like I'm late. You've already showered—*alone*."

"Yep, guess you're going to need to work on your timing."

I flopped back onto my bed. "My imagination is fucking you like crazy right now."

Harlow gave me an easy smile as she sauntered over to my bed. "Give me your hand."

Offering her my hand, I cocked a brow. She gripped my hand in hers and then lifted the towel revealing her bare pussy. *Holy Christ.*

Harlow positioned herself over my hand and then eased my middle finger inside her. She worked her hips finding the perfect rhythm. Her skin smelled like my soap and the wet heat of her body was intoxicating.

Watching her fuck my finger was one of the hottest things I'd ever seen in my life. Somehow I tore my gaze from where our bodies were connected meeting her hooded hazel eyes. Harlow's teeth grazed over her plump bottom lip. The zipper of my shorts bit into my balls, the aching friction sent my need for her into overdrive.

"Touch yourself," she murmured. "I want to watch you stroke your cock."

"You are such a demanding dirty girl." My eyes never

left hers as I unzipped my shorts and gripped my cock. She hummed and moaned as my hand grazed up and down my shaft with long slow strokes. A lazy smile tugged the corners of her mouth. Her movements managed to loosen the white cotton from her body and I watched it slide down exposing her breasts.

A long moan slipped from Harlow's lips sending electricity charging through my veins. She picked up her pace using my finger for her pleasure.

"More *please*."

My thumb teased over her clit, and I felt her walls tighten around my finger. When the towel hit the floor, Harlow's free hand cupped her breast. Her other hand held my finger in place, and I felt the tremors pulsing against me.

"Fuck, *Harlow*, get on my dick and let me fuck you."

She shook her head and that lazy grin returned. The wicked gleam in her eyes alone nearly had me coming undone. Harlow was enjoying the power of control. It was hot as hell.

She was wild, raw and opened to me. *Fuck.* She looked beautiful—her auburn hair swayed back and forth as unintelligible words slipped from her lips.

"Don't stop, Grady," she groaned, as the spasms rolled through her body.

My hand pumped my cock faster and I thrust my finger deeper inside Harlow giving her just what she wanted.

"Yes, yes, oh yes . . ." she chanted, shaking and riding my finger through the muscle-weakening orgasm. Waves of my own release tingled in my balls when her arousal slid down my hand. *Jesus.*

I let her ride my finger until her legs threatened to give out. In a swift motion, I pulled her on top of me. What surprised me next was when she slid down my body, and popped the button of my shorts. She gave me a wicked smile before taking my cock into her mouth. I watched with extreme fascination as my dick slid between her perfect pink lips. Her tongue swirled around the tip of my dick, teasing the underside and sucking my balls into her mouth.

"Harlow, sweetheart, I'm going to come." My voice was strained with warning.

She stared up at me, not caring, sucking me deeper. My hips shot up, and she tested her gag reflex. "Fucking hell, your sweet mouth."

Teetering on the edge of losing it, my fingers tangled in her dark hair. My eyes screwed tight as my head fell back against the pillows. Gripping my length with two hands, she sent me over the edge exploding into her mouth.

"My God, you're amazing." I blinked up at the wooden beams taking a quick moment to regain my breathing.

Her fingers brushed up my thighs, sending a shiver rattling through my bones. My gaze returned to her and I wrapped my arm around her lower back bringing her closer. She curled into my side, nuzzling the crook of my shoulder.

"I think I need another shower," she murmured, tracing her finger along the tip of my half-hard cock.

"Keep doing that and I'll have no choice *but* to fuck you—here on my bed *or* in the shower."

She rolled onto her stomach, propping herself up on her elbows. "Should I expect to become familiar with every flat surface inside this place or the entire property? I think I saw an *outdoor* shower."

"You're crazy."

"I thought we established that your ex-wife was the crazy one and you really shouldn't tell a woman that she's crazy," she said with smile.

"There are two definitions to the word, crazy," I informed, zipping my shorts. "Number one—unhinged. That one's mental state has manifested in a wild or aggressive way. Two, extremely enthusiastic and I'm particularly fascinated by the way you passionately mentioned the outdoor shower."

She shot me a pointed glance. "I'm not sure that you're expressing the term correctly, rather twisting it to fit your narrative."

"Hmm, I'd like to see you twisting that beautiful body of yours again."

"Are you some kind of sexual deviant or is everything an innuendo to you?"

"Not a deviant. But if you leave the sexual innuendo door open even a fraction, I'll come barreling through like the Kool Aid Man."

She snickered, dropping her forehead to my chest. My hand brushed up and down her back and she tossed her arm over my stomach. We laid on my bed in silence, listening to the sounds of The Harbour and my ceiling fan. My fingers continued to skim over her skin, the sight of Harlow's naked body atop my bed with sunlight splashing over her curves had a profound effect on me. If I had any talent, I'd take a photograph or paint a portrait of her capturing this moment.

"How did your meeting go?"

"Fine, I'm investing in a high-tech system complete with a security detail."

"It's probably a good idea."

"Yeah, I have another good idea—how about you accompany me to a wedding?"

"I already agreed to go to Ronan Connolly's wedding with you."

"Ronan and Holliday are a flight risk. I'm not sure the wedding they're planning is the *real* one. Knowing Connolly, he probably has decoy wedding invites out to throw off the paparazzi and gossip hounds. Those two could be getting married in Ireland tomorrow for all I know."

"I'm actually talking about his sister, Ella," I whispered. "She and her fiancé, Alex, are getting married on the twenty-fourth."

She tilted her head to look at me. "I wish I could, but I'm finally launching my website the day before."

"Congratulations, that's awesome news."

She busied herself with her phone. From the corner of my eye I saw her calendar. Yep. It was filled with meetings in New York and California. I was happy for her, but I couldn't help feeling some disappointment that she wouldn't share her good news with me. Even with all the casual sex, I thought we were at least better friends. *I sound like a douche canoe.*

"We should sync our calendars. I'm texting Haven to do that for us. Now, give me some details about the wedding."

I laughed. "You know that I can't do that, if you want details you should come as my date."

She rolled up to her knees, swinging her hair over her right shoulder. "Okay, at least tell me this, what's the dress code?"

"Formal," I answered, watching as she slid her long legs over the side of my bed.

"Location?"

"Hmm, yeah that's off limits. I'll tell you afterwards or text you during." I rolled onto my side, propping up on my forearm. "If you're looking for the wedding invitation, you won't find it."

"I figured that you'd have that locked up somewhere. I

know you have a copy of the *Preppy Handbook* somewhere here, Grady."

"That's cute, as if I needed some book to tell me how to dress."

She opened my nightstand drawer and rummaged through its contents. All my books were in my study, and the *Preppy Handbook* was not on the required reading list.

"You think you've got me all figured out, sweetheart." I stood up from the bed, stretching my arms over my head. "How about you take that shower and meet me downstairs. It's time to take the boat out."

As she zipped past me, I gave her perfect ass a quick smack. She yelped, before blowing me a kiss over her shoulder.

Chapter
Twenty-Seven

Harlow

It was a great afternoon for sailing. The waves of The Harbour were smooth as glass. I hadn't been on a sailboat since Harry and I vacationed in Capri. But, this wasn't Capri and I wasn't with Harry. Not that I needed to remind myself who was steering this vessel.

I glanced over my shoulder sneaking a peek of Grady at the helm of the boat looking devastatingly handsome in a pair of grey shorts and a dark blue t-shirt. The wind tousled his brown hair and his baby blues were hidden behind a pair of aviators

Damn. My phone was vibrating like an unbalanced washing machine. That could only mean one thing—trouble.

Zanita: Harry had a presser today. He was asked point blank about your breakup.

Zanita: He played fantastically today, by the way.

Zanita: He was about to answer when . . . someone cleared their throat.

Zanita: His entire demeanor changed. He said, "It's been a rough go of it personally, but I'm trudging on and determined to win this for England."

Harlow: What the fuck? Is he being coached by his PR team and using our breakup to gain sympathy?

Zanita: Yes, I am afraid so. My sources tell me that Harry was actually at a private party with a number of people over the weekend and cozying up to a few women. Then, he played a round of golf yesterday at a private club.

Harlow: So, it seems that he's not going to admit that he broke up with me? Fine. Fuck him.

Harlow: What are the tabloids saying about me now?

Zanita: The latest headline: Harry Brackman Crushed Over Grady James and Harlow Trembley—Lonely and Heartbroken. (Don't read the comments.)

Harlow: Seriously?

At that point my blood was boiling. My fingers twirled the ends of my hair. Where the fuck was the post about Heather cheating on Grady? Now, it seemed as if I needed to get in the game and clear the air.

I was so engrossed in my text conversation with Zanita I barely registered that Grady had anchored the boat. Shoving my phone into my pocket I contemplated my next move. Or maybe it should be *our* next move.

Grady approached me bring up a bottle of wine and two glasses. "Ahoy there."

"Hello, Captain." I took the bottle of wine and the glasses from his hand as he dropped onto one of the many cushions that decorated the bow of the boat. He poured a hefty amount of wine into my glass and I wasted no time guzzling the contents.

"What's wrong?" he asked, taking off his sunglasses and clipping them to his shirt.

"Huh?"

"I can tell there is something weighing on your mind."

"How so?"

"You crossed and uncrossed your legs at least ten times that I counted, and you twirl the ends of your hair when something is bothering you. It's your tell."

Averting my eyes, I stared into the waters of The Harbour concentrating on the ripples. I swallowed the remnants of my glass. "You're observant."

"Talk to me, Harlow. Tell me anything, you want. Even if it's, fuck off, I want to enjoy the view."

I huffed a laugh, tracing the rim of the glass with my index finger. "Where should I begin—let's see, my mother died a few months after I graduated college, after suffering a long battle with Alzheimer's. My father dumped her in a nursing home, because he couldn't handle watching her deteriorate from the disease. Personally, I think he did it because she was no longer the useful trophy wife he needed. Then my father dumped me and my brother, Nicholas—disowned I think is the proper term." My fingers fluttered in the air.

"Ah, yes, the Daddy issues you mentioned."

"He isn't a good man. He wasn't a great father in the least, but he was the only one I had." I glanced at him. "Why didn't you ask me about it that night? The night I mentioned it, I mean."

"Everyone has a chapter they don't read out loud." He threaded his fingers with mine. "I knew that was a delicate moment and when you wanted to talk about it you'd let me know or give me an opening for the conversation. Besides that, I don't think talking was *really* on your mind at that time."

He wasn't wrong. I appreciated not having the pressure to discuss the heavy stuff.

"And, do you remember that episode of *Friends* where Rachel asks Ross for some ill-advised sympathy sex?"

"Yeah," I laughed. "Ross was all like, I treated you with respect and understanding. Rachel's face—that's *so* hot!"

"See if I hadn't obliged, you would have been feeling embarrassed and mad at me."

I tapped my finger to my wine glass. "You really can associate everyday life to an episode of *Friends*. Ross did so many things wrong."

"So many."

"I'm glad you are a fellow *Friends* fan. Where do you stand on the Ross and Rachel controversy? Were they on a break or not?"

"They were on a break and here's why—because the next morning when Rachel shows up at Ross' apartment, she asks him if she can be his girlfriend, *again*, which implies that she wasn't his girlfriend previously. Case closed."

"That's a logical explanation. He still shouldn't have slept with her though."

"Uh, no, that was a terrible idea—that was never going to end well for Ross."

Time drifted by, the sounds of birds, the hum of boats filled the spaces of silence. The tension that had been residing in my neck and shoulders no longer existed. "What is it about the ocean—is it the water itself—the sounds of waves lapping against your skin, the boat, the shore?" I breathed in the salt and sun, getting my fill and letting the calm wash over me.

Grady pulled me into his side. "Never underestimate the

healing power of the ocean."

"Is that why you love The Harbour? Why you bought a home here?"

"My parents had a home here. I spent many summers in East Harbour, even a few winters. Mom loved The Harbour in the fall and winter."

"You parent's *had* a home here, where do they live now?"

"My mom lives Fenwick, Connecticut. She sold their home here after my father died. I wished she'd kept it, but it was too hard."

"Oh, I'm sorry to hear that your father died. Was his death recent?"

"No, Dad's been gone about ten years now. He died in his sleep—massive heart attack. It was Fourth of July weekend, I'll never forget because I'd just played in the Stars and Stripes Polo Challenge. They left after the trophy presentation and I'd gone out to Castle Hill to celebrate with Ridge and some of the guys. My mother and sister left the house to pick up last minute essentials for the cocktail party that evening. The day had caught up to him, I guess my father had been up late the previous evening writing his latest novel and he went to take a nap. When they came home, he was already gone."

I reached for his hand and squeezed. "That must have been a complete shock."

"It was a difficult time." He kissed the top of my head. "My father, he never saw me act. I'm not sure if he was ever proud of my career choices. He never said outright, but I don't think he was happy with my modeling. It started out as a way to pay the bills during college."

I could relate to Grady's story; my mother never saw any of my modeling work. She passed away shortly after I earned my degree.

"I didn't know that you went to college. I mean I assumed as much, but . . ."

He chuckled. "I get it believe me, I get it. I have a degree in English from Brown University."

I pulled back, shifting to face him. "Did you want to become a writer like your father?"

"I gave it the old college try for sure," he said, tucking a wayward strand of hair behind my ear. "I've written several short stories and I started a novel, but I never showed him. I've always felt like I was kind of a disappointment."

Saying nothing I grasped his hand, once more, I listened as Grady talked about his father and his summers here. He kind of had the all-American family experience, those were things that I dreamed about as a kid before the realization that my father was just not into a family experience.

"Don't get me wrong. I had a wonderful relationship with my father. He taught me how to sail, and ride a horse. I took up polo because of his encouragement and he never missed a match."

"This is going to sound silly, but what are some of the books your dad published?"

He paused for a moment, and a small smile tugged the corners of his mouth. "His name was Ian Reed."

My mouth dropped open. "Ian Reed is your father? Ian Reed, the famous novelist?"

"One in the same."

"But, *your* last name is James."

"What? You're kidding," he mused.

I tossed a pillow in his direction, and he caught it, and then tossed it right back onto my lap.

"My father was born Ian Reed James. He was advised to drop James, and go with Reed. Apparently, it was more marketable, since James is such a common name."

"And Reed isn't?"

He laughed, before taking a drink of wine. "What's in a name anyway?"

That was something we'd shared. My father's last name was Sinclair and after he disowned Nicholas and me, I started the process to legally change my last name. Luckily for me it all came together when I started my modeling career. Trembley was my mother's maiden name and Constance was pleased when she found out I was changing my name. She said that it had an air of sophistication. I didn't know about all that, but I'm pretty sure she was trying to be supportive.

The boat rocked gently over the waves. Another boat anchored about fifty feet away from us and I wondered if it was the paparazzi.

Folding my legs beneath me, I inhaled a deep breath. "My mother died not knowing about my career. She wasn't lucid when I graduated from NYU and her conditioned worsened over the summer. She passed away that fall, just before the Nadia's Dream Fashion Show was televised."

The images of my mother fading away in the expensive nursing home came into view. Armed with a cosmetics bag and her favorite magazines—*Town & Country*, *Real Simple* and *Vanity Fair*, I'd visit my mom. I spent time reading articles that I thought would be of interest to her and sometimes I'd have to read them twice in a visit. Other times she'd change her mind and want to walk in the garden or listen to the Beach Boys. On occasion when she was feeling extra sparkly, we'd paint our nails and she'd tell me stories, mostly about her youth. Mom loved to talk about my father and how he loved playing golf. I could hardly stomach listening to her ramble on about Monty Sinclair, the greatest love of her life.

Some days she remembered they were divorced, other days she asked when Monty was coming home for dinner and proceeded to ask me to make her a vodka martini.

"I'd taken a job as an assistant with *Bella Magazine*. I'd been there about seven weeks, and one morning I was asked to help with a shoot. Constance Kimball happened to be there that day. Fifteen minutes in, she stood up yelling for everyone to get the fuck out and then directed the photographer to start shooting me. Constance signed me to her agency on the spot, and told my boss that I was quitting effective immediately. Everything passed in a blur—I couldn't believe how my life shifted after that day. She took me under her wing, and taught me every aspect of the business. My first modeling job was Miami Swim Week. It was sensational. I only wished my mom could have been there."

"Some days are harder than others, huh?" he asked, refilling my glass.

"Yeah." I bobbed my head.

We sat in a comfortable silence watching the boats drift along the water. It was refreshing to know that we didn't have to resort to idle chit chat. I liked that—it was a welcomed relief that when I'd shared my sad story, instead of feeling terrified Grady would run the other way our conversation somehow provided a sense of recognition. Even though our stories were completely different we had an understanding.

The two of us knew what rock bottom looked like and we were determined to crawl from beneath the rubble and not let it destroy us. Despite our failed relationships or our family struggles, we knew it didn't define us, we had to keep going.

"Apparently, we've killed the mood once again," I joked.

"No, but we have killed this bottle of wine. Should I grab another or do you want to head back in?"

My stomach rumbled and I knew that I should eat before I drank anything more.

"Let's head back in, I'm starving. We should maybe work on that good eats list of mine."

"That sounds like a very good idea."

Chapter
Twenty-Eight

Grady

It had been a long time since I had an afternoon of meaningful conversation with a woman. When it came to family history, Heather was slightly closed off and with good reason. Family was a source of negativity for my ex-wife, and ended up driving her to drink or get high, sometimes both.

I'd listen as she told me horror stories of growing up in southern Missouri. Her family ran a local gas station, but when things got tough her brother started dealing and cooking meth among other drugs.

When she was eighteen, she skipped a local party that ended up getting busted. Heather had driven two hours to Branson to sing at an open mic night hoping that someone would recognize her talent. When she got home her best friend, Tish was waiting for her, said she was real proud of her and that they should celebrate. Heather found herself out in the woods with a rope around her neck being accused of being a snitch. Luckily the cops tailed some of the teens the rest of the weekend and had been able to save Heather's life. That night, she packed a bag, bought a bus ticket and headed straight for Hollywood.

When her brother, Randy, showed up at our place in Manhattan demanding money, it sent Heather over the edge.

"I don't understand why this motherfucker tells you how to spend yur money. I'm 'er family—'er kin. We are blood, Kandi . . . excuse me, Heather. I know you got the money livin' up here in yur big fancy penthouse and we know you got a mansion out there in Hollywood too."

"How the fuck did you find me?" Heather screeched.

"Money talks, even Missourah money in the Big Apple. I paid some guy selling celebrity maps five hundred dollars to tell me where you lived. Cuz even if I gave him half the money I had on me, it's worth it to get my payday from you. You owe us, Kandi girl."

I stood up, and my fingers carefully buttoned the jacket of my Burberry suit. Words formulated in my brain as I studied this jackass wearing khaki cargo shorts and a Psycho Circus concert t-shirt. And yes, I stood in judgement of him, and my problem was his entitlement and lack of respect for his sister.

"She's my wife, my family. She doesn't owe you a dime. You never gave a damn about Heather, and she left Missouri to get the hell away from you and your family. In between auditions, she put herself through acting classes by working at Vacancy. She did it all by herself without any help from any of you."

"Fuck you, Hollywood! Why don't you go fuck your sister or your cousin?"

"Randy, I'm going to breakdown my answer in simple terms so you'll understand. That kind of shit isn't legal where

I come from. Now, maybe in your part of the world it's okay to call your sister a fucking bitch in front of an Applebee's on Mother's Day and fuck your family members, but where I'm from that's called being a fucking redneck."

After security escorted him out, I left for a meeting. Heather said she was just fine, but she'd gone on a bender—pills, booze, and cocaine. Dazed and drunk she went to the Union Club and confronted Holliday during fashion week. I knew I had to get her to rehab and once I had her sobered up she agreed to check herself in.

Some celebrities embraced their roots as a source of strength. For a lot, it was a reminder of how far they'd come, but Heather's past was a source of pain and embarrassment.

My heart ached for Heather. And as she slowly opened up to me about her life—the life that brought her shame and flooded her with pain. I wanted her to know that she'd come a long way, our past lives did not define us, they only strengthened us. But the demons never left her, they stayed and she dealt with it the only way she knew how to cope.

Where Heather tucked her emotional pain way down deep, Harlow spoke freely. Nervous of course, but she wore it like a badge of courage. Saying to the world, "This was where I've been and this is how far I've come."

"We need to talk about our arrangement," Harlow said, pointing her fork at me. This was the second . . . possibly *third* time she'd positioned a utensil in my direction. "For starters, why haven't the details of Heather cheating on you circulated yet? I mean, what is Haven waiting for?"

I shrugged. "I'll text her again."

"Do better and call her," she demanded, stabbing another chunk of chicken and pineapple on to her fork. "She works for us."

The tone in her voice reminded me of earlier in my bedroom, and my dick seemed to be recalling that moment as well. I wanted to fuck her perfect mouth, and then fuck her.

"You don't need to remind me of that."

"Here's what I do need to remind you of then, the press is sinking us. They're not impressed with our 'love story' we need to do something *bold*."

"What do you suggest? I've already done the Vegas celebrity wedding thing."

She tossed a blueberry into her mouth. "I'm surprised that you'd consider marriage again after Heather."

"Hey, first you marry for love then you marry for money—my next marriage will be all about the dolla dolla bills. I'm going to be a kept man."

She eyed me as if I was serious, but before I could respond, Nancy Brooks, the owner of the diner where the two of us were currently stuffing our faces tapped her finger to the table.

"How is everything this evening?"

"Delicious as always, Nancy," I answered, dipping another fry into the special spicy Cajun sauce. In addition to the best breakfast you'd ever had, Nancy was famous for mixing in some of her classic southern recipes with traditional east coast seafood dishes.

"I'm glad to hear that, sugar." Her smile grew wider, and her gaze drifted to Harlow.

I leaned back into the booth, draping my arm across the back. "Nancy Brooks, I'd like you to meet Harlow Trembley."

"Harlow, it's lovely to meet you. Are you new to The Harbour?"

"Nice to meet you as well, I've visited The Harbour frequently over the years. By the way, this salad is delicious."

"Thank you," she said, placing a hand on her hip. "The summer salads are a customer favorite around here. Next week, it's blacked chicken with fresh strawberries."

Harlow's eyes darted to mine. "Yum, I guess I'll be coming back here soon."

"Well, you two enjoy the rest of your meal. You better bring her back here, sugar." Nancy patted my shoulder, and gave me a wry grin.

I leaned forward, resting my elbows on the table. "I'm not bringing you back here for fucking salad, at least not until you've had the French toast with maple syrup as a sweet indulgence."

"Is *she* sweet on you, sugar?"

"You jealous?"

She leaned forward. "Not even a little bit."

"When her husband, Phil, was laid up and too sick to work, I'd help Nancy out by fixing things around this place and their house. I mowed their lawn and replaced the sink in their kitchen."

"That's really sweet. I bet the neighbors sat outside just to watch you push a lawnmower."

That forced a deep laugh from me. A few of the patrons turned in our direction.

"See that booth over there?" I pointed to the one in the corner. "That is where I sat with my dad. We'd come here after my horse riding lessons. Nancy would bring us two slices of fresh peach cobbler, a vanilla milkshake for me and black coffee for my dad." I leaned forward crossing my arms underneath my chest. "Nancy's like a second mother to me. When I bought my place here, she and Phil brought me groceries. Nancy was afraid I'd wither away—she always tells me I'm much too thin."

Harlow laughed. "My grandmother—my mom's mom, she was the same way. They lived on a twenty-acre farm in northern Vermont, with an apple orchard and cherry trees. When we'd visit, she'd take Nicholas and me out to the orchard to pick our own apples and then she'd make pies, muffins, and doughnuts for days. She shoved food in front of us every chance she got."

"I can't picture you on a farm."

"It happened. I may even have a few pictures to prove it."

At the sound of chiming bells, I swung my head towards the front door. A couple of teenagers walked in grabbing seats at the counter. They started discussing milkshake flavors and for a moment I swore I saw my father sitting in the booth with his notepad.

I blinked up, pulled from my daze. The screen on my phone lit up, a message from Jennifer appeared: *Buchanan Beauty photo shoot details have been emailed. You leave for Bermuda next week.*

"Everything okay?" she asked, nodding towards the phone.

"No worries, it's not Heather drama. Just work. Apparently, I'm going to Bermuda—Buchanan Beauty calls."

"Oh my God, you are so lucky. I've been dying to go to Horseshoe Beach. I've got to see for myself that pink sand exists."

I tapped my finger to the table. "Why don't you come with me, and we'll make that beach fantasy of yours a reality."

Her brows rose. "Intriguing proposal, but in case you've forgotten I am launching a website in the next few days. I don't think I can jet off to some Caribbean island with you."

"Actually, Bermuda is in the Sargasso Sea not the Caribbean Sea, although it is often considered part of the

Caribbean region. In 2003, Bermuda became an associate member of the Caribbean Community or CARICOM. I won't bore you with the details of the organization, you can Google it sometime."

"Wow, impressive. I'm glad that Ivy League education of yours is doing you *some* good."

I chucked a fry into her salad. "I am a wealth of knowledge, and don't you forget it."

"Uh, huh," she said, before popping the French fry into her mouth.

And my dick was back to thinking about her mouth being wrapped around it.

"So, what do you say?"

She shook her head, all that hair swirling around her shoulders. "I can't, what if something goes awry with the site?"

"I'm pretty sure the hotel we're staying at has Wi-Fi, if not we'll find you a café and that way you can check in on things. It's only three days."

"In our original deal, you promised me a Caribbean vacation. My fantasy is specifically tied to a Caribbean romp. I'm standing firm on this."

"Original deal? Have we renegotiated terms and I am unaware?"

She flashed me a wry grin. "If I go to Bermuda with you, then you and I are going to pop over to Aruba."

"Pop over, huh? It's at least an eight-hour flight." At present I was plotting the perfect Caribbean escape in my head and I would be calling in a favor. "If it's a Caribbean vacation you want, I'll make it happen. Now, back to the matter at hand—our arrangement."

"Have you been online since this morning?" she asked,

before taking a sip of her iced tea.

I shook my head. "Why have there been some new developments?"

"Yeah, I learned that Harry is being coached by his PR team. He's using our split to garner sympathy for the World Cup. Apparently, he has a plan of his own, and according to my friend, Zanita, he's having the time of his life though— parties, women and golf."

She swiped the screen on her phone, and then handed it to me. My eyes scrolled the headlines settling my focus on one with my name attached.

Harlow deserved better than this fucking guy allowing the press to drag her name through the mud.

England's Brackman Hiding Secret Heartbreak

"Pussy." A few of the teenagers turned in our direction. "Redirect, I think the Caribbean vacation will be a bold enough move. In the meantime, I have a few other ideas."

Chapter
Twenty-Nine

Grady

Curling my fingers around my mallet, I listened to the umpire rattle off the same old rules and regulations. The sky was cloudless with a light breeze rustling the tall grasses that lined the pristine field of The Harbour Polo Club. My gaze swept over the crowd scanning for a glimpse of Harlow. Despite the fact that she was wearing a yellow sundress, I couldn't spot her anywhere.

Elsa bristled with energy, waiting for my signal to strike and tear up the untouched field. Beneath my helmet, I looked towards Ridge. He nodded, tugging his glove tighter. Our eyes focused on that tiny white ball. My teammates held up their mallets in salute, and when the bugle sounded we charged the field ready for battle.

"Great match," Ridge said, as we led our horses to the stables.

Today was the first time in a long time that I didn't feel the slightest bit sad after playing in the Stars and Stripes Polo Challenge. Our team has won the last four years which normally puts me in a good mood, but then the nostalgia washes over me making me miss my father.

"You too, man."

"Should we celebrate at Rum Bar or Castle Hill?"

Wiping the sweat from my brow, I laughed. "I think I'll be celebrating at home."

Ridge slapped my shoulder, and then wiped off his mallet. "Understood, man, if I had a beautiful lady at home, I'd never want to leave."

It wasn't just that Harlow was my girlfriend—she was my friend. These moments were that much more special because I had her in my life.

"Yeah, I don't know that there's a woman out there to keep you from being a forever bachelor, Stephens."

"That's true enough," he replied, through a hearty laugh.

Once we'd put our gear away, we walked back towards the polo grounds for our interviews and trophy presentation. I was in desperate need of a shower to rinse away the dirt and grime. Whistles of appreciation and cheers erupted as Ridge and I entered through the gate. Walking briskly, I darted through the crowd in an attempt to find Harlow.

Instantly, I recognized her copper hair, the warm breeze whipped at the hem of her skirt, inching it ever so slightly up her thighs. As I turned the corner, a portly man with greying hair nearly white around the temples came into view. Harlow folded her arms over her chest, as the man inched closer to her.

I strode up to her side. "Everything okay here?"

The man's hazel eyes shot daggers in my direction. "Ah, Grady James, you won today's matches by a fair margin, not bad. Although, your defensive game could you a little work."

Who the fuck is this man?

"Grady, this is Monty Sinclair. I can't say that I'd like to introduce you."

This man is Harlow's father. My fists balled at my sides, at the recognition. "No, I suppose this is not a pleasant introduction for you, sweetheart." I pulled Harlow behind me, squaring up to the motherfucker.

Dragging his gaze over us, a booming laugh erupted from his lungs. "Harlot, is this the polo player that you're spreading your legs for?"

"Excuse me?" I said, moving a step closer.

"Slow your roll, hot shot, this is between me and *my* daughter," he said, scowling in Harlow's direction. "*This* is a family matter."

"Let me shed some light, Harlow is your nothing," I replied, shaking my head. "*She* is an independent woman free of the likes of you."

Monty inhaled a sharp breath. "Well, well, looks like someone finally wants to take up with your fat ass, Harlot."

He would not talk to her like this, not now—not ever. As much as I wanted to, and it wasn't without epic restraint, I opted not to smash his face into the table or my fist. Instead, I used my words, like an adult.

"Sinclair, you have ten seconds at best to move your ass from this spot. Harlow Trembley is none of your concern, not while I'm around. You don't think about her, and you don't come near her ever again. You got me?"

He puffed up his chest. "And just what are you going to do about it?"

"The answer to that question—I can assure you is one that you do not want."

Dragging his glaring gaze over us, Monty's lips curled into a devilish grin. He held up his hands in mock surrender. "She's all yours, kid, I hope you know what you're in for with this one."

In a hurried movement, Harlow scooped up her wine glass. "Go fuck yourself, *Dad*," she hissed, tossing the drink in his face. "You don't get to be a part of *my* life."

Her smile was so big that I couldn't help but laugh. Standing next to her witnessing the moment as she took the power back from the bastard filled my heart.

Scrubbing a chubby hand down his face, he laughed a belly shaking laugh. "That's good." He grabbed a linen napkin from the table and then wiped his face.

"The next time you find yourself at an event with Harlow," I said, taking her hand in mine, "walk the other way."

I led Harlow through the onlookers some whose mouths hung open in shock, others whispering hushed musings. My singular priority was getting Harlow away from her father.

"My hero," she gushed, bumping my arm with hers.

"The way you tossed that drink in his face, and spoke your mind—sweetheart, *that* was badass."

"It was pretty badass of me," she agreed. "I feel so light right now, like I could do anything."

"That feeling, it's called, closure—*healing*."

She smiled over at me. "Thanks to you, I'm going to be fine."

I hooked my arms around her waist. "You're going to be better than fine, all on your own."

Chapter
Thirty

Harlow

The past two weeks had been all business, which kept me from going away with Grady. I launched my website and it couldn't have gone more perfectly. After Bermuda, Grady ended up going to Los Angeles to shoot a television pilot leaving us with zero staged outings for the tabloids. As far as arrangements go, ours had seemed to be working against us or not working at all.

England ended up dominating both the United States and France in the World Cup. Analysts now have them favored to win it all. From the look of things, Harry didn't have any excuse for poor play. I mistakenly turned on ESPN and watched the highlights. As one announcer said, Harry Brackman was on fire. It was true enough. I'd never seen him play so well. Perhaps he was correct in ending our relationship.

In other news, reasons for the James/Young divorce

cheating scandal circulated and the tabloids took a different direction with Heather's accusations.

Grady James and Harlow Trembley Relationship Rebound—Revenge of the Ex's.

At this point, the entire scheme felt ineffective, and I'd seemed to have lost sight of why we were even doing this in the first place. I wondered if Grady was feeling the same way.

The only thing that I was sure of was that I missed him when he wasn't around. I missed our talks, and I had little desire to hit up any of the local restaurants or coffee shops without him. I craved his intellectual notes and fun facts.

Grady: I may be seated next to a killer on this flight. Thinking an assassin.

Harlow: How do you figure?

Grady: His hands are stained reddish-orange and he looks as if he's been crying.

Harlow: Maybe he's a painter.

Harlow: A sensitive artist.

Grady: I'm going with murderer fleeing the country. Let's see if he's going straight to New York or has a connecting flight.

Harlow: If he was a murderer fleeing, I think he'd pick Australia.

Grady: He's going to London. I see why you would think Australia.

Grady: But, he said he just filmed a scene for a movie and his character had been killed off.

Grady: Apparently, there was no time to shower.

Grady: Dammit. Now, he wants to talk to me.

Harlow: That's what you get for peopling.

Grady: What's peopling?

Harlow: In layman's terms, basically being social.

Grady: You kids and your new words.

Harlow: I resent that. I'm just hipper than you, old man.

Grady: How old are you?

Harlow: Remember how I told you to never call a woman crazy?

Grady: Yeah.

Harlow: You should never ask a woman her age.

Grady: You sound like my mother.

Harlow: I would be offended at that comment, but I haven't met your mother.

Harlow: She sounds like a pretty classy lady who has manners.

Grady: Wikipedia says that you are thirty.

Grady: My mother is definitely a classy lady. You'd like her. I think you should meet her sometime.

Grady: Will you be confirming your age?

Grady: What if I told you that I'm 33? Does that help matters? A share for a share?

Harlow: Maybe.

Grady: Flight is taking off. I'll text you when I get to NYC.

Harlow: Safe travels.

Grady suggested that I should meet his mother. Was that how far he was willing to take this faux relationship? With a smile, I set my phone onto the counter and returned to the task in front of me.

I couldn't decide which cocktails to feature next. At the moment, I was trying to decide between simple syrup and triple sec for the pineapple margarita recipe I was concocting. Definitely wanted a lime and pineapple garnish.

I sipped the cocktail with triple sec and then the one with simple syrup. They were both yummy.

Choices. Choices.

And I did need to make a choice. After sampling multiple times, although tipsy, the choice was certain. The orange of the triple sec was just too much and confused the flavor profile. Once I fashioned together a few glasses, I grabbed my camera and took several photos.

Grady: Just landed in New York.

Grady: I have twenty-seven minutes before my flight to East Harbour.

Harlow: Are you going to make it to the wedding on time?

Grady: I should. Are you sure that I can't pick you up on the way to the ceremony?

Harlow: I've been working on a few cocktail recipes today. I'm a little drunk.

Harlow: I don't want to show up wasted to your friend's wedding.

Grady: Understandable. Day drinking is an art form.

Harlow: Definitely a marathon, not a sprint.

Grady: How are things with Cocktails & Couture? I'm guessing good, if you're drunk.

Harlow: I can't believe the views that it's getting.

Grady: I enjoyed the travel packing tips post.

Harlow: You read that post?

Grady: I'm sure that I've read all of them. And I signed up for your newsletter.

Grady: Is the bikini in the photo one that you'll be wearing in the Caribbean?

Harlow: Perhaps.

Grady: Fantastic. For the second part of our trip, we have a private beach.

Grady: Clothing is optional.

Harlow: I'm not sunbathing nude.

Grady: Topless?

Harlow: How private is this beach? Are you going to tell me where you're taking me?

Grady: Nope. You need to embrace the element of surprise.

Grady: How about you send me a picture of you topless right now?

Harlow: Haven't we discussed nude photos already?

Harlow: No nude selfies. Ever.

Grady: Get a Snap Chat account.

Harlow: No.

Grady: Redirect.

Grady: How much convincing do I need in order to get you into my bed naked tonight?

Harlow: You're going to be exhausted after traveling and the wedding.

Grady: I'll never be too exhausted to fuck you.

Grady: Time to board. Give some thought to spending the night with me. I want to see you.

Grady: I don't think I can wait until tomorrow to kiss you.

Grady: Redirect.

Grady: I'm not waiting. Want you in my bed tonight or I'll be in yours.

Grady: I have to admit. This wedding is rather romantic.

Harlow: Aren't all weddings romantic?

Grady: I suppose.

Grady: What are you doing? Still drinking?

Harlow: No. I went for a swim to help sober up.

Harlow: Now, I'm eating pineapple and shrimp tacos.

Grady: And you didn't send me a picture of you in a swimsuit?

Grady: How much do you love pineapple?

Harlow: You didn't send me a picture of you in a suit.

Harlow: Pineapple is sweet and juicy. What's not to love?

Grady: Fair point.

Grady: BTW, the innuendo door is wide open for me about your sweet and juicy expletive.

Harlow: I love it when you talk dirty to me, especially when you censor yourself. Hot.

Grady: I'm sweating my balls off. Beach weddings are hot as fuck, even at dusk.

Harlow: Tell me about the bride's dress.

Grady: Ivory I think. Could be off white. Strapless.

Grady: I have a picture of Alex and Ella. I can show you later.

Harlow: I haven't said yes, to spending the night with you, yet.

Grady: You said yet. That implies you will.

Harlow: Perhaps.

Grady: You will.

Harlow: I was thinking. We need to get a couple of rafts.

Harlow: For your boat and for your pool.

Harlow: Like a pink flamingo or I found a pineapple shaped one.

Grady: Anything you want. You got it.

Grady: The bride and groom just left.

Grady: Am I on my way to your house or are you coming to mine?

Harlow: I'm out the door. You need to sleep in your own bed tonight.

Grady: Sleep? That's cute. I won't be doing much sleeping in my bed tonight.

Grady: My headboard is going to punch a hole into my wall tonight, sweetheart.

I parked my car and tossed my keys into my handbag. Hauling my overnight bag higher onto my shoulder, I walked up the stone sidewalk. It was a gorgeous summer evening, storybook perfect, no humidity and the smell of chlorine and oriental lilies hung in the air. Squinting, I tapped the code into security pad and then pushed open the door.

"Grady, I'm here."

The entryway was dark, a little bit of light illuminated the kitchen. As I stepped further into the house, the glint from the moon splashed over every fixture and surface. I dropped my bag to the floor and set my laptop and handbag on the island.

"Whoa." A voice said—*his* voice. I'd know Grady's voice anywhere.

I turned around to face him. The moonlight passed over his face, when he stepped in front of the window. I studied his neck, and his five o'clock shadow. Dirty thoughts surfaced, thinking about his face between my legs with that scruff rubbing against my most sensitive spots. I pressed my thighs together, averting my eyes to concentrate on the buttons of his dress shirt, two at the top, unbuttoned with his tie draped loosely around his neck.

One . . . two . . . three . . . four strides and he was on me, pushing my back against the cool glass of his refrigerator.

"You're in a bikini."

"Well, you did say that you wanted to see it."

"You drove to my house wearing a bikini in the middle of the night." His finger teased under the thin strap of my top brushing across the rise of my breast. "You're such a weirdo, I love it."

Brushing my hair to the side, his eyes met mine. He leaned into me, kissing his way up my neck and over my jaw. He sealed his mouth over mine, kissing me deeply, sucking all the air out of my lungs.

"I'm the weirdo, you've been texting me perverse and filthy things all day." He nipped my bottom lip making me moan.

"You don't mind, though." His fingers dipped inside my bikini bottoms. My cheeks heated, feeling the rush of wetness pooling between my thighs. A groan rattled his throat, when his fingers pushed inside me.

His hands slid to my ass, spreading my arousal along my hip. When his lips kissed below my ear, while gripping and kneading my bare flesh, I nearly lost my mind. My fingers dug into his shoulder, and everything tightened inside me.

"You're so hot," he murmured against my skin.

Grady lifted me up onto the island, the sound of my thighs slapping against the surface was the only thing that I registered before his mouth was on me again. I managed to knock the fruit bowl over sending whatever was in there rolling onto the floor.

"Sorry, about that," I laughed against his lips.

His hand slid under my top, caressing my breast. "Not a problem. Are you clumsy around all fruit?" he asked, his finger pinching my nipple.

My hands gripped his forearms. "It seems that way."

"Except for pineapples," he mused.

"Yeah, pineapples."

Snaking my arms around his neck, I wanted to say something dirty, something depraved but words were lost in a haze with Grady's fingers sliding up and under my thighs. He took me by surprise when his chest pressed against mine propelling me backwards.

"Now, I'm going do something that I've fantasized about since the day I saw you at Buchanan Beauty." With a snap of his wrist he removed his tie from around his neck and tossed it onto the counter. My breath hitched at the possibility of him using it to blindfold me or tie me up. Parts of me wondered if I'd even like that—if I could let go and give up control.

My hips jerked, when I felt the ties of my bottoms fall away. "Lift up, I want you bare."

I arched up, and Grady removed the fabric from my body. I was opened and exposed to him in the most vulnerable way.

Goosebumps splashed across my body when his warm breath fanned across my skin. I levered up onto my elbows watching him as he rolled up the sleeves of his shirt.

"I'm going to eat you so well that you'll get wet tomorrow just thinking about it and then I'm going to fuck you in a way that makes you throb when you have flashbacks." His voice was rich and full of promise.

"Good, because I want to hug your face with my thighs."

Teasing me, his lips trailed up my stomach as his fingertips grazed my thighs. His tongue lashed over my skin, rubbing my clit with his thumb and driving me out of my mind.

"Oh, fuck—*your* mouth." My fingers twisted and pulled his dark strands while I murmured inaudible pleas and hummed moans of satisfaction.

"You look just as beautiful as I imagined you would."

Two long fingers pushed inside me as he continued licking me into an epic orgasm. Searing pleasure wound its way through me at the primal way he ate and licked my pussy. This was a man who knew his way around a woman's clit. Grady James was both a scholar and a gentleman when it came to all things foreplay and fucking.

"I love the taste of you on my tongue."

"*Grady.*" His name came out in desperate plea wanting him to soothe the needy ache deep inside me. The ache he created.

I wanted more—more of this, more of him. Increasing, his rhythm, his lips and tongue worked a delicious friction making me hot and slick. The scrape of his stubble against my thighs made me drunk with lust and I rocked against him.

"There's my dirty girl," he groaned against my skin. "Does it feel good when you rub your gorgeous pussy against my face?"

Fucking hell. His teeth nipped and sucked my folds, biting the tender skin ever so slightly.

"Please," I moaned feeling my muscles tightening and pulsing.

He twisted his fingers inside me, and his tongue lashed over my skin making me cry out as my orgasm ripped through my body. Toe-curling, mind numbing explosions unleashed and a tidal wave of heat crashing over me.

"Grady!" His name bounced off every wall and beam in his home. He tongue fucked me through another orgasm and I had to push him away, it was too much. Multiples were his specialty, as if further convincing was needed. If my legs weren't jellied I'd stand up, clap, and cheer giving him the proper ovation he deserved for that performance.

I gazed up at him, watching as Grady pushed his dark hair away from his eyes.

"Is it okay to kiss you after, that?"

"Mmmm hmm."

He dipped his head, crushing his lips to mine. My tongue stroked against his. A shiver moved through me, tasting me on him. His hands threaded through my hair, gripping at the base of my neck pulling me up to him. "Now since you've wrecked my kitchen, let's go wreak havoc in my bedroom."

Chapter
Thirty-One

Grady

"Tell me about the pineapples."

"Is this code for something sexual?" Harlow asked, nuzzling her face into the crook of my shoulder.

"No, it's about your affection for the fruit, which I hear that the government made some of them pink."

"Yeah, they're totally cute."

"You're totally cute." My fingers skimmed over the curve of her hip, drifting up her ribcage. Cupping her breast, my thumb traced her nipple, coaxing it to attention.

She hummed in response, scratching her nails up and down my abs. "It's a silly childhood story."

Smiling, I kissed the top of her head. I liked knowing that part or parts of her childhood held some happiness for her. Everything I'd learned about Harlow's past held pain and sadness.

"Silly childhood stories are my favorite. Remind me to tell you about the time I peed on the kitchen floor in front of my mother and her friends."

Her face twisted up. "Was this recently?"

"Yes, it was just last month as matter of fact." I waggled my brows. "No, I was seven, and that night I was dazed and confused. I made the mistake of walking into the kitchen instead of the bathroom. Without missing a beat, I dropped my Underoos and pissed all over the wood floor."

Her hands covered her face as she giggled. "Oh my God, was your mom mortified?"

"It was hard to tell. I remember the laughter bringing me out of my daze. When I finished, my mother handed me a roll of paper towels and told me to clean it up."

She shifted her position in bed to look at me. "My story is a different kind of silly."

My lips traced the smooth expanse of her shoulder. She twisted out of my hold, rolling up to lean against the headboard, which was still intact despite my best efforts to make good on my earlier promise. It was probably better that way I wasn't in the mood for any home repairs.

She shoved a hand through her auburn strands, sweeping them around her shoulder. "In sixth grade, I hit a growth spurt. I was the tallest girl in my class and I was taller than most of the boys too. Having hair the color of a tomato didn't help matters, the teasing was relentless. My classmates made fun of me and called me names—Giant, sometimes Jolly Red Giant, Stretch, Chewy, and Big Bird. You can guess where I'm going with this. It made me feel more awkward than I already did." She released a long sigh. "I came home in tears one afternoon after finding out my best friend, Marie, had made a scrapbook with my face plastered on a giraffe's body, a bronto-saurus, an anaconda, even Chewy from *Star Wars*."

Harlow glanced over her shoulder. "Somehow Marie found out about the movie *The Fifty Foot Woman*, and glued my face to her body. Bright pink and yellow fliers were taped up in the girls' bathroom and all over the hallways."

I searched my brain and my vocabulary wanting to say something more than just "sorry." I wasn't subjected to any teasing in school that I could recall. However, in college, I took my punches when people found out I was modeling. That was nothing compared to what Harlow went through. Teasing at a young age, especially during the awkward and formidable years, can stick with you and carry into your adult life.

Harlow slid down and rolled onto her side, her hazel eyes boring into mine. "After I shared everything with my mom, she told me to embrace my height. She said, 'Harlow, be a pineapple—stand tall, and pretend that you're wearing a crown. No matter what, always be sweet.' Then she babbled on about having a prickly skin, but unlike the pineapple my spikes didn't show but I would need it to survive in the world." She laughed and rolled the pineapple charm between her fingers. "The advice stuck with me and the rest is history."

My hands tangled in her hair, and I pulled her face to mine. "I think what your mom was saying, is that you are fierce on the outside and sweet on the inside."

She leaned in, kissing me softly. "I think you're right."

"Stick with me, sweetheart, you'll find out that I'm right about a lot of things."

As it turned out, Harlow stuck with me that weekend and the next and by mid-July the two of us had slid into a comfortable routine. There were Saturday morning trips to the farmers' market, afternoons on the boat, Sunday brunches for two and daily workouts. She cheered me on at my polo matches and I had become the official taste tester for new Cocktails and Couture recipes.

Over the last few weeks we slowly checked off places on her "Good Eats" list. We had her coffee place locked in—North Harbour Coffee Shop's salted caramel iced coffee had erased memories of her time in Italy. Although, she said it felt sacrilegious to dare even admit. Pastries, specifically double chocolate muffins from The Bake Shoppe, were her new obsession, and we were still on the hunt for the perfect cheesecake. Most Friday nights consisted of meals with an assortment of fried foods and then going back to my place to binge watch *Vampire Diaries* and her new favorite, *Riverdale*.

Not once did we search the gossip sites for our names, although, Zanita and Haven both sent texts with headlines of interest.

Heather Young believes in Morning Sex and Yoga—breakfast of champions.

Grady James and Harlow Trembley Dating: New Couple PDA Farmers' Market Date.

Harry Brackman and England Fall Short of World Cup Victory—No More Ex-cuses.

Heather Young Wants Grady James Back from Harlow Trembley.

Harry Brackman Spotted in London Night Club with Unidentified Blonde.

We hadn't officially discussed our arrangement or

revisited the original terms. Whatever this was, felt like an actual honest relationship. A relationship free of Hollywood drama, it felt so fucking awesome. Except that we were both celebrities and the shadows of Hollywood were never far behind. I couldn't help but wonder what was lurking around those dark shadows for Harlow and me.

What social media drama would pop up? Would a crazy fan threaten her life? Would someone hack our phones and find something sacred to the two of us and make it public knowledge?

Exposed.

Ironically, those in between moments the ones the cameras or onlookers didn't capture were my favorite. Stolen kisses and hand grazes. The whispered compliments, alternated with dirty promises we'd fulfill in the bedroom or nearest unoccupied space.

Droplets of water rained over my chest. "What are you thinking so hard about?" Harlow asked, running her finger over my lips and chin.

I smiled over at her from my position on the giant pink flamingo raft that we were drifting around on the ocean waves. "Honestly, I was thinking about us."

She propped her chin onto my chest. "Us, I like the sound of that."

"What do you think about the possibility of a *real* us?"

"I'm going to need you to elaborate." Her palm smoothed over my shoulder and down my chest. "Because *this* feels real."

"Okay, how about we toss the arrangement and you and I date for real?"

A slow smile spread across her lips. "That's cute."

"Why is that cute?"

"It's cute, the way you asked me to be your girlfriend, just now."

I leaned into her, kissing her effectively sealing the deal. "Well, I'm glad we had this talk."

Chapter
Thirty-Two

Harlow

"Tell me something odd, really out there."

Grady stretched his long legs, and I snuggled into his side. His hand massaged slow circles into my hip. "How out there are we talking?"

"Nothing is off limits."

"Is it an off-limits topic or just sharing a strange fact?" he asked, kissing the soft spot between my neck and shoulder.

"Is there a difference?"

"Well, let's see how out there we can get—my ex-wife has never been to this house."

I stared up at him. "Oh my God, I might need a drink if you're going to bring up your ex-wife in bed."

"I'll get you anything you want, sweetheart." Grady untangled our limbs, and slipped out of bed hobbling as he made his way out of the room. My guess was that his body was still a little jellied from the morning sex which led to shower sex. After all that we found ourselves starved and making peanut butter pancakes—a secret family recipe, he told me. We did unspeakable, filthy things to one another with the maple syrup and that landed us right back in the shower and then here to his bed. We haven't made it to the outdoor shower, yet.

Sundays were fast becoming my favorite day with Grady. The two of us would lie in bed—I'd check my website stats, read "Sex Diaries" from *The Cut*, and then channel surf for a guilty pleasure movie. Lifetime and Hallmark served up some fabulous favorites starring Tori Spelling, Kellie Martin, and Candace Cameron. Those movies led to discussions of ridiculous plotlines and lessons learned.

He'd read *The New York Times* and the *Hollywood Reporter*. We'd discuss my love for old Hollywood glamour and his passion projects. He'd tell me about his desire to save the oceans and his charity work. Then we'd make our way downstairs and prepare a fabulous feast, everything was fresh from our Saturday trips to the farmers' market. After breakfast, depending on our mood, we'd lounge by the pool or take his boat out.

Today was a rarity, the rain kept us inside, but that didn't matter because we were together. Much like the weather outside, there was a storm brewing between Grady and me. It was powerful, it was magnetic, and it was like catching lightning in a bottle. I wanted to show the whole world that we were together—*plot twist!* The fact remained that we *were* together—a legit couple, not something staged for Hollywood or good press.

"Okay, I've got wine for you and beer for me. And the snack menu consists of pretzels, mixed nuts, Vermont cheddar slices and an apple," Grady announced, carrying an ice bucket and a serving tray. "I re-stocked the upstairs bar, so this should keep us well fed and satisfied for at least two hours." He tossed me a knowing glance over his shoulder. I pressed my fist to my mouth, hiding a grin. Grady set the tray and ice bucket on his dresser and then poured two glasses.

"Your rosé, my dear," Grady said, handing me a glass.

"How is it that your ex-wife had never been to your Hamptons hideaway?"

Grady slipped back in between the covers. "She never wanted to come to the Hamptons. Heather didn't like the scene. She said it was too quiet. When we were looking to buy a house together, I asked her to tell me about her ideal place, she told me it would have to be somewhere with a lot of noise. It made sense, our house in LA was always filled with people—she needed the noise. I suspected that when it was quiet, she wound up in her dark places."

It was mind-boggling. Even if Heather hated the Hamptons, shouldn't she have given it some effort to spend time with Grady in a place that meant so much to him? On the other hand, at least this place isn't laced with memories of her or the two of them here.

"Okay, now you tell me something," he requested, as his fingers traced the back of my knee.

"I saw my father in Palmetto Bluff." I swallowed a gulp of wine. "He was at the polo match with his latest trophy—expensive extensions and pumped full of fillers."

"Lips and tits?"

"Lips and ass, the tits were real as far as I could tell."

"Did you speak to him?"

My head bowed, as I started at the pink liquid in my glass. "Unfortunately, yes."

Grady tipped my chin forcing me to look at him. "Is he

the reason that you left the polo match?"

Nodding, I placed my wine glass on the nightstand. "Seeing him in the flesh, it tore at my old wounds, cutting the stitches that I'd used to close up those feelings. It's embarrassing. I'm still his verbal punching bag—fat ass, stupid, worthless, whore. Those were a few of the endearing names he likes using to torture me emotionally."

Grady wrapped his arms around me, pulling me closer. "I suppose that I don't have to tell you that you are none of those things." He dropped a kiss to my shoulder.

"I appreciate that," I said, grasping his hand in mine. "My mom used to tell me stories about my father's glory days playing golf. He was an average player—never accomplished anything of significance like winning a major tournament. My brother, Nicholas, he excelled at everything, sports and academics. I had my share of accomplishments with academics and choir competitions. My athletic skills were limited to running and swimming purely for survival and beach volleyball when the mood struck. Nicholas has a theory that dear old Dad has some kind of jealousy towards us, which is why he cut ties with us. Some studies have shown that one reason a parent might hate their child is because they're the embodiment of everything the parent is unhappy about with their own life."

Grady stroked his knuckles up and down my arm. He didn't offer any apologies or advice he just listened and that was how I knew that he understood. Most people listen to reply, they don't hear the other person because they're constantly thinking of things to say. I didn't need advice for the sake of making me feel better.

"Your brother, are the two of you close?"

"Yeah, he's one of the best people I know. Nicholas is

amazing. When we were in high school we used to cook together. At that point, our mom had days where she would spend days in bed. She drank a lot once she found out our dad was cheating on her. So, we had to take care of ourselves. We were pretty much on our own for dinner. He'd make these amazing grilled cheese sandwiches, sometimes adding a slice of tomato."

"Grilled cheese is the staple of any diet rich in comfort foods."

"Totally, and then we figured out how to make grilled cheese with sharp cheddar, Granny Smith apples, and mustard. He perfected that recipe at our grandparent's house."

"The ones who live in Vermont," Grady interjected.

"Yep." That made me smile knowing he remembered little facts about the stories I shared. "Nicholas is finishing up his residency in emergency medicine in Chicago. We don't get to see each other very often, but we schedule times for regular phone calls and video chats."

"A doctor. That's impressive."

"Yeah, sometimes I can't believe that he saves lives. Nicholas spent two weeks at our father's financial firm the summer after his freshman year of college. He hated every minute of it. One morning before work, he was sitting at the coffee shop across the street and a guy, who he thought was intoxicated, sat down beside him. As it turned out, the guy, who was only twenty-two, was having a heart attack and Nicholas called 911. Luckily there was an EMT standing in line when Nicholas yelled for help. They were able to get the guy to the hospital and save his life. Nicholas walked into our father's office that day and told him that he wanted to be a doctor. Changed his major and that was that."

"Lucky guy."

My fingers brushed against his forearm. "What about you? Are you and your sister close?"

"Definitely. Willow and I keep in contact fairly regularly. She's pretty active on social media. My sister loves Instagram." Rain tapped against the glass and Grady slid out of bed to close the window. "After Willow graduated from college, she opened a luxury bath shop in Fenwick. She's always sending me pictures of fabrics and cool fixtures. That's why all my bathrooms are 'so tricked out' as Willow likes to say—she designed all of them." He crossed the room back to the bed, bringing along the bowl of pretzels.

"Your sister has an eye for design. Maybe I should consult her when I remodel my home."

Grady shot me a pointed glance. "Did you buy a house while I was away?"

"Oh, did I not mention that?" I asked, popping a pretzel into my mouth.

"Did you really buy a house?"

I shook my head. "No, but I found this amazing home. It's so dreamy and I am in love with the kitchen. The tile backsplash is teal."

Grady took the bowl of pretzels from my hands and then placed it back onto the tray of snacks. "I've been thinking about incorporating some color into this house." Shifting my knees, Grady settled between my legs. Even though I was starving for food, I was hungrier for his touch so I didn't complain when he took away my snack.

"Don't you dare change a thing in here, Grady. This place is perfect."

"Speaking of perfect, that's what you are, sweetheart."

I was hardly without my own faults. Often, I'd forget friends' birthdays. My only reminder was Facebook, which on some level seemed sad. I used to be very good at keeping a calendar of important dates—weddings, anniversaries or the occasional mitzvah. The last few years, I'd sent New Year's cards to make up for missing important dates or perhaps it was a way of starting the year off on a good foot.

Presently, my own foot was firmly in Grady's grasp as he kissed his way up my thigh. The swipe of his tongue sent me arching up and crying out. When he added a finger and sucked my clit into his mouth I was convinced I'd crack the headboard. Primed and ready, I wasn't sure that I'd survive the exquisite torment from his perfect oral skills.

He knew that that smooth slide of his tongue against my folds and the gentle scrape of his teeth against my skin sent fine tremors of pleasure zapping through my body. Each stroke set my nerves on edge with anticipation. My moans bounced off the walls, and my hands gripped the sheets when his tongue wrapped around my clit.

He looked up at me, pleased with his efforts, the shiny evidence of my arousal on his lips and chin. He crawled up my body. With one hand buried in my hair, he angled my head to the side, his mouth trailing down my throat and his tongue sliding over my pulse.

I needed him.

His lips drifted across my chest, licking a line between my breasts. Tugging my nipple between his teeth, my back arched off the bed. His fingers curled inside me hitting all the right spots. On a thready cry, my first orgasm rolled through me.

"You look sensational when you come. *Beautiful*," he rasped in my ear.

Goosebumps splashed across my skin, and my legs shook as Grady circled my clit with his thumb drawing out my orgasm. My eyes opened to see Grady smiling down at me, his cock sliding between us.

This man, this gorgeous, hot as sin man revved me up better than any porn or a smutty book could do. Lean muscles, strong brows and a set of lips I could kiss for days. On paper, Grady James fit every relationship qualification I envisioned. In and out of the bedroom, he filled every desire of mine. This was dragging me under. He was pulling me into something deeper than I ever imaged was possible between two people.

Shifting his body, Grady dragged his fingers through my hair and kissed me. My inner muscles tightened as he notched the head of his cock between my slick folds. With one thrust, he filled me burying himself to the hilt.

"Oh my holy . . . *fuck*." The last word came out in a gasp.

"You okay, sweetheart?" he asked, scraping his teeth over my earlobe.

My arms found their way over his shoulders. "Yeah, you're just . . . so *deep*," I whispered.

Grady's laugh filled the space between us. "I'll take that as a good sign. You feel so good."

I hooked my legs around him, drawing him closer and his hips rolled against me. We rocked together, moans of pleasure and our hushed sighs wrestled with the crashing rain and thunder booming outside.

The heavy ache of my orgasm built with every pulse pounding thrust and my fingernails dug into the muscles of his shoulders and back.

"You are incredible, all I feel is your pussy squeezing me," he gasped, stilling his hips and relishing the moment. "You're perfect, *this* is perfect. Being here with you just like this."

Grady pushed deeper. I wrapped my legs around his

waist, my heels digging into his back. His lips found my neck, shoulders and lips and my orgasm slammed into me and then Grady came with a roar as he fucked into me harder. As if the moment wasn't monumental enough, a thunderous boom dropped shaking the house.

Grady cocked a brow, a smirk tugging the corner of his mouth. "You think that was applause from the man upstairs?"

I couldn't help the laugh that bubbled in my throat. "It *was* something."

Chapter
Thirty-Three

Grady

"**I**'m not ready for summer to end," Ronan muttered as we crossed the street to the Rum Bar.

"Summer is hardly over," Alex argued.

The humidity was unusually high today, and it was hard to imagine that July was sliding into August. I was hit with a cool blast of air as I pulled the door to the restaurant open.

Ronan signaled to the bartender for three beers. "Maybe not, but where has the time gone? I feel like I haven't had a moment of peace."

I slapped his shoulder as we approached an open four top. "That's because you're getting married, renovating a house, flying back and forth from New York to Los Angeles and isn't your youngest starting kindergarten?"

"Not to mention, his real estate hobby," Alex added, sprinkling salt onto his napkin.

Ronan scowled. "Jesus, are two you stalking me?"

Alex chuckled, scanning the menu. "He's not wrong, you just need to take a few days and relax. Pump the brakes and enjoy life."

"For the record, I'm not stalking you. It's called *peopling* and I am engaging and being social."

Ronan's hands rubbed at his forehead. "What the fuck is peopling?"

The bartender dropped off three cold beers and Alex ordered the appetizers. "Did you learn that term from your lady friend, James?"

"As a matter of fact, I did."

Ronan turned to me. "When do we get to meet this fine woman?"

"Their pictures are all over the internet," Alex informed, jutting his chin in my direction. "Or call your sister. She'll fill you in on his love interest."

I took a swig of my beer. "Our relationship is still new and I'd like to get to know her better before I let you hyenas near her."

"What?" Alex lifted his hands in surrender. "We're harmless. It's our counterparts you might have to worry about."

"Nonsense," Ronan said, waving off Alex's comment. "As long as you're not back with Heather—Ella and Holliday will welcome anyone with open arms."

The bar started to fill up with weekenders and a few locals. The helicopter fans started to inch closer to our table. Alex subtly waved anyone off who looked as if they were about to approach and ask either of us for a selfie.

"Mr. Robertsen, would you prefer a private table upstairs?" the manager asked.

He shook his head. "No, in about an hour, they'll all

forget that these two are even here."

She huffed a laugh. "Let me know if you need anything."

"How about you bring her out to our house for the end of summer party?" Alex suggested.

I held up my hands. "I'm not making any promises.

"So, this is it, my big send off into married life?" Ronan mused.

Our server dropped off the plates and silverware for our appetizers. "What would you prefer, Connolly? Strippers? Vegas?"

He ran a hand through his hair. "Oh hell no, I do not need that shit showing up on TMZ."

"And that is no way to start off a marriage, Vegas is fucking overrated. Just ask James." Alex smirked.

"I went to an audition the next week, and the director asked me if I had coke on my pants. Sure as fuck, I did. Apparently, wifely duties hadn't kicked in yet for Heather."

"Well played Vegas," Alex said, before taking a sip of his beer. "Reason number forty-seven why Vegas is a bad idea."

"When I confronted Heather about the cocaine, she had another form of blow in mind."

"So not all bad then," Alex asserted.

"Right and honestly, I was giving you guys shit, *this* is great." Ronan glanced at his phone. "Shit, okay, Matt is coming in, he's parking his car."

"Maybe no one will recognize him." Alex offered, signaling the bartender for another beer.

"Right," Ronan scoffed. "Barber has the number one film in the world right now."

"He's more popular than voice enabled technology, Cuba, and gin and tonics."

They looked at me as if I'd suggested we go out kicking

puppies for fun. It was an article on Harlow's website, the biggest trends of the year. She asked me to read it, so I did.

Matt walked in with his Chicago Cubs ball cap tugged low and his sunglasses shielding his eyes. Matthew Barber was one of Ronan's oldest friends. As the story goes, they met at the VMA's when they presented an award together. The prank wars between them are legendary. A few years back, Ronan set up a crowd of fans outside Matt's hotel in Toronto, and had them chant "Ronan" all night long. For that stunt, Matt countered by telling various interviewers at the Venice Film Festival that Ronan was a very serious actor and when interviewing him, it's best not to make eye contact or tell jokes, because he would become very upset.

"Hey, guys, sorry I'm late," he said, slapping a hand to Ronan's shoulder.

Our appetizers came out just as Matt situated himself on a barstool. Our server's hands shook as she set the first two baskets onto the table.

Ronan spoke up. "Kacie, hi, I'm Ronan and these are my mates," he said, tilting his head to meet her eyes. "I promise that we put our shoes on one foot at a time. We're not here to make you feel on edge."

Her cheeks flushed crimson. "Okay, Ronan," she said, dropping the basket of poppers between Matt and Alex.

The three of us ordered another round of beers and Matt ordered one too and asked for a bottle of hot sauce. The guy put it on everything. Matt slid his sunglasses off his face, and then rubbed his palms together. "This looks fucking delicious. I could eat the ass end of a horse right now."

After about fifteen minutes of devouring food and listening to Matt discuss his latest film shooting in Australia, I had serious vacation envy.

I cleared my throat. "Is anyone using the house in Sapodilla Bay next month?"

Alex raised a brow giving me a smug smile. "You're taking her to T and C?"

Matt glanced between Alex and me. "Who is *she*?"

"James is wooing a lady," Ronan said, swiping his phone to life.

"Not just any lady," Alex announced, lifting his beer in my direction. "A lingerie model, former WAG."

"Robertsen, you have got to stop talking to your wife about celebrity gossip. I want the old Alex back, the one who rattles off baseball stats and explains the unorthodox hazing rituals you'd put today's youth through."

"For your information, it's called data collection." Alex pointed a finger at the three of us. "It's one of the ways I stay abreast of all the situations surrounding you chuckleheads—unless you've forgotten that you're all my clients."

Matt wiped his hands with a wet nap. "Whoa, okay, Alex can read anything he wants, *InStyle* or fucking *Home and Garden*."

"I have a feeling I'm going to have to hire extra security for your wedding." Alex shot Ronan a pointed glance. "And you and Holliday better not try to give my team the slip either."

Ronan tapped his finger against the table. "The house in Turks and Caicos is available all month, so it's all yours, James."

"You're not going to come back married, are you?" Matt asked.

I glowered at him. "No, I'm not going to come back married."

"It's a fair question, you have a history," Alex pointed out.

"One woman. One marriage. That's hardly a pattern of behavior. Now, Connolly on the other hand," I suggested, dipping a few fries into ketchup. "He's someone you should worry about."

And under the bus goes the Irishman.

Chapter
Thirty-Four

Harlow

Grady: Where are you?

    Harlow: I had to go back to Afton's.

    Harlow: Laundry day.

    Grady had begged me to stay the night with him after his guys' weekend. They ended up flying to Chicago and stayed at a house on Lake Michigan. Apparently, Alex had a buddy with a house somewhere on the lake near or in South Haven.

    Grady: You could have done your laundry here.

    Harlow: Thank you. I appreciate that.

    Grady: Are you coming back? I'm going to need you in my bed tonight.

    Harlow: We'll see.

    Grady: Harlow.

    I could practically hear him growling my name.

    Harlow: Maybe, I want you in my bed tonight.

Grady: Interesting counter offer.

Harlow: Let me sweeten the deal, Afton is out of town.

Grady: For a moment, I thought that you were going to suggest a threesome.

Harlow: Not that I don't find Afton attractive, but hell no.

Harlow: Although, if you're into that, I know a girl.

Grady: Oh really? Tell me more.

Harlow: Tara from Castle Hill Beach House.

Harlow: I have it on good authority that she is into that kind of thing.

Grady: Is this you giving me the gist again? I need details.

Grady: Use your dirty words, and please be explicit, sweetheart.

Harlow: She told my brother that she'd be into it.

Grady: Um.

Harlow: She didn't know he was my brother, if that helps.

Grady: It doesn't.

Since I'd killed the fantasy, I decided to do something I'd never done before—I sent Grady a picture of me wearing a new piece of white lace lingerie. I positioned my arm, so that you couldn't see my face.

Grady: Oh fuck. That's hot as hell.

Grady: I'll be in your bed tonight. Don't take that off or move from that spot.

I barely paid attention to any news headlines over the past few weeks, but England had won the World Cup. Part of me was very happy for Harry and his teammates the other part of me may have given the middle finger to the ESPN announcer.

The buzzer on the washing machine rang out and I hummed along with the song. After I hung up my delicates, I pulled out the tray for the detergent and fabric softener and dumped the excess water into the sink. I had twenty minutes until my conference call with the lingerie company who sent me a few pieces to try. I really liked the brand and I hoped that they'd allow me to keep the samples.

Knock. Knock.

"Hey, girl, you here," Afton called out, sliding the door open.

"Hey, I thought you were out of town on business? Are you here to collect the rent?"

Afton laughed and twisted the gold anchor bracelet on her wrist. "Ah, no, you're a wonderful house guest and this place is . . . is paid for, no . . . no . . . *need* for money."

I shot her a sideways glance as she stuttered through her words. Crossing the room, to the kitchen, I asked, "You want some coffee or tea?"

"No, nothing for me," she replied, crossing her arms over her chest.

"Are you okay?"

She smoothed her palms over her floral pencil skirt. "I guess that I am. I'm actually happier than I've been in a long time."

I poured some coffee into a mug, and walked back into the living room. Something was off with Afton. I'd never seen her on edge like this before. "That's great news, so what's with your weirdness?"

She took a seat on the couch. "Well, I guess I have some news. Some really, *really* big news—huge."

I took a seat beside her, tucking my feet underneath me.

"Okay, then out with it."

Afton grabbed the mug from my hands and set it on the coffee table. "Can't have any hot beverages in your hand while I tell you my news."

"Out with it, Afton. Quit dragging this out like a damn soap opera."

She sucked in a deep breath. "I'm . . . I got married over the weekend."

My eyes bugged out of my skull. "*What?* To who? I didn't even know that you were dating someone." I jumped to my feet in a rush, nearly spilling coffee onto the white rug. "Oh my God, you eloped—how romantic. I need the details. I'm a little pissed that you didn't invite me, but wow, I'm so happy for you."

"Well," Afton began, rising to her feet. "You know him actually, and he's someone that you like . . . and care about *a lot.*"

Shrugging, I furrowed my brow. I followed Afton's gaze, and saw my brother walking up the steps. He pulled open the sliding glass door. "Hey, sis."

I didn't give Afton or Nicholas another moment of my time. Mad didn't even begin to describe my feelings. With only one destination in mind, I zipped my Lexus through the streets of East Harbour. I rescheduled my conference call, which was completely unprofessional but I knew that I was in no condition to be talking business.

By the time I made it to Grady's, my mood had gone

through a cycle of emotions. Once I parked the car, I slammed my hand against the steering wheel. I was hurt, frustrated, angry and teetering on elated. Two of the most important people in my life were in a relationship and didn't tell me. And now they were married. It was a hard pill to swallow. Giving myself a moment to compose myself, I grabbed my purse and then hopped out of my car.

"Grady, are you here," I called out crossing through the kitchen. It occurred to me that I should have called him before barging over here unannounced.

"Harlow," Grady called out, his voice laced with confusion. "This is a surprise—a very good surprise." Even in my salty mood, I still took notice of the way this man filled out a grey v-neck, t-shirt. It was unfair for a man this sexy to have a charming personality and the brains to back it all up. *Fuck.* Why Heather ever cheated on him was beyond my comprehension.

Pushing the lustful thoughts aside, I took a moment to focus on my current issue. My eyes scanned over the water watching the sailboats rocking back and forth. The water was inviting, and I was in desperate need of its healing power. Grady bent to meet my eyes, his hands framed my face. "What's happened, sweetheart? Did your meeting not go well?"

"It's worse. Afton and my brother got married." The words tasted bitter on my tongue, which filled me with shame.

"And this isn't happy news for you?" he asked, dropping a hand to his hip.

Stalking towards the kitchen, I threw my hands into the air. "Good guess, Sherlock."

"Sorry I asked." Taking a step back, he shoved his hands into the pockets of his jeans.

Shaking my head, I paced around the island. "I'm sorry." I blew out a harsh breath and cocked my hip against the edge of the counter.

He pulled a chair away from the breakfast bar, urging me to take a seat. "How about a drink? And you can tell me why this has you so upset."

I nodded, drumming my fingers against the cool surface. "I'm so mad at both of them. I don't even understand how this happened." Grady set a glass and the bottle of Simi chardonnay in front of me. "I am trying to wrap my brain around this idea of the two of them married, and them doing *marital* things." I took a big swallow of wine.

Grady stood in front of me, pouring a can of Harbour Brew pale ale into a tall glass.

"At one point, I was convinced she was having a fling with Ridge. I haven't been this mad at anyone in a long time."

Grady emptied the contents of the can into the glass and then tossed it into the recycling bin. "What about your ex?"

"What about *your* ex." I retorted, and then polished off my glass.

Grady smirked, refilling my glass. "Does this mean that your brother will move here?"

I cocked a brow. "What?" The word came out more sarcastically than I intended.

"Silver lining."

"Screw your silver lining," I said through a laugh. "I just don't get why they didn't tell me?"

"Maybe they didn't tell you because they didn't know if it was going to go anywhere."

A deep sigh, escaped me as I propped my elbows onto the counter. "Ugh, why are you making sense?"

"Look, Harlow, I get it, he's your brother and she's your

best friend. They kept a secret from you—something huge and then they cut you out of their big day. I'm sure it brings up feelings of abandonment, how your dad left you, your mom and more recently Harry."

I let his words roll around in my head, because it all made a lot of sense. Every damn bit of it.

"Go talk to them, let them share their story."

"Is it wrong, if I push it off until tomorrow?"

He shook his head. "Not one bit."

Chapter
Thirty-Five

Grady

Afternoon settled into dusk over The Harbour. Harlow worked out her feelings, staying mostly silent. I suggested she take a bubble bath, but she refused citing that she didn't have any clean clothes or toiletries. Instead, I made her bacon, shrimp, and corn chowder and kept her wine glass full. Although she didn't eat or drink that much at all.

"Do you want me to go over to Afton's and pack you a bag?" I asked, clearing the dishes.

She shook her head, wiping her mouth with a napkin. "No, all I need is to run into town and grab a toothbrush and a few miscellaneous beauty items."

I should have extra toiletries on hand. I'm making a mental note to have Thora stash them in all the bathrooms.

Closing the dishwasher, I nodded. "Do you want me to

go with you?"

She rolled up to her feet. "That's fine."

I wished there was something I could do to improve her mood. My cellphone rang. The screen showed it was Chelsea from the polo club.

I lifted the phone to my ear. "Hey, Chelsea, what's up?"

"Grady, it's Elsa. The vet is in with her now, she has colic. We noticed she didn't eat much last night, and this morning she was pawing at the ground and didn't eat at all."

Feeling my shoulders tense, I rubbed at the back of my neck. "Is she lying down? How about drinking water?" I didn't' give Chelsea time to answer. "Never mind, I'll be right there."

I ended the call and grabbed my keys from the bowl on the hutch. Harlow's hazel eyes narrowed. "What's going on?"

"My horse, Elsa, she's sick with colic. I need to go . . . and be with her." My heart hammered in my chest.

Harlow took my keys and set them back onto the counter. "I'll drive you."

Harlow

My heart tumbled into my stomach watching as Grady paced with Elsa in circles outside the stables. "Elsa girl, you need to stay on your feet."

She kept pawing at the ground making several attempts to roll. The vet told us that Elsa didn't have a twisted bowel, which came as a welcome relief to Grady. Dehydration and possible shock was the vet's diagnosis. As for the reason Elsa wasn't drinking or eating, that was unclear. I learned that with colic it could be anything, often there is no clear answer.

"Come on, Elsa girl," Grady said, rubbing her forehead and snout. "Just go to the bathroom and this will all be over."

Grady's eyes met mine. The pain filling them, tugged at my heart. I've never had pets, not a cat, dog, or even a goldfish. I couldn't imagine the way he was feeling at this moment.

"Can I help with anything?"

Grady shook his head. "Just having you here is all I need."

I patted Elsa's hindquarters like I saw Grady doing earlier. "Can I just say, Elsa, your house is gorgeous."

Reclaimed brick lined the walkways, making you feel as if you're strolling through a part of history. Stone columns and iron railings enhanced the classic aesthetic appeal. The stalls were immaculate with their sliding Dutch doors. There was even a lounge area complete with flat screen televisions anchored on the walls. My first apartment in Manhattan wasn't this chic.

Grady chuckled. "Yeah, only the best for my girl."

"How did you come up with the name Elsa?"

"I didn't, my mom and sister flipped a coin for their name choices. My mom won and Elsa isn't named after the Disney character, her namesake is Elsa Peretti."

I laughed, rocking back on my heels. "And what was your sister's name selection?"

"Pat, short for Patricia, but she really just wanted me to introduce her as Pat, the horse."

"Are you thirsty?" I asked, stepping onto the grassy area beside the stables.

"Actually, yeah, could you grab me a bottle of water? Go

up to the clubhouse. Use the code I gave you earlier, the player's lounge is three doors down on the left. There's a refrigerator in there stocked with everything."

I trekked up to the clubhouse pausing for a moment when I heard Grady talking to Elsa. Turning back, searing pain wound through my heart when I saw him step in front of her, and then kiss her nose.

I made my way into the clubhouse and then found the lounge Grady mentioned. My phone vibrated in my pocket as I snagged two bottles of water from the fridge.

Zanita: Harry wants to talk to you.

Harlow: Then he can call me, but honestly, I'm not interested in hearing what he has to say.

Zanita: I figured as much.

Harlow: After all this time, why?

Harlow: You know what, fuck that. I'm happy and we're over.

Zanita: Bravo, girl. I debated on whether or not to tell you.

Zanita: I'm of the mind better to have all the information.

Harlow: And I appreciate that about your friendship.

Zanita: Want me to tell him to piss off?

Harlow: Nah, not worth it. Goodbye, Harry, have a splendid life.

Harlow: I know that I will.

And that was the end of that—officially closed the door. No room for this back and forth bullshit. He dumped me. I pulled up my big girl panties and moved on with Grady. It had been a few months, but it all felt so right—so fucking right.

I opened the door and then reset the code to the clubhouse. Whatever crap life dished out for the two of us, I was confident that Grady and I would handle it—there was no doubt in my mind.

"Hey, Harlow! Watch your step, Elsa's feeling better!"

My face scrunched up and I couldn't help the cackle that erupted from my chest. "Way to go, Elsa!"

Chapter
Thirty-Six

Harlow

Afton becoming Mrs. Nicholas Trembley was an issue that I needed to address. I didn't know where to begin with this line of questioning. How? When? My fingers hovered over the screen of my phone as I attempted to dial Nicholas. Last count, I had half a dozen messages from Nicholas and double that amount from Afton.

Grady plucked my phone from my hands. "Sweetheart, you need to go back to Afton's and look her in the eyes. This isn't a phone call situation."

I folded my arms across my chest. "Seriously?"

"Seriously," he repeated, handing me a travel mug filled with coffee.

On a groan, I took the mug. "Fine, I'll do it. Why do you make so much sense?"

His lips brushed against mine and he hummed. "I'm

very wise."

Taking the long way, I drove around East Harbour cruising up Main Street over to Harbour Drive. When I reached Afton's place, I thought about turning around and driving right back to Grady's house. I sat in my car, gathering my thoughts but everything was jumbled.

What am I going to say to her?

How long have you been screwing my brother? How long have you two been sneaking around? Ugly was not a good color on me.

The smell of white lilacs and Casablanca lilies filled the air with a sweet scent as I pushed open the front door. Vases of white hydrangeas were staggered throughout her kitchen and dining room. Afton loved white.

"Afton, are you here?"

I walked around her kitchen staring up at the coffered ceilings admiring the clean lines. My fingers traced the edge of the white marble countertop. I studied the shaker cabinets and the glossy white subway tiles. Lines, they surrounded me everywhere. They were beautiful, untainted by cracks and went on forever. A line—a path had led Afton to Nicholas and vice versa.

"Hey, Harlow," the voice belonged to my brother.

Expelling a heavy sigh, I pivoted to face him. As he approached me, the morning sunlight glinted off the platinum band that hugged his finger. It had never been more difficult to formulate words.

"Did you two register somewhere so I that can at least buy a gift?" The words finally tumbled out of my mouth.

Shifting the newspaper from one hand to the other, he rolled his eyes. Nicholas wanted to laugh, a hint of a smile played on the curve of his lip. "It's good to see you, sis."

I stared at his wedding band, a circle that represented love and a lifetime commitment. It wasn't a line. A line could only be intersected, a single spot at a time, a fleeting interaction before continuing. A circle . . . a circle was infinite, and infinitely connected, never to be broken.

I didn't know what hit me, but in that moment, I realized that Nicholas had made a commitment to his person—Afton, my best friend. My brother had married my best friend. Suddenly tears carved paths down my cheeks. My heart stuttered in my chest and then I was full on sobbing. I was crumbling in front of Nicholas and I hated that I wasn't part of that moment when he married Afton. I hated that I wasn't part of the moment when she married Nicholas. Even more I hated that I'd been pissed off when he had something monumental happen in life.

He reached for me, pulling me into his frame. The rustling of newspaper mixed with the half-sobbing, half-hiccupping messy sound that flooded the kitchen.

"I'm sorry, Nicholas," I managed to choke out. "I'm happy for you really, I promise."

"Is that why you're crying?" he asked, stroking my hair.

"Yes, these are happy tears," I retorted, untangling from our embrace. "I'm fine, I swear."

"All right, you're okay." Nicholas stepped around the corner.

Smoothing my palms down my cheeks and blinked through my tears.

Nicholas handed me a tissue. "Thank you," I sniffled, and replied. When Nicholas pulled out a chair from the breakfast nook, the tears started all over again. He set the entire box down on the table and urged me to take a seat.

"I've never known you to be a crier, Harlow."

"Well, you ran off and married my best friend and you look so damn happy," I said, before drying my eyes and gracefully trying to blow my nose. Looking at my reflection in the microwave I was a serious hot mess. "Can I ask you a question?"

As he stepped up to the coffee maker, he nodded. "Always." Nicholas poured two mugs of coffee and then handed one to me.

"How the hell did this happen?" When the question dropped from my lips, Afton sauntered into the kitchen wearing a pink and white striped pajama set. Her fishtail braid fell over her shoulder, as she leaned in to kiss Nicholas.

"I'd be happy to answer that question—every gory detail," she said.

I blew the steam away from my mug. "No thanks, I just need the PG version."

Afton approached me, and then pulled me into a hug. "For the record, I wanted you there but your brother wanted to elope. Blame him."

We both laughed. "It's all Nicholas' fault."

Chuckling he folded his arms over his chest. "I get the feeling a lot of things are going to be *my* fault." Nicholas pulled a mug from the cabinet and poured a cup of coffee for Afton, adding a splash of skim milk.

Tears streamed down my face. "Fuck," I blurted out, throwing my arms in the air. "You know how she takes her coffee."

Before I knew it, Afton was crying and Nicholas was handing her the box of tissues. "Okay, I love you both, but you have got to stop crying."

Pushing her shoulders back, Afton swiped away the tears. "All right, all right, we can do this."

With fresh mugs of coffee, the three of us gathered around the table. My phone buzzed, it was Grady asking how it was going. I swiped the screen and typed a quick message letting him know it was all good.

Wrapping my hands around my mug, I said, "Tell me everything—PG version, please."

Chapter
Thirty-Seven

Grady

Our drive from the airport to Sapodilla Bay was brief. No sooner than I had our luggage hauled into the master bedroom, Harlow was already in her bikini.

"It's beautiful here," she said, dabbing sunscreen on her creamy skin.

"I'm glad you approve."

After the Sundance Film Festival last January, Ronan received a tip on an island property. He proposed the idea of buying the estate to Alex, Matt, and me. Naturally, the three of us jumped at the chance to have a piece of tropical coastline at our disposal. I had the money. It was a no brainer investment.

"It's five o'clock somewhere," she said, pouring a glass of champagne.

"When you're on vacation you can drink anytime you like."

"I guess that's true." She lifted the glass to her lips. "Did your sister decorate the house?"

"Actually, she doesn't even know about this place."

Ronan hired a design company for revamping some features. Alex took care of all the security arrangements and it was almost certain, Holliday and Ella had their hands in the interior decorating. The house was a mostly neutral color palette, with azure blue, teal and coral splashed throughout the house.

I loved everything about this place. The views from each balcony and terrace were incredible, but the double day bed lounger suspended over the water's edge was my favorite spot. We stepped onto the main terrace walking past the infinity pool down the wooden walkway inching us closer to the vibrant, calm blue waters.

Harlow rested her hip against the railing. Needing to touch her, I leaned forward, brushing her hair out of the way to kiss the soft spot between her neck and shoulders.

Her hands snaked around my neck. I kissed her long and hot, sliding my tongue against hers, tasting and savoring the feel of her soft lips against mine. I inhaled deeply getting my fill of salt and sand and Harlow. I wanted to remember this moment, catalog it to the index of my life.

Without sounding like a real estate agent, I explained the layout of the compound to Harlow, because that's what it was—15,000 total square feet with nine bedrooms in total, including a master pavilion that housed five bedrooms and two guest pavilions with two bedrooms each. As we walked the property, she held my hand listening to me ramble on about the history and culture of the island.

I took her through the movie theater, and to the gym. "Here, you can work off the extra calories consumed from eating conch fritters, jerk chicken with rice, and my personal favorite, coconut crusted snapper tacos."

We made our way back to the main house. "If indoor activity isn't your thing, there is basketball, tennis, paddle boarding, and kayaking."

"Well, if this acting and modeling thing doesn't work out for you, Grady, I think you can find a career in real estate development."

"What do you want to do first?" I asked, hooking my thumb over my shoulder. "Are you hungry?"

Her mouth curled up into a sexy smile. "Not for food."

I cocked a brow. "Where should I fuck you first?"

Harlow gazed around the property, but I didn't give her a chance to think about it a second longer. I hauled her up onto my shoulder, carrying her to the outdoor shower. With one hand buried in her hair, I tilted her head back.

"*Ahhh, Grady,*" she gasped, digging her nails into my shoulder blades. "I want you."

My mouth trailed down her throat, my teeth scraping against her pulse. I cupped her ass, fisting at her thong, the scrap of fabric that separated me from the Promised Land between her legs.

Crushing my lips to hers, I flipped on the spray. Using my hand, I tested the temperature before pushing her back against the wall.

"It's important to shower before getting into the pool."

"Yes, of course," she agreed, smiling against my lips.

Thank fuck, for bikini bottoms that tie at the sides. With a swift tug, the material fell to the ground. I spun her away from me, and she gave me a devious smile over her shoulder.

Using my foot to widen her stance I rocked against her, my cock, hard and straining against my board shorts.

She tilted her head back into the spray, water sliding over the expanse of her back and gliding over her perfect ass. *Fuck me.*

I pushed my shorts down over my hips, gravity did the rest. Steam curled around our bodies as she whispered my name while removing her top. Licking every inch of her neck and shoulders, my hands glided up her ribcage palming her breasts.

Arching against me, I groaned when she rubbed her ass against my cock. The sounds of her moans, and the feel of our wet slick skin gliding together made my dick hard as steel. I guided my cock against her, and she moaned. It was music to my ears—loud and needy.

My fingers circled her clit, and with the snap of my hips I pushed inside her sweet pussy. "Hold on, sweetheart, this will be fast."

Pleas and moans alternated with breathy whispers as I thrusted deeper.

"Oh, yes," she cried out.

"That's it, sweetheart," I growled. "Let the whole island know that I'm fucking you." Over and over I pounded into her, giving us both the release we're craving. Fine tremors of pleasure built in my balls.

"Ah, yes," she groaned, pushing back. The sensation was almost too much to take.

Her hands slapped against the stone tile, and my fingers dug into her hips. A scream left Harlow's lips heralding her orgasm. The sound unleashed something possessive inside of me.

She is mine. Only mine.

In the deep recess of my mind, I knew what Harlow and I had was something special. This might have started even before the hair-brained scheme of mine. We were friends who needed each other in a bigger way than I expected. I don't know how or when it happened, but Harlow had helped me heal the parts of my soul that needed it most.

"Mr. James, welcome back to the island." The voice with its musically accented English and Creole came from Augustin Lightbourne, the caretaker of the property Ronan had hired. I sat up from my position on the sundeck pulling Harlow with me.

"Augustin, how are you, my man?" I asked, gripping his hand.

"Very well, sir, just glad to have some people back here buzzing about." His dark eyes shifted to Harlow. "And who is this stunning woman?"

I laughed. "Augustin, I'd like you to meet my girlfriend, Harlow Trembley."

"Ah," he replied nodding. "Trembley, that's French Canadian."

Her cheeks tinged pink. "Yes, that's correct."

My brow scrunched. *French Canadian.* I'd never given much thought to Harlow's last name. After all this time, had I not taken the time to really get to know her? Impossible.

"Have you found everything to your liking, Mr. James?"

"We have."

"Mr. James, if you and your lady need anything—food,

drinks, please let me know. Anything at all, it's my pleasure."

"Augustin, there's one thing, would it be possible to get some fresh pineapple?"

"Of course, Mr. James, right away, sir."

Harlow looked up and smiled at me. "You think of everything."

My lips brushed against her temple. "When it comes to you, I do."

Chapter
Thirty-Eight

Harlow

I t's been a long time since I felt complete and total relaxation. At least I had been relaxed until Heather Young burst through doors of the main house chased by Augustin and two men wearing grey shirts and dark shorts. Neither of whom, I'd seen before.

"Heather, what the hell are you doing here?" Grady yelled.

Heather struggled against Augustin's hold, as he brought her front and center like a prisoner. Grady nodded to Augustin who then released the hold he had on her. I stood motionless, rooted to my spot. Stunned, was the most accurate feeling I could describe seeing Heather standing mere feet from me. The bags under her eyes were visible. She looked as if she hadn't slept in days. Her blonde hair was pulled up in a messy ponytail. Red marks donned her neck and chest.

A sick feeling spread through me, making me cold. Suddenly I understood—she was high.

How did she know that we were here?

Heather shot me an icy glare. "Yeah, you stay right there—slut," she spat. Her words were delivered harsh and slightly broken.

When Grady approached Heather, she attempted to step back only to find herself stumbling into the back of the couch. "Heather, I'm going to ask you again, what are you doing here?"

Shaking her head, and pushing up from the back of the couch she inhaled deeply. "You brought her, here," she sobbed, pointing at me. "You have the nerve to bring her *here?*"

Grady shook his head. "You aren't a part of my life anymore. We're not married."

Confused I stared at Grady, irritation and sadness passing over his face. Heather's eyes darted between the two of us and I swore my heart stopped for half a second. *She is unwell.*

"But, *why* here?" she asked, the words were half-whine, half-cry.

"Because she is my girlfriend, that's why I brought her here."

Heather's hands spread wide in front of her. "That's just great, Grady, bringing your mistress to our vacation home," she cried, sounding the same level of insane.

"Heather, we're not married anymore, remember?"

"We spent our anniversary here, we are married!"

Dread sank into the pit of my stomach, the feeling eerily resembling the moments before Harry dumped me. Grady rushed to me, gripping my wrists. My eyes fell to his forearms, something about those shirtsleeves rolled up showcasing his strength knocked me out of my headspace every time.

"Harlow, look at me," he said, his eyes filled with concern. "Trust in me, please."

Hearing his words, I nodded. "Of course."

"Thank you," he whispered, his hands framed my face. "I'm sorry she's here. Did I mention that I own this place?"

"I think you left that part out of the tour." I reached for him, weaving my fingers through his hair. "I want to kiss you, but given the current situation, I'll refrain."

His eyes brightened. "I have words. So many things I want to say . . ."

My hands fell to his shoulders, kneading the thick cords of his muscles. Tension lingered, but I felt it all evaporating under my touch. "I know, me too," I whispered.

A sharp thunderous crack echoed. My head jerked to find broken pieces of white porcelain surrounding Heather's feet. Augustin lunged at her just as she picked up a jagged piece from the vase she'd destroyed. Knocking it from her grip, Augustin held onto her as one of the men slapped flex-cuffs around her wrists. The other man, who I now realized was a security guard, had moved to stand by Grady and me, that's when my eyes focused on his gun.

"Let me go!" she screamed, thrashing and kicking her feet against the tile.

Grady's blue eyes searched my face. "She's not my responsibility, anymore, but . . ."

I nodded, smoothing my hands over his grey t-shirt. "But, it would be cruel not to get her the help she needs." My fist pounded against his chest. "I understand, Grady. I do," I said, reassuring him.

"God, I . . . how . . . *how* did I get so lucky to have you in my life?"

I knew what he wanted to say, but he couldn't for

obvious reasons.

"Is there anything I can do to help? Call anyone?"

Lifting my hand to his mouth his lips brushed the back of my knuckles. "No, but thank you."

He looked over towards the seating area. I followed his gaze. Heather writhed against Augustin's firm grasp, tears spilling down her face. My heart went out to her. Grady raked a hand through his hair, and then turned away from me. Goosebumps swept across my skin, I'd never seen him look so pained.

Grady

After I persuaded the highly-recommended doctor with an expensive fee to leave his golf game to give Heather a drug test, my security team took her to a guest house to sleep it off.

I didn't want Harlow to be here while I dealt with this matter, so I had Augustin arrange for her to spend the remainder of the afternoon being pampered. Harlow offered to stay. She even offered to talk to Heather—woman to woman. In Heather's mental state, I wasn't willing to risk it, although I appreciated the thought.

I walked into the study, and then fired up the laptop. This was a delicate matter and I needed it handled with as much discretion as possible. A message from Haven lit up my phone, it contained all the details for the treatment facility. It had all been arranged. *Thank you, Haven.*

Swiping the screen on my phone, I dialed Heather's assistant, Drew. I didn't wait for him to speak. "Heather's in Turks and Caicos, and she's using again. There's a first-rate rehab facility in Georgia, she's going there as soon as possible. I'm sending you the information, and I need you to be there when she arrives."

"I don't work for Heather anymore," he informed me.

"Since when?"

"Since she fired me," he said hoarsely. "After the cheating story came out."

I took a deep breath. "I'm hiring you for the foreseeable future. If you have plans cancel them."

Once I squared things away with Drew, Alex was next on my call list. I walked over to the bar in the corner of the room and then poured a glass of scotch.

"Is the vacation that bad that you needed to call me? Are you in jail? Fuck, you got married, didn't you?"

"You're a funny guy, Robertsen," I said, staring down at the liquid in my glass. "Actually, my ex-wife is here, she showed up unannounced, obviously."

Instinctually, the man trained with superior interrogation skills launched into a fuck ton of questions. I filled him in on the whole insane debacle.

"That's fucked up, how did she even know that you were there?"

"Harlow's Instagram."

"Damn social media, one of the best and worst inventions ever."

"Yeah, no kidding," I laughed a humorless laugh. "Would it be possible to send a jet here so that I can get Heather back to the states?"

I heard tapping against a keyboard. "Sure, anything you

need, man. You okay?"

"Fine for a guy whose ex-wife crashed his vacation with his current girlfriend."

Alex laughed. "And how's your girl?"

"Well, she didn't runaway or kick me in the balls," I replied. "Harlow is . . . the best—understanding, caring, and supportive."

"Ah yeah, I've been there my friend, there's nothing better than a woman who can handle a difficult situation with compassion rather than with jealousy and animosity."

I knew that Alex understood. He'd gone through a difficult time during the beginning of his relationship with Ella. Instead of giving up on him, she stayed knowing that he needed her. As my grandmother used to say, "Work on me, before becoming we."

"Okay, you are all set," he said, "I've just emailed the details and the flight itinerary. Heather will be out of your hair in a matter of hours."

"Thanks, man, it can't come soon enough." I ended the call and tossed my phone onto the desk. I swallowed the remains of my drink. "Time to have a chat with my ex-wife."

I instructed Harvey and Isaac, the security guys, to stay close. I found Heather sitting on the terrace, a plate of untouched fresh fruit and a mug of coffee on the table. I settled into the chair across from her, still unsure of where to begin. Her hair was wet from the shower, and she'd changed into neon pink t-shirt with "Turks & Caicos" printed on the front and a pair of denim shorts.

"Do you feel better?" I asked, sliding a bottle of water across the table.

She hadn't looked at me since I walked onto the terrace. "Not really."

"No, I suppose you don't." I leaned back, tapping my finger to the table. "I fast tracked your drug test. The doctor said, with the amount of drugs in your system, he's concerned that you're heading down a path to overdose."

With her eyes still trained on the floor, she lifted a shoulder. "Would you care if I did?"

"If you don't care enough about yourself, how am I supposed to care?"

"I know that you hate me, and you don't owe me a thing."

"Heather, I don't hate you—it takes a lot of energy to hate someone. It's exhausting."

"Don't," she breathed. "Please don't be nice to me. I don't deserve it." Tears dripped onto the t-shirt, as she wiped her nose with the back of her hand. "I told myself I wouldn't cry, but here I am . . . *here* I am in Sapodilla Bay stalking you and your new girlfriend like a psycho." She finally looked up at me.

"You said it not me."

That made her laugh, but the dam broke unleashing a fury of tears. I jogged to the bathroom and grabbed the tissues. As I crossed the living room to the terrace, I pulled a few tissues from the box.

She sniffled and blew her nose. "That's going to be the headline. Heather Young, actress turned stalking psycho flies to Caribbean disrupting ex-husband's vacation."

I sat silent for moment, while she collected herself.

Sure, I could pile on and kick her while she's down, but that wouldn't do any good. I didn't know if Heather would tell me the reason, the real reason that she was here. Was she lonely? Was she heartbroken? Was she in love with someone else and that freaked her out?

"What caused this psycho stalking episode?"

"Honestly, I don't know, I just snapped," she said, taking the cap off the water. "I was sitting alone in my condo, drinking a cheap bottle of wine and scrolling through Instagram and there it was a picture of the two of you in the pool, so happy."

"Being happy is a very personal thing, Heather. It has nothing to do with anyone else."

"I'm miserable and alone."

"You did it to yourself."

She nodded, returning her gaze to the ocean. "I did, I know that. I think that I've been holding onto my memories because it's all I have." Her hands shook as she lifted the water bottle. "I need help," she admitted. "I'm an addict and I need help."

I nodded. "It's all been arranged. I booked you into a treatment center in Georgia. I called Drew and he's going to be there when you arrive."

She tilted her head to look at me. "You're not coming with me?"

"No," I replied firmly. "You're going to heal yourself on your own."

"I'm broken. I don't think I'll ever be over you." Her fingers picked at the label on the water bottle. "I don't know how to forget you. Sometimes, I forget that we're divorced, and I think about what our life would be like now. I'm scared I can't move on and that I'll always wonder what might have been."

"It's important that you separate your feelings from your reality. This thing we once had, it's over. It's done."

That's all the advice I needed to give to Heather. She wouldn't heal a life time of pain overnight.

Dusk had settled over the island by the time I stuffed Heather into the back of the SUV with Augustin. Harvey escorted the two of them to the airport, while Isaac stayed here at the house.

I was exhausted, hungry, and fuck, did I need a drink. This was not how I planned this vacation to go, not at all.

Augustin said Harlow returned from the spa just before dinner. I found her lounging on the terrace by the pool.

"Hey," I said, dropping to the chair beside her.

"Hey, would you like me to make you something to eat?"

"Yeah, but first I just want to sit here with you, is that okay?"

She nodded. "It's more than okay. How's Heather?"

I stretched, folding my arms behind my head. "Honestly, I have no clue. She said some stuff about holding onto the past wondering what things might have been like for the two of us if we'd stayed married."

Harlow rolled onto her side to face me. "She wants you back?"

"She can want all she wants, but I don't want her. I made it very clear to Heather that she and I are over, forever."

"And she was okay with that?"

"She has no other choice," I said, moving to sit on the end of her lounger. "I've fallen for someone else."

"*Grady*," she breathed my name like a prayer. I hauled Harlow to her feet claiming her lips putting a cap on this conversation.

Chapter
Thirty-Nine

Harlow

A black cloud hung over our Caribbean vacation. We tried, but nothing seemed to scrub the memory of Heather's visit. Grady and I seized every opportunity to make the most of our days left here, but with my period coming a week early and the threat of Hurricane Dionne looming. Side note, the locals were referring to her as one nasty bitch of a storm. I was certain Grady would want to call game over any minute.

"Ronan, chill, you need to relax," a feminine voice ordered.

Glancing up from my magazine, I listened to the voices carrying through the house.

"Have you checked the weather report?" The rough rasp of Irish brogue asserted. "I'm not sure it was a wise choice to fly into the oncoming path of a hurricane. Let alone with my baby sister who happens to be having a baby and my soon to be wife. I'd like to see these moments happen. Alex, back me up."

"My wife is carrying my baby, I'm lucky she's still talking to me in this heat." A deep male voice called out.

What the hell is happening?

Grady was out in the middle of the water paddle boarding while I nursed my cramps alternating between green tea and a glass of Remy Martin. I stood up from the daybed lounger, waving my arms and jumping into the air trying to get his attention. I probably looked like one of those giant inflatable advertising props you see in the front of car dealerships.

By the voices I'd heard and the conversation, I'm guessing the Irish male voice belonged to Ronan Connolly. He mentioned his baby sister, which would be Ella, who is married to Alex, the security guy. The feminine voice that spoke first must have belonged to Holliday Prescott, Ronan's fiancée.

Glancing over my shoulder, I saw Grady paddling up to the shore. Confusion passed over his face, and he shrugged. I jumped off the platform and into the water.

I waded towards him. "We have guests," I whisper yelled, hooking my thumb towards the house.

He jumped off the board, and handed me the oar. "What are you talking about?"

Looping my arm with his, I said, "Listen."

"If it's a vacation you want, I have it on good authority that Europe's nice this time of year. No chance of a hurricane or any other natural disaster," Ronan quipped.

"Sure, let me check with Interpol first, and get the latest threat assessment. Europe sounds much safer than an isolated Caribbean island," Alex mocked.

"Fucking shit," he said, tugging me close. "Sweetheart, you're about to meet some friends of mine."

We trekked up the stairs to find four pairs of eyes on us.

"Well, well, look at this motley crew," Grady said, spreading his arms wide. "Everyone, this is Harlow. Harlow, this is the Riot Club."

"The Riot Club?" I asked, glancing at Grady.

"Fuck," Ronan muttered. "Are you bringing that back?"

"Is he allowed to bring it back?" Ella asked.

Grady waved his hands in front of him. "Honestly, there is no better way to describe us, and I'm not calling our little group of misfits a fucking 'tribe'—Riot Club stands." While the group of four argued amongst themselves Grady pointed out everyone to me.

"Hmm, is this because Breakfast Club was taken?" Ella asked.

"The Riot Club is an actual club at the University of Oxford," Ronan informed.

"Noted for its wealthy members, impressive banquets, and rituals of trashing restaurants," Alex quipped.

"I believe that Grady is referring to a night out in Park City, with three stolen snow mobiles and the smashing of one A-list celebrity douchebag's car windows," countered Holliday.

"Yeah, he fucking deserved it," said Alex.

"He really did," Ella agreed.

"Best night of my life," Ronan stated.

"I beg to differ," Holliday retorted.

"Okay enough," Grady shouted, clasping his hands together. "What the fuck are you all doing here?"

"We wanted to meet Harlow," Ella replied, motioning to me.

Grady folded his arms against his chest. "You flew all this way—*pregnant* to meet a woman I'm bringing to their wedding in a week?" His head bopped between Ronan and Holliday.

"Twelve days, to be exact," Holliday interjected.

"This is our babymoon," Ella said, nudging Alex with her shoulder.

"How can you have a babymoon, when you've already got one son at home?" Grady asked. "I'm not convinced."

"It's *our*,"—Holliday gestured between she and Ronan— "Pre-wedding vacation."

"You mean a pre-honeymoon, honeymoon?" Grady chided. "Nice try."

Holliday threw up her hands. "Fine, if you're going to make us spell it out—we were worried about you and the whole debacle with Lululamoan's like a whore, so here we are—The Riot Club at your service."

"Lululamoan's like a whore," I repeated doubling over in a fit of laughter. "That's Heather's nickname?"

Ella smiled. "Yeah, perhaps we shouldn't be making fun of her anymore?"

"Are you kidding me?" Holliday shook her head. "I'm all for sympathy, but no matter how you dice it, she's a one-woman train wreck."

And then they started talking all at once again, it was like watching a live episode of *Grey's Anatomy* or *Friends*. They'd make a great ensemble cast.

"Speaking of train wrecks, we should make those," said Alex.

"Oh yeah, one of my college friends she used to make train wrecks. Beer and Boone's Farm, right?" asked Holiday.

"Yeah, my sister, Amy, taught me how to make them. She got the idea from a college bar at Indiana State," Alex inserted.

"We should make Irish Car bombs," Ronan suggested.

"You are all a bunch of booze hounds," stated Ella.

"We should have our signature drink, Riot Rum Runners," Holliday stated.

"Ella, you can have a glass of wine, it won't hurt the baby," said Ronan.

"I'm fairly certain my mother had liquor during all her pregnancies," Alex quipped.

"Didn't Portland have a rum riot?" asked Holliday.

"Maine or Oregon?" asked Ella.

"Maine. In 1855, citizens of Portland stormed the steps of City Hall. They were convinced that the mayor was stockpiling and selling confiscated liquor," Alex replied.

I turned to Grady. "Aren't historical fun facts *your* thing?"

"With this group, it's a toss-up," he said, scratching the back of his neck. "We don't have a labeled set of norms—the pretty one, the smart one, or the funny one. We're as much a group of unlikely friends as we are likely friends."

"We should go to Maine and sample some of their craft cocktails," suggested Holliday.

"Yes," Ella agreed. "When we go, let's make sure that I am *not* with child."

"I think you and Alex are the ones in control of that situation," Ronan stated.

"Oh, so now I'm a situation?" asked Ella.

A slow smile spread across Grady's face. "Well," he said, turning to face me. "What do you think? Should we toss them out?"

"No," I answered, bopping my head. "I really like them."

Cheers erupted and I was swarmed by this awesome unlikely, likely group of people.

Grady

After everyone settled into their rooms, Alex and Ella went to work in the kitchen prepping a feast while Harlow and Holliday made the drinks. Ronan had every television in the house on and set to a news channel or weather except for one which had music playing.

I shouldn't be surprised that the fearsome foursome traveled all the way to the Caribbean to check up on me. The day the house in Los Angeles sold, the four of them showed up, along with Matt and Tinley—beer and pizza in tow. That day, I'd put on my "just fine" face, today I was more than fine with them being here—I'd never known friendship like they'd shown me.

Sure, I'd had friends, but those relationships lacked a genuine quality. People always wanted something from me, at first I'd been happy to help, but once I figured out they were ladder climbers I started looking out for number one. After a while, I began putting up walls. It left me feeling bitter and resentful.

My attitude reflected in my work, which led to Ronan grabbing every fashion campaign and the reason I'd been booked less and less. Heather urged me to take up yoga, saying it would help improve my mental state. She believed it would allow me to focus and heal.

It's funny, my friendship with Ronan—Heather and

Holliday had been our link. Where Heather broke that link, Holliday mended it.

Ronan handed me a glass of Irish whiskey. "From my personal stash, Midleton, cheers." He lifted his glass to mine.

"Excuses for babymoons and pre-honeymoons were extremely clever."

He chuckled. "Yeah, I told them that you'd see right through that load of bullshit."

"Should I be expecting Matt to arrive soon?"

Ronan sipped his drink. "No, he's otherwise occupied." He steered me towards the great room. "How's Heather doing, really?"

I lifted a shoulder. "Drew called me to let me know that she checked in, but as you know we won't know anything for a while."

"And when she was here?"

"Erratic, confused—at first, she thought we were still married and that I was cheating on her. I've seen Heather at her worst, or at least I thought I had. The level of drugs in her system had the doctor concerned."

His brow crinkled. "How so?"

"Well, enough that he thought she might be heading for an overdose."

He pointed a finger at me. "You did the right thing booking her treatment. Now, you know what you need to do, step away."

"She has no family, no friends," I pointed out. "I know I can't be responsible for Heather, that's why I sent Drew. He's always cared about her and not because she was paying him."

"Is there a romance there?"

"No."

That was one thing that I was sure of, and Heather didn't

need a romance complicating her recovery. If she was going to get clean, she had to do it all on her own. Everything would have to be different than the times she's tried and failed to get sober before.

"Hey, you two," Ella called from the kitchen. "Break up the bromance and join the party!"

"Or do we need to call off the wedding because you've fallen in love with Grady?" Holliday teased.

"He is not my type," I said, slinging my arm around Harlow's waist.

"Awww," Ella and Holliday drawled in unison.

"Okay, okay," I said, squeezing Harlow tighter. "Pipe down and let's get this babymoon, pre-honeymoon, buddy-moon, romantic vacation celebration underway."

"Here, here," Alex interjected, raising his glass. "To old *and* new friends."

Various terms of agreement and elation wound through the air.

Harlow clicked her glass to mine. "Is it okay if I tell you that I love your friends?"

"More than okay, I kind of love them too," I whispered into her skin.

Harlow pulled me out of the kitchen and onto the terrace, crushing her lips to mine the moment we were out my friends' line of sight. Everything and everyone else floated away. All that remained was the two of us and the passion between us. She backed me against one of the pillars, smoothing her hands down my chest. "Grady, is it okay if I tell you that I love you?"

"More than okay," I replied. "I love you too, Harlow."

Chapter
Forty

Harlow

For two people who loved using their words, the only form of communicating Grady and I had been doing since leaving Turks and Caicos was the physical style. It was half past six in the morning and my inbox was jammed with a mountain of unopened emails, and I had three articles that demanded my attention. Grady's body, his mouth, and his cock were too tempting. Not that I didn't love being around him, but my lady parts needed a break.

I stood in the living room admiring the stunning view as the sun rose above the trees on the horizon. Hints of summer's end and shades of fall would soon weave their way into our lives. Over the dunes, Grady came into view with his board in tow and his wet suit slung low on his hips. I admired his muscular legs, his rippled abs and those fucking arms—superbly defined. He propped his board up against the side of the boathouse and shook the water from his hair and then slicked it back.

Watching him was a dangerous spectator sport and my traitorous body ached with the need to touch him. *No, you have to work today, Harlow.*

I shoved my laptop into my bag and then checked my calendar with all my appointments and meetings for the week. After my conference call with Haven, I was going over to the North Harbour Coffee Shop to work.

Grady came into the house, freshly showered wearing nothing but a towel. My fingers twisted the ends of my hair as I studied every line and angle of his lean body.

"What are you thinking so hard about?" he asked, wrapping his arms around me from behind.

"A few things—work, finding a place to live, and summer coming to an end." If I told him what I was really thinking about he'd have me naked and on my back in a matter of seconds, and I needed some self-control. Not a total lie though, all those things were on my mind.

"So, you only have a few things on your mind, huh?"

Our lips met for a long slow kiss. He shifted, pinning me against the breakfast bar. My white blouse and lace bra pushed down, exposing my breasts. Our kisses escalated into to tangle of tongues as his finger teased my nipple. Every part of him was hard, his blue eyes brimming with lust. A hand pushed beneath the waistband of my jeans.

"*Grady* . . ." The need, I felt it in his touch as his erection pressed against my belly.

"Let me have you, Harlow," he whispered, his lips grazing over mine.

Taking back my willpower I shoved at his chest. "You can have me tonight, but right now, I have to call Haven."

He stepped back smirking and then tugged the towel so that it fell to the ground. His hand fisted his cock, his big, thick, beautiful cock, and I had to walk away.

Fuck, adulting is overrated.

I grabbed my car keys and waved to Grady, who stood in the living room gesturing to his cock.

"*Harlow,*" he growled. "You're seriously going to leave me while I'm hard and waiting for you?"

"Yes, I'm seriously leaving you," I replied, opening the door to the garage. "But if it helps, you look damn good naked. It's *really* difficult for me to walk away."

Gingerly, he reached for the towel on the floor.

"Bye-bye, I love you," I called out, just before he snickered tossing the towel in my direction.

Harlow: I'm claiming North Harbour Coffee Shop as my territory.

Grady: So, it's a no-fly zone for me?

Harlow: Consider this place my Crystal Castle.

Grady: Did you just make a reference to She-Ra?

Harlow: I did. You are exiled from Skydancer Mountain.

Grady: Forever?

Harlow: Not forever. It's been three days and I'm getting so much done.

Harlow: We can renegotiate terms at a later date.

Grady: We'll work them out naked while you ride my cock.

Harlow: Is there anything else? Be explicit.

Grady: Roses are red. Violets are blue. I'm using my hand and thinking of you.

Grady: Picture my fist wrapped around my cock, my cum splashing onto your stomach.

Harlow: Yes, I'm picturing it.

Grady: And for some reason I now have an image of you in a Princess of Power costume.

Harlow: Okay, enough. You cannot turn my childhood hero into a dirty whore.

Grady: You started it.

Grady: Get back to work.

Smiling, I shoved my phone into my pocket. After ordering my coffee and chocolate croissant, I found a quiet spot in the corner. I opened my email sifting through several press inquiries. My eyes landed on an invite to a special event for *Bella Magazine.*

"Hello, Harlow," a voice whispered. Not just any voice, the posh in his English accent was completely recognizable. "Is this seat taken?"

I lifted my head from my computer's screen to find Harry standing there with a cup of coffee in hand. I blinked twice, thinking I might be hallucinating. The sunlight reflected off his silver Bulgari watch, drawing my eyes to meet his. He was dressed in a white tee and dark denim jeans with his ball cap tugged low over his brow. I doubted anyone would have recognized him here.

"Harlow, can you hear me?" he asked, waving a hand in front of my face.

"Uh, hi," I drawled.

He slid into the chair across from me. "How have you been?"

My arms folded over my chest. "How have I been?" I

repeated. How in the hell did he know that I was here?

Nodding, his lips pulled into an amused smile. "Yeah, that's what I asked."

"How did you find me?"

Leaning back into the chair, Harry stretched out his long legs under the table. "Instagram. You've been checking into this place for days."

Confusion washed over me. I thought I had turned off my location settings after the Heather incident. I pulled out my phone, swiping it to life. "So what, you're a stalker now?" I snapped.

How the hell do I turn off my location settings?

"Not a stalker."

My head was still buried in my phone. "Well, what would you call it, Harry? Let me guess, you just happened to be in the neighborhood?"

"Actually," he began, tapping his finger to the table. "I was in New York with some of the guys, taking in a game and some of the culture. Francisco's family, his mum's an American. Well, they summer here, so we came out for a few days."

I glared at him. "How convenient for me."

"I wanted to talk to you," he said, leaning forward. "And even though Zanita told me to piss off, I needed to see you."

"You don't take direction very well, do you? That's why you played so poorly during the opening matches against Team USA." I rubbed my temples, annoyance taking its toll. "How could you do that to me?" I hissed.

His lips twisted into a frown. "I'm not proud of that, but you know how it goes—do whatever it takes to get people talking, tuning in, or buying what you're selling. Right, Harlow?"

There was an edge to his voice that I hadn't noticed before—ominous yet, somehow telling. I studied his face as the look in his brown eyes took on a knowing smugness.

"I trusted you Harry and I loved you," I said solemnly. "You dumped me, and basically ghosted me. Then, when the rumors swirled, you didn't even have the decency to defend me."

"They wouldn't let me." He swallowed thickly. "I wanted to tell the press every fucking time that my poor play was me and me alone."

I'd imagined this conversation a few times in my head, the moment when I'd confront Harry and lay it all out.

"Aside from the business of you throwing me under the bus with an entire country," I said quietly. "Why don't you tell me the real reason you broke up with me?"

His arm reached for his cup, most likely filled with English tea. The hem of his t-shirt inched up over his biceps, revealing the dark ink of his tattoo—a lion with Celtic knots, some kind of emblem. I remember he had explained the significance of the design to me once, but its meaning was lost on me in the moment.

"I broke up with you because you . . . you were becoming the bigger star. I couldn't let you overshadow me during the games. It was advised that I end things."

The words were sharp, slicing right through me, and with the pained expression on his face—I'm not sure who they hurt more.

"Bigger star?" I asked. The words tumbled out with a hysterical laugh. "Are you fucking kidding me?"

Heads that had been bent over laptops perked up like prairie dogs in the desert spooked by the threatening noise of a predator. Harry's eyes dropped to the floor, the shame passing over his face was immeasurable.

"And I might have been a tad jealous."

"Lame. Really lame."

"I fucked up, Harlow, I'm sorry," he said, looking up at me. "I wanted to tell you that much at the very least."

That was my closure, but as it seemed I was already over it. It was an odd feeling. He didn't ask for me to forgive him, and I wasn't sure he wanted me too. It was done. There was nothing more to say.

"You've said your apology. Is there something else?"

"Yeah," he answered, his eyes never leaving mine. "I came here to tell you that I still love you. I want to marry you and build a life with you."

Shaking my head, I stood up. "How dare you, Harry," I spat, gathering up my belongings. "This thing that was between us, it's done. It's *over*. I was in bed for weeks crying over you, and I had to get over you because you left me—there was nothing but a 'see ya, don't let the door hit you on the ass' from you." I shoved my laptop into my Tyler Ellis tote and got the hell out of there.

I walked and walked, my feet hitting the ground harder with each step along Harbour Drive. Needing quiet, I turned off my phone. My feet throbbed, and I realized I didn't have the right shoes for taking a long power walk. The black shirt I had on didn't help matters as it seemed to be a heat magnet for the afternoon sun.

I stopped for a moment, ducking into a store to cool off.

The boob sweat was at a serious level of annoyance. When I leaned over a rack of white and pink frilly blouses, I felt a hand grasp my shoulder.

"Harlow?"

I turned around to see Ella Connolly standing before me wearing the most adorable white, wide leg jumpsuit with billowy flutter sleeves. Her red lips accented her beaming smile. Pregnancy glow was no joke, because she had it in spades. I hoped to look this good when I was pregnant.

"I thought that was you," she said, giving me a tight hug. "That auburn hair of yours is a dead giveaway."

"It *has* always been my trademark."

"What brings you to my store today?" she asked, looping her arm with mine.

"This is your store?"

She nodded, leading me around a table of scarves towards the seating area with a sleek modern couch and two black leather club chairs. Ella gestured for me to take a seat, while she grabbed a bottle of San Pellegrino and two glasses.

"I should definitely do a feature of this store on my website. Maybe, even a few 'look of the day' posts."

She handed me a glass, and then took a seat beside me. "I'd love that, you just let me know what you need."

"I had no idea this was *your* store."

"It is, I just love the location," she said, tucking her fist under her chin.

And that was all it took for the tears to slide down my cheeks. The word "love" apparently triggered an avalanche of emotions.

"Oh no, sweetie," Ella whispered, handing me a box of tissues. "Tiffany, finish up with those two clients. Hang the closed sign up and then you can take your lunch."

I blinked up through my tears. "Tiffany? Tiffany Buchanan?" My eyes were playing tricks on me, Afton's little sister was not so little anymore.

"Harlow? Oh my God," she cried out, hugging me. "I can't believe you're here."

Drying my eyes, I pushed to my feet. "You've grown up," I said, taking a step back.

Ella stood and clasped her hands together. "I take it you two know each other."

"Tiffany is my best friend's younger sister," I answered. "Afton told me you were spending the summer in Greece."

Ella patted my shoulder. "I'll let you two catch up while I finish up with the clients. Then we're having a chat about the waterworks."

"I just got back from Greece last week," she said, rocking on her heels. "I have to be on campus next week, but Ella said I could pick up hours here anytime."

While Ella helped the customers, Tiffany and I gabbed about Nicholas and Afton's surprise marriage news.

"I haven't seen Afton in a few days," I admitted, closing my fingers tightly around the tissues.

"Afton is leaving for Chicago to see her hubby," she replied as she glanced at her watch. "Correction, she left about an hour ago. I'm staying at *her* place this weekend. I can only stay at Daddy's so long before my mind is overrun with memories and I don't know whether to cry or scream. I'd like to keep my sanity."

I nodded. I couldn't imagine how hard it must have been for Tiffany losing her father at such a young age. On top of that, she was still a teenager and her mother wasn't even around. As we chatted about the upcoming school year and her trip to Greece, Tiffany busied herself with the task of finger spacing hangers on the built-in rack.

Ella strode up beside us, rubbing at her shoulders. "I'd ask if you want to grab a drink, but how about going for ice cream, instead."

I hauled my bag onto my shoulder. "That sounds great."

"Thank you for this doughnut filled with ice cream," I said, before popping the last bite into my mouth. *Yeah, I ate the entire thing.*

Even though the food I just devoured wasn't healthy, having girl time with Ella was much needed.

"So, what's got you feeling blue?"

I wiped my fingers with the napkin. "I just ran into my ex at the coffee shop. Actually, he stalked me via Instagram."

"Girl," Ella said, giving me a knowing glance. "You've got to turn off your notifications."

"Duly noted." I held my phone up. "I can't figure it out."

She plucked the phone from my hands. I watched in awe as her fingers flew over the screen. "Done, and now you don't have to worry about him any longer."

I shrugged. "Maybe, but he professed his love and desire to marry me."

Her blue eyes went wide. "Are you serious?"

"As a heart attack." I reached for another napkin. My fingers danced along the smooth edge and then I started to rip the paper.

Ella sipped her water, watching me destroy the napkin. "Usually I'd call a man a douchebag, but given that your ex is an Englishman, he's a total wanker."

"Do I tell Grady?"

She nodded. "Yes, you tell him everything, but the declaration of marriage is irrelevant. Grady doesn't need to know about that, it's a moot point."

"It's like a cow's opinion, it's moo," I said.

That threw us both into a fit of laughter.

"Thank God, you're a *Friends* fan," Ella mused. "I don't trust anyone who isn't."

"Same." I liked Ella. She was so easy to like, and I was drawn to her genuine demeanor. Sweet Ella, with her perfect topknot and her chic pregnancy outfit.

She slid off the barstool and grabbed her purse. "Come on," she said, tugging my elbow. "I need to walk off these calories. Let's go look at adorable baby clothes."

Our heels clacked against the sidewalk in unison.

"Clothes are so much cuter when they're tiny."

"Agreed," Ella said, looping her arm with mine as we crossed the street.

My afternoon with Ella was wonderful, we ended up going to the spa and I walked into the kitchen and pulled a bottle of wine from the refrigerator. I had a good feeling that we were going to become fast friends.

"Long day?" Grady asked, tossing a newspaper onto the island.

"Yeah, you want?" I asked holding up a glass.

He approached me, and I stood in front of him, drinking

in his beautiful face. Hitching his arms around my waist, he pulled me close. I buried my face into his chest, breathing in his fresh clean scent like the ocean water. It was uniquely Grady, and his hold on me was warm and familiar.

He kissed the corner of my lips. "I'll grab a scotch."

"Yeah, you'll need a stiff drink for what I'm about to tell you."

He stopped in his tracks, and turned back to face me. "What's going on?"

"Join me on the sofa and I'll tell you all about it."

After he poured his drink, he dropped onto the sofa. I joined him, curling up and tucking my legs under me. Warmth slid through my veins as he pulled me into his side.

"I saw Harry today," I said, staring into my glass.

"Go on," he murmured into my hair.

I took a drink of my wine and continued. "He said he was sorry, told me his still loved me and admitted he fucked up."

"He wants you back?"

I looked up at him. "He can want all he wants, but it's too late because I've fallen for someone else."

He touched my face, his fingertips swept down my cheek. "This guy that you've fallen for, he's very lucky to have you in his life."

Chapter
Forty-One

Harlow

"Zip me up," I coaxed, glancing at Grady over my shoulder. I stared at my reflection falling in love with the dress all over again—a cornflower blue, sleeveless, lace midi. I even found adorable floral print heels and a gorgeous set of off-white baubles for flair.

"Gladly," he said, stepping into the bathroom. "You look fucking stunning."

I fluffed the ends of my hair, adding a few more curls with the iron. "I'm not upstaging the bride, am I?"

"That's a loaded question," Grady replied, adjusting his silver cufflinks.

Splashing some perfume onto my wrist, I laughed. "Yeah, I know that's not a fair question to ask. But, I've got to say, James, you have a body designed for tailored threads. That navy suit is giving me too many reasons to skip this wedding."

It was true. I swore he was even more handsome than I'd ever seen. Designer suits, casual jeans and tee, or even a towel, Grady was the epitome of male perfection. I was a lucky girl.

His hands slipped over my shoulders. "This dress is the only reason I need to skip this wedding," he whispered, his lips drifting up my neck. "Actually, what's underneath it has me crafting a lengthy list of all the ways to get you out of it."

I batted his hand away and turned on my heel to face him. "I paid way too much money for this dress to let it sit in a garment bag, but, yeah, you are so getting laid tonight."

His hands danced over the curve of my hip. "As much as I love the idea of messing you and this dress up, I'm proudly showing you off tonight."

I laughed. "Remember when this wedding was just part of the original deal?"

"Seems like a lifetime ago," he replied, banding his arms around my waist.

Grady grasped my hand when the string quartet played Michael Bublé's "Everything." We stood as Holliday emerged onto the expertly manicured lawn at the De Belles Estate Vineyard. A vision in an ivory, charmeuse sheath, atelier dress with an illusion beaded v-neckline; the smile on her face had all of us grinning like we'd slept with hangers in our mouths. As Holliday passed our seating row, the back of her custom gown was equally as stunning as the front adorned with jeweled appliqués at the shoulder. The groom was outfitted in a black four-button Prada tuxedo.

I imagined the headlines that would be splashed across the glossy magazines at super markets from coast to coast. Rumor had it that *One Park Avenue* magazine was the highest bidder for the exclusive wedding photos—price unknown. It had to be more than the $14 million *People* and *Hello!* magazines dropped for the exclusive photos of the Jolie-Pitt twins.

No one needed to point out that the groom was absolutely taken with the bride. Everything was beautiful, the couple dropped a cool $100,000 on flowers alone, which may not seem like much, but everything was covered in roses, wisteria, and plenty of greenery, and looked like something out of a true fairytale.

It was dreamy and romantic and we hadn't even heard the vows, although they were beautiful and poignant. Declarations of love and protection mixed with humorous promises—Holliday vowed to wake Ronan up and urge him to come to bed whenever he fell asleep reading by the fireplace. Ronan promised to start the Christmas festivities as soon as the clock struck midnight on Thanksgiving.

Before we knew it, the ceremony was over. U2's "All I Want Is You" played as the newlyweds walked down the aisle taking a shot of Irish whiskey and then smashing the glasses to the ground.

Grady snaked his arm around my waist, his lips coasting against the nape of my neck. We made our way towards the terrace for cocktails and hors d'oeuvres.

Dusk fell away to evening and toasts went on forever, but no one seemed to mind because it was more like dinner and a show and that went over well with this crowd.

After Ronan and Holliday completed their first dance, chatter erupted once more and the bubbly flowed.

With the mic in her hand, Holliday stood. She had changed into a cocktail dress adorned with floral appliques along the bodice and sheer long-sleeves. "Okay, so most of you know how Ronan and I met."

Cheers and applause erupted from the crowd along with whistles and the occasional "Ow, Ow."

"What you might not know is that our first official fight was not clean," she admitted, grasping Ronan's shoulder. "In fact, it was *dirty* . . . and it involved many shots of Irish whiskey, but Ronan, my love . . . you'll always be as smooth as Irish whiskey too me and sweet as a chocolate kiss." She bent to kiss him. "Babe, I have a surprise for you. Ladies and Gentleman," she shouted and pointed to the left of the stage. "Cash Knight of Rebel Desire."

Ronan's face was priceless, all I could make out was— "*Oh my God*"—when Cash emerged from the Tasting Room stepping onto the terrace plucking the strings of his guitar.

"Could they be any cuter?" I whispered to Grady.

He nodded. "They're going to be very happy together."

Even though the bride and groom had long said their good-byes, the party continued well into the night.

Grady pressed his hand to the small of my back. "Dance with me," he whispered, kissing just below my earlobe. The rush of bubbles tickled my throat. Breathing in his scent, I pressed my cheek to his shoulder.

The Robertsen's glided casually across the dance floor laughing and holding each other close. Alex dipped Ella, and then brought her up for spin. *Very smooth.* Matthew Barber had led Tinley Atkinson to the far side of the dance floor where they swayed to the beat of the music.

With one hand at my back, Grady took me in his arms and we sailed around the dance floor. "When I get married, this would definitely do," I breathed. "Tasteful and elegant, it's perfect."

"I suppose that it is," he murmured.

"You prefer something different?"

"No, I don't plan on getting married again," he said, matter of fact.

Heat spread like wildfire across my skin and my heart slammed into the pit of my stomach. What? He joked about a second marriage earlier this summer. Was he serious about not marrying again?

Reigning in my emotions, I formulated my questions. "So, you don't want to get married again?"

He pulled back to look at me. "No, I don't need piece of paper to dictate my love for another person."

Sharp panic spread through me. His mouth was tender as he brushed his lips over mine, but I couldn't shake the harshness of his words.

I want to get married.

How could I have not seen this coming?

Maybe, he's messing with me.

"Ha, ha," I mused, grasping the lapels of his jacket. "You almost had me there, James."

We stayed on the dance floor through two more songs. We walked back to our table and I grabbed my clutch. A visit to the ladies' room was in order.

Grady grasped my elbow. "What I said out there, Harlow, it wasn't a joke. I don't intend to marry again."

My hands flexed around my clutch. "Then, what's this all been for Grady?"

"What do you mean?"

I knew better, that was the sad part. I was just a distraction to mend his heartbreak, but unable to heal his soul. All along I'd known better than to take up with someone who'd been jilted by love.

"How, I am so stupid, *fuck*." My fingers splayed against my forehead. "You let me fall in love with you!"

My heart splintered into a thousand pieces as I stomped down the steps and onto the grass. Grady grasped my arm, spinning me to face him. Those blue eyes pierced through my soul. I loved this man and the shock to my system was too much to bear.

"I didn't lead you on, Harlow. I love you. I don't understand why a piece of paper is make or break for us. I've been there and trust me it's not all it's cracked up to be."

We glared at each other under the twinkling lights, the sounds of upbeat music drowning out the ugliness of our tone.

"Are you kidding me right now?" I seethed. "We're at the wedding of two of your best friends and you have the nerve to stand here and tell me that marriage isn't worth it?"

He shoved his hands into his pockets. "Marriage isn't for everyone."

I threw up my hands. "Marriage *is* for me, you bastard." I scowled, pointing my clutch at him. "Keeping the fact that you didn't want to get married again, isn't fair to me."

"So, the *fact* that I love you," he said, taking my face in his hands. "That I'm *in love* with you means nothing?"

Tears slid down my cheeks. "How can it hold any value, if we don't want the same things?"

He kissed me through the sobs of my tears. "Harlow, *please*," he breathed, pressing his forehead to mine. "I love you, please."

"I can't, Grady. I want a marriage and a family." My hands gripped his collar, and my knees buckled. "Falling for you was the easiest thing I've done, but its killing me to be near you right now."

I stormed off with the little dignity I had intact, but the further away I walked from him—from us—the floodgates burst. My heart felt as if it was being ripped from my body, as I rushed to the ladies' room. Unable to catch my breath, I pushed open the door feeling my chest tighten.

As I held onto the door handle, I blinked the tears from my eyes bringing more focus into the room. I stumbled to the vanity, and dropped to the chair.

Staring at my reflection, I thought to myself that I should be the last fucking person in the world who wanted to get married. My father cheated on my mother, on top that he left her when she was sick. *In sickness and in health, it's part of the vows.*

"It's just a piece of paper." Dabbing the wetness under my eyes, I swipe away the smudged mascara. "Is it really that important?"

"Yes," a sweet voice answered.

I stood up and peeked around the room. Ella was sitting on the love seat with Tinley Atkinson. Ella formally introduced me to Tinley and we exchanged the usual small talk, getting all that out of the way.

"In case you're wondering, we're hiding out," Ella said, picking a piece of lint from her skirt.

"Here," Tinley said, pointing a bottle at me. "You look like you need this more than I do."

I laughed, it was a miserable laugh. "Thanks," I replied, lifting the bottle to my lips and swallowing a big gulp.

Ella patted the cushion of the empty seat next to her. "This is the second time I've seen you wiping away tears in less than a week."

"Yeah, instead of auburn hair being my trademark, it seems crying in public wants that label."

"What did Grady do to you?" Tinley asked, fluffing the ends of her blonde hair.

"Oh, he just told me that he doesn't plan to ever marry again."

"*Fuck*," Tinley exhaled. "We need something stronger than champagne."

Ella sighed. "What the hell is the matter with him?"

"Heather Young," Tinley answered. "She fucked him up and broke his heart."

"She did," I admitted, taking another pull from the bottle. "He said marriage wasn't for everyone—which I understand that it's not, but it *is* for me. At least I think that it is."

Tinley stood and plucked the bottle from my hands. "No, don't do that, don't bargain or settle for something based on someone else's choices."

Tears welled in my eyes. "He made me fall in love with him. He was . . . *is* charming and thoughtful." My words were heralded by a wave of sobs. "What I have with Grady I don't want with someone else. I want him." The words echoed around the room, each one hitting me in the chest harder.

Ella leaned forward, wrapping her arms around my shoulders. Tinley bent down in front of me, squeezing my knee and offering me more tissues.

Ella swiped the tears from my chin and handed me the bottle of champagne. "Sweetie, you love him and he's totally in love with you, maybe he needs time."

I sniffled, my gaze darting between the two of them, my hands wringing the tissues. "He seemed pretty firm in his decision."

The three of us stood and I attempted to pull myself together. I loved Grady that was true enough, and maybe that in itself was enough.

"Clooney said he'd never marry again," Tinley pointed out, slicking her lips with a blushing pink color. "Look at him now, married *and* a father."

Ella stood, and joined Tinley at the vanity. "That's true. People change their minds as fast as they change their underwear."

"That would imply that I would be waiting for something that might never happen," I argued, swiping the bottle from the vanity.

Eyeing me in the mirror, Ella arched an eyebrow. "You could always marry that ex of yours. He apparently wants to marry you."

I laughed. "I'm not looking to get married anytime soon. I know that marriage doesn't guarantee a forever. It's the work that you put in day in and day out, and a combination of love, respect, trust, friendship, and understanding. I think it's about making the other person happy and vice versa."

"I get it," Tinley said. "It's the little things in life that really are what love is all about."

We exited the bathroom and I knew that I couldn't face Grady, not tonight any way. I needed time to think and I didn't have the strength for a counter-argument. This had to be a world record for heartbreak twice in less than five months. It was a special kind of hell being a hopeless romantic stuck in a hookup culture.

"Aren't you coming, Harlow," Ella asked.

"No, I'm just going to catch an Uber and call it a night."

Tinley marched up to me. "You are not taking an Uber," she disagreed, pulling her phone from her clutch. "I'm calling my driver, Anthony. He will take you home or anywhere you want."

I nodded, wrapping my arms around my body. The chill of the evening air danced over my skin. As we stood waiting, my eyes drifted back to the terrace and the vineyards. Was Grady still out there or had he gone home? This wasn't at all how I saw this evening ending.

The limo pulled around, and Tinley instructed Anthony to take me anywhere that I wanted.

"Harlow, hey, where are you going?" I whirled around to see Grady bounding down the stone steps towards me. Shaking her head, Ella stopped him in his tracks. He skidded to a halt, his blue eyes met mine. By the look passing over his face, I could tell that Ella had instructed him to let me go. Swallowing the lump in my throat, I turned away from his gaze blinking back tears. My legs vibrated as I climbed into the limo. The weight of the evening and the entire summer started to crush me. The sobs grew stronger as I dropped into the seat sinking lower.

"I still can't believe the two of you are married," Tiffany squealed, unfolding her napkin.

"Yeah, sometimes I can't either," Afton admitted, snuggling into Nicholas' side.

"In my wildest dreams, I don't know how I got so lucky to find this woman," he said, giving Afton a chaste kiss on the lips.

"The lobster salad here is terrific," I said, interrupting their love fest. My mood was sour. Afton and Nicholas chose Nancy's Diner as this Sunday's weekly brunch spot. It was much too soon to be brunching with the newlyweds.

Tiffany babbled on, recapping their love story. Afton and Nicholas bumped into each other at Eataly in Chicago. She was in town on business and he was out having dinner with friends. Blah. Blah. *Shut up.*

"It was the one night," Nicholas chimed in, "that I had off in weeks and it was good luck this lady was sitting at a table by herself."

"No, it was painfully embarrassing," she said, picking up her menu. "You rescued me from being gawked at as if I was a sad, single woman eating alone. I hate being a cliché."

My eye rolled into the back of my skull. I had heard this story at least five times in various narratives. *Over it.*

I needed to get my hands on a margarita rimmed with salt to compliment my salty mood.

"Tara had been an excellent cover during Pour Fest," Nicholas boasted.

"A year and a half of dating, and Harlow never suspected a thing." Tiffany stated, flipping her menu over.

Nicholas shook his head. "Nope, but then again, Harlow was in Europe for the majority of our relationship."

"We were almost busted the morning after, when I was in the kitchen," Afton recalled, gripping her coffee mug with both hands. "I'll spare you the details, but my back bumped against the light switch . . ."

Gasping, Tiffany covered her mouth with her hands.

"That's when Harlow texted and asked if you were making coffee."

They nodded in unison. Nicholas kissed her cheek. "I knew that weekend that I wanted to marry her."

"So cute," Tiffany gushed, resting her chin on her palm.

"Yeah, yeah, it's a cute story. Can we please order?"

Our server had been by our table at least three times, but we were still chatting and hadn't had the time to "make a decision." Only, I *had* made a decision, food wise anyway. I wanted the French toast with a side of crispy bacon. All other decisions outside this moment were minute by minute, day by day.

I needed to hurry this brunch along and get the hell out of here before Nancy, or worst yet Grady, spotted me. I wasn't ready to face him. On the way to the diner, I tried to come up with at least half a dozen excuses to bail. However, with Tiffany home from Yale, and given the fact that this was the last weekend of the summer season, it felt wrong to cancel. My mood would have been improved if Nancy's served booze. Could you really call it brunch if Mimosas and Bloody Marys weren't involved?

"So, Harlow, how's the business going?" Nicholas asked.

I plastered a smile. "Wonderful, just *really* great."

Afton cut me a narrow glance and I chose to ignore her.

Our server skirted up to the table and before she asked, I rattled off my order. "It will be one check," I added. "On them." I nodded towards the lovebirds across the booth.

After our server walked away, Nicholas leaned across the table. "I want to talk to you about selling Mom's place in the city."

"Okay, let's chat."

"We don't have to do this in front of them."

"Why not?" I lifted a shoulder. "She's your wife and Tiffany is your sister-in-law now. Um, hello they're family."

Nicholas raised his hands in mock surrender. "Fine with me," he said, blowing out a harsh breath. "Since Afton has a place in Manhattan, there's no need for us to hold onto Mom's."

I tapped my finger to the table. "I disagree. You two are married and that's fine if you want to keep a place in the city, but when I come to visit or if I want a getaway where would I stay?"

"With us," Afton replied brightly.

"No thanks, I like my space," I grumbled.

"Sorry, I mentioned it," Afton said, before taking a sip of her coffee.

"It's just that," I began, ripping the edges of my napkin. "What if I get married and my husband doesn't have a place in the city? I think it might be nice to have the family home option—it's a lovely place for holiday gatherings."

Nicholas shook his head, draping his arm over the back of the booth. "And when exactly was the last time you were there?"

I'd stayed there for a few days when I returned from Italy, but I didn't tell anyone. I spent the first few days lying in my mom's bed ordering takeout, watching episodes of *13 Reasons Why* and *Frontier*. When I felt the urge to do more than be a slug, I went through Mom's closet trying on her vintage Halston and Dior couture gowns.

As the week progressed, I spent time ripping my father's face out of several photographs while listening to Beach Boys records and drinking red wine from our mother's private collection. When Trudy, my mom's longtime personal secretary stopped by to let the cleaning crew in, she found me face down on the sofa in nothing but my underwear. Mortified didn't even begin to describe my state of mind. That's when I cleaned up, packed up, and called Afton.

"Before I took up residence in Afton's guest house," I replied. "I dropped in, and happened to see Trudy."

There was a long silence, and then our server re-appeared refilling coffee mugs and water glasses.

Nicholas cleared his throat. "About that, *you* staying in my wife's . . . *our* guest house. Have you found a permanent place of residence yet?"

Afton's eyes went wide. It was the kind of expression that told me they'd discussed the subject, but at the same time, she wasn't ready to call attention to the matter.

"Nicholas," Afton nudged his arm. "Harlow can stay as long as she wants."

I slapped my hands to the table. "Actually, Afton, your husband brings up a good point. I should be getting a place of my own. In fact, there are several open houses this afternoon for properties I'm particularly interested." I slid out of the booth and dropped twenty dollars onto the table. "For my part of the tip, I hate being a mooch. And I'm not selling Mom's place, but I'll buy you out, since you're so very eager to unload that property."

"Harlow, wait, come back," Afton called after me.

Waving her off, I walked out of Nancy's with my head held high. On the inside though, I felt as if someone had taken my heart, tossed it into a blender and pressed crush.

Chapter
Forty-Two

Grady

The last weekend of summer, and instead of being out hitting the final party circuit, here I sat like a chump camped out in front of my television in my grey sweatpants. This all seemed vaguely familiar.

Alone. Alone. Alone.

This time the reason for my loneliness, it was all my own doing. Pain flooded my heart, and the ache was excruciating. I missed Harlow.

There was a loud buzzing noise coming from somewhere inside the house. I had no idea where my phone was, because I hadn't seen it since last night.

Grabbing a bottle of Jameson, I climbed the stairs. It was day . . . one . . . five thousand without Harlow. Shuffling towards the shower, I saluted my bed with the middle finger along the way. I hadn't slept in it in days. Not when I'd come to the sobering reality that she wasn't coming back here, possibly forever. Everything lingered with her scent—honey and peaches.

"Grady, you need to let her go."

"She's hurting and she needs time to think."

Ella's words echoed over and over in my head. Thinking back to that night so many times, it haunted me, but I thought being honest with Harlow was the best thing. I knew it was a risk telling her that I never wanted to get married again. I didn't anticipate her reaction, and I should have, that was my mistake. The matter should have been handled differently.

Had I led her on? The possibility was real and I had to live with that and maybe live without her.

I never wanted to hurt her, ever.

"Mr. Grady," Thora said, from the kitchen. "It's Friday, payday."

I pressed my palms to my eyes. "What?"

"Friday, payday."

"Oh, okay." I stood up from the couch. "You didn't wash my sheets, did you?"

She shook her head, and continued putting my groceries in the refrigerator.

After I retrieved the envelope marked with her name from my safe, I walked back into the kitchen. "Thanks for taking such good care of me, Thora," I said, handing her the money.

"Mr. Grady, it is a pleasure to work for you," she said, tucking the envelope into her bag. "You know, love is a tricky business," she continued. "But if you cannot live without her, you need to tell her how much she means to you. You are young and in love, be happy." She slapped her palm to my face. "Go get your lady."

The task of getting my shit together and Harlow back into my life was a daunting one. Getting Daniel Craig to agree to two more Bond films was far easier. Since that night, I made several attempts to call, text, and message her via Instagram, none of which were returned. I had run out of options.

In between work and polo practice, I checked her favorite places hoping to accidently run into her. The North Harbour Coffee Shop was becoming my second home, but Harlow seemed to be avoiding it like the plague. I drove by Afton's place every day, but I never turned into the driveway.

"James, quit being a pussy and go talk to her," Alex shouted, his voice vibrating through my Bluetooth speakers.

"I'm pretty sure that your wife advised me to give Harlow some space."

"Do you love her?"

"Your wife? Of course, I love Ella, it's only a matter of time before she leaves your sorry ass for me," I joked. Apparently, I had no filter today. I could almost hear the sound of Alex ordering a tactical team to my exact location, kidnapping me and bringing me to some secret compound, and inducing various forms of psychological torture. He's probably cleaning his gun as we speak.

"I'm going to give you a pass on that little joke, James,

because I know that you're in a fucked-up head space and not completely in control of your mental faculties."

"Got it."

"So, the question on the table—do you love *Harlow*?"

"Yes," I replied, as my hand glided over the steering wheel. I turned into my driveway and then punched the button to lift my garage door.

"Then that is all that matters. The rest will work itself out."

I slid out of the driver's seat, disconnecting the Bluetooth from my car. "I don't know," I said, blowing out a harsh breath. "She wants to get married and I can't see myself going down that road again. Harlow doesn't want to waste her time with someone who is never going to give her what she needs. I can't say I blame her." I tossed my keys on the counter and sifted through my mail. An invite to the 3rd Annual Elizabeth Atkinson Foundation for the Arts Celebration caught my eye.

"James, I'm going to impart some wisdom," he declared. "Just because it didn't work with Heather doesn't mean a marriage won't work with someone else."

Unconvinced, I stared at the invitation mentally flipping through memories of my ex-wife and our failed marriage. Moments of clarity smacked me hard. I walked towards the window in my living room and stared out at the ocean waves. Heather cheated on me. I honored the vows we took and gave her everything she wanted. There was nothing I could have done to stop her from cheating.

"Love, hell, even marriage—it's not about who you see yourself with—it's about who you can't see yourself living without."

"Yeah," I sighed, dragging a hand through my hair. "I've heard that somewhere before."

But was it enough? Was I enough for Harlow without the official vows of marriage?

"Go get your lady," he advised. "Don't overcomplicate the matter. Life's too short. If there's a sliver of hope that you're open to the possibility of marriage, you need to consider it. Don't lie or manipulate the situation to get her back and don't tell her want she wants to hear. Say what you mean, and mean what you say."

"How did you know that Ella was the one?"

"There wasn't one moment that hit me and said, 'Alex she's the one don't let her go.' It was a series of moments. When I'm weak, she's strong. Hell, even when I'm not weak, she's strong. When I looked at my life and Ella wasn't there, it was like I couldn't breathe. She's my light, and I'm a better man when I'm with her."

I refrained from making a smartass comment. There was a real possibility that Alex had a set of wires with my name on them—charged and ready to shoot ten thousand volts of electricity into my body. For his own amusement, he'd probably attach them to directly my balls.

"That sounds about right," I agreed.

"Next time you want to have a heart to heart, James, let's do it over beers. Don't call me like I'm one of your fashionista gal pals."

"Noted."

I ended the call, turning my attention back to my very empty house. The emptiness that I once craved no longer made sense. Don't get me wrong, solitude had its benefits, but isolation was another story altogether.

Chapter
Forty-Three

Harlow

I sipped my champagne and studied the image hanging on the wall. Each of the photographs portrayed a certain degree of vulnerability, but there was hope in the woman's expression. I knew because that woman was me.

Days after Ronan and Holliday's wedding, Tinley contacted me and asked me to be a part of her annual charity fundraiser. How could I say no to something that was not only important to funding the arts but also her mother, Elizabeth's legacy? I couldn't which was why I staring at four pictures of myself shaded in green and blue hues.

Blue, the color of his eyes and the water he loved so much here in The Harbour. The swirls of aqua and azure blue, held a striking reminder of the Caribbean waters in Sapodilla Bay. The green was loudest—a canopy of palm leaves surrounding the outdoor shower where we shared a profoundly intimate moment.

Moving on, I stepped in front of the black and white photos anchored on the wall in a blocked cluster of four. *Breathtaking.* Gavin Lacourt knew his way around a woman's body, photographically speaking—although the Frenchman was a known ladies' man and the rumor mill was extremely complimentary of his bedroom skills.

"There you are!" Ella's toned arms wrapped around my shoulders. "Fabulous, isn't it—a total smash."

"Ella, you look stunning," I said, admiring the lace detailing of her cranberry colored gown.

Her hands drifted over her barely there bump. "Aren't you sweet," she replied, grasping my hand and then entwining our arms. We stared up at the photos. There we were, naked and on display for the whole world. Gavin had an idea for a collection of photographs featuring Ella, Holliday, and myself. A figure brushed past the two of us, slapping a red "sold" sticker next to Ella's portrait.

"Well, that's a blow to my ego," I joked, taking a sip of champagne.

"My husband purchased it," she remarked.

"How do you know?" I asked, shaking my head.

"I thought for sure they'd cover the photos up once they were purchased," Alex said, from behind us.

"Told you he was the buyer."

"You're goddamn right I'm the buyer. I don't need this portrait going in another man's house where he can jerk off to it every night."

Ella rolled her eyes, a smirk playing on her lips. "Babe, where are you going to hang a nude photo of me? In the guest house?"

"I haven't decided, yet," he answered, taking a long drink

from the tumbler in his hands. "Maybe, I'll hang it in my office, better yet our bedroom."

A young woman breezed past us, marking Holliday's portrait with the red sticker.

I threw up my hands. "What the hell?"

"Not too worry, love." Ella nudged me. "I have a feeling the buyer of your portrait is standing right there."

Following her gaze, my heart thumped out of sync. Grady stood before me in an ink black suit and matching tie. He looked undeniably handsome. Was it possible that he'd become more so, since we'd been apart? His blue eyes held that same smolder that I'd seen many times. I wondered how I'd lived without seeing his beautiful face these past weeks.

Ella squeezed my arm, as she turned on her heel. "Talk to him."

Grady maneuvered his way towards me, sidestepping patrons with effortless precision. His eyes locked on mine, captivating me.

The overwhelming feeling took hold, tugging my need for him. Adrenaline coursed through my veins, winding its way to my heart pouring weeks' worth of emotion into it—misery, frustration, desire, and excitement all brewing together making me dizzy.

"Harlow."

"Grady."

Grady

I stared at her for a long moment, studying every line and curve of her face. If this was the last time I'd ever see her, I needed to catalog it to memory. Harlow was breathtaking in a silver beaded, floor-length gown. When she arrived, I saw . . . *felt* her immediately. The lights from the gallery seemed to follow her everywhere. Her dress was like liquid metal sliding all around her as she walked from one display of art to the next. All those copper waves shiny and thick, cascaded down her back.

I reached for her, sliding my hand down her arm taking her hand in mine. Touching her, being this close, allowed me to breathe again. I took a slow, deep breath, feeling the air in my lungs. Abandoning all my planned speeches, I went straight for the three words that mattered most.

"I love you." My shoulders sagged with relief as the words poured out of me. "I don't know what the future holds, but the one thing that I do know and it's with great certainty— is that I love you. There's this huge important thing that you want, and I can't promise it to you today or tomorrow or a hundred tomorrows from now," I continued, my hands sliding into her hair. "I love you. *That* I can promise you. And I never lie, so you know my words are true."

She gazed at me with heavy-lidded eyes. "Okay," she breathed.

"Okay," I repeated, as my heart beat a bruising rhythm against my ribs.

"I love you, Grady," she said, squeezing my hand. "I promise to listen to all your fun and historical facts. I can't promise that I won't roll my eyes from time to time. I promise to cheer you on in everything that you do. I promise to . . ." Her voice broke into a sob. "I can't think of anything more at this moment, but I will, I promise."

I laughed, swiping the tears from her cheeks. "It's okay, we can revise and revisit anytime you want."

Closing the gap between us, I tipped her mouth to mine. Desperate for her, I sealed my mouth over hers. I kissed her, sliding my tongue against hers. I claimed her mouth. Harlow was mine for as long as she would have me.

I needed her, needed to feel her skin. I needed her beneath me, hearing her say how much she loved me. "Do you want to get out of here?"

"I do," she whispered against my lips.

I set the palm of hand to the small of her back as we walked towards the door.

"Almost forgot, wait one second," I said, as we passed by front table. After I made my donation, I turned Harlow back towards her photograph. Wrapping my arms around her waist from behind, we watched as they posted the sold sticker. "That's going on the wall in my office," I whispered, kissing just below ear.

"A wise choice, you made a very good investment, Mr. James."

"Yes, I did," I agreed, pulling her out the door.

Epilogue

Grady

"It's Friday night. Remind me again why we're going out?" Harlow asked, scrolling through the calendar on her phone. "I don't have anything on the schedule for tonight."

With Harlow preoccupied with Met Gala and Cannes fashion business, it gave me plenty of time to plan this evening. Summer was fast approaching and before the crowds descended bringing the excess of Manhattan here to rest behind the neatly groomed hedges of our seaside town, the time was now.

We reveled in the comfort of drinking wine on the deck, boat rides at dusk, and quiet dinners with friends. Our ultimate bragging right: "Oh, we *never* go out." We were firmly in The Harbour Hermit Camp by choice, of course and we're not alone. We decided our personal motto this summer will be, avoid Route 27 altogether on weekends. We never go out, *ever.*

I'd be lying if I said that we didn't attempt an evening out occasionally. Rum Bar, Castle Hill Beach House, and the occasional yacht brunch were needed. With new restaurants popping up and food trucks in abundance, we seemed to find new fried foods and desserts to try all the time. I mean we weren't complete recluses. *That* would be crazy.

Speaking of crazy, Harlow's website has grown exponentially. Recently, she was asked to work with a popular fashion brand—a collaboration for a new line of lingerie and swimwear. She purchased her dream home, the one with the aqua tile in the kitchen.

As for my career, solid and going strong. The pilot I shot last year was picked up by HBO. Filming would begin this summer, and I would be splitting my time between The Harbour and Los Angeles. I sold my loft in Manhattan. As much as I loved it, the better investment was Harlow's Mom's penthouse. It had taken a while for Harlow to really get over Afton and Nicholas' elopement, but we spent Thanksgiving in the city with Nicholas, Afton, and Tiffany. Christmas in Fenwick with my mom and sister, and then drove up to northern Vermont where Harlow and I convinced the new owners of the apple orchard that once belonged to her grandparents to let us walk the property in the snow. They thought we were insane, maybe we were. A snowstorm kept us in Vermont a little longer than expected, but we made the most of our stay snuggled up in a cozy inn.

Harlow and I adopted Elsa, because it was time for her to retire from the sport. Alex and Ella welcomed a new baby right after the New Year and in the middle of a snowstorm. Trying to get Ella to the hospital was a feat only Alex could pull off. I guess eight inches was just a light dusting compared to the several feet of snow the Great Lakes dumped on Grosse Point when he was growing up.

I pulled up to the Hutton House. After stepping out, I handed my keys off to the valet who traded me for a basket with a few special items—bottle of champagne, two glasses, and a cashmere blanket.

"What are we doing here?" Harlow asked, stepping out of the car, the sound of gravel crunching under her high heels. She looked beautiful in a blue strapless dress, the warm breeze tousling her auburn strands.

I came around the front of my Range Rover, taking her hand in mine. "Do you remember, about a year ago, on a night particularly reminiscent of this one, you and I took a rowboat out for a spin?"

She sighed, looking up at the sky. "Yes, I think I remember."

"Call me sentimental, because I wanted to take my lady for a moonlight boat ride."

"How romantic of you."

We walked across the newly cut grass to the beach where she balanced her hand on my shoulder to take off her heels. I helped her into the boat. Once she was settled, I handed her the basket.

I rowed a good distance, but close enough to the shore where we could still see the flood lights from Hutton House. In one . . . two . . . three . . . soft blue lights flashed in the distance and that was the cue I'd given myself. I pulled the ring box from my pocket—the same color as the lights wrapped in a white ribbon.

"*Holy crap*," Harlow whispered, as I placed the box in her hands.

"Harlow Trembley, is it *okay* if I ask you to be my wife?"

Wrapping her hands around the box she stared at it for a long moment. Her hands shook as she lifted the lid with her thumbs. Tears slid down her cheeks. My hands framed her face, swiping the tears away.

"But, I thought you didn't want to get married?"

"Loving you is the easiest thing that I've ever done and at the end of the day you're the person I cannot live without. Loving someone, truly loving them, means you work day in and day out making that person happy. I love you and you make me happy, that's what you've done for me and it's important to me that you're happy."

Seconds turned into minutes and my throat felt as dry as sandpaper. Finally, Harlow looked up at me, one shaking hand covering her mouth.

"Sweetheart," I said, pulling the canary diamond from the box. Yellow, the same color of pineapples—the fruit she adored. Call me cheesy, but I knew that Harlow would appreciate the sentiment.

"Will you marry me?"

She shook her head. "No."

"No." I repeated.

Fuck. No. She said no. She doesn't want it. Should I jump overboard now and drown myself in the ocean or get drunk? Better yet, I could drop by the stables and have Elsa kick me in the balls.

"What do you want? Do you want the moon? The Ocean? Anything you want, sweetheart, name it." *Was the panic in my voice obvious?*

"Wait this is all wrong . . . ask me again," she murmured. "The *original* question, just like you said it the first time—all the words."

I huffed out a laugh. Without hesitation, I knew exactly what she needed to hear. "Is it okay if I ask you to marry me?"

"More than okay," she breathed, tears cascading down her cheeks. "My answer is yes."

My heart jackhammered in my chest as I slid the ring onto her finger.

She smiled, as the pad of her thumb brushed over the center stone. "I can't wait to marry you, Grady James."

THE END

Books by Christy Pastore

The Weekends Series
Fifteen Weekends

The Scripted Series
unScripted
Perfectly Scripted

The Harbour Series
Bound to Me
Healed by You
Return to Us

Be sure to sign up for my newsletter at
christypastore-author.com for the latest news on
releases, sales, and other updates.

Acknowledgements

I can get a little wordy when it comes to saying thanks, as I never want to leave out a thank you or a nod of appreciation. Writing a book can be a very lonely process at times, but for the people who love romance and adore this genre none of this would happen without your love of reading.

To my hubby, Kevin, thank you for keeping the ship in order while I'm locked away in the cave. More importantly for keeping my drink glass filled.

My Editor, Missy Borucki, you my dear, deserve a star on the Editors 'Walk of Fame.' I cannot thank you enough for your insightful feedback and honest suggestions. More importantly thank you for catching my "dumbass mistakes." It's the most entertaining part of the editing process. #Lightening #Jealously

Special thanks to the people who made book look so damn gorgeous—Sara Eirew, this cover blows me away. It's perfect. Once again, Stacey Blake you've outdone yourself with the formatting of this series.

Kelly, it's never been a better time to support me and my books. When the crazy train is barreling down the terminal at full speed, you're always there with the comic relief and/or supportive nudge. {It's always a toss-up.} Also, thank you for all your history of horse knowledge. I'm so happy that degree of yours was put to a good cause. "Dear God! This parachute is a knapsack!"

Andrea Joan, Fabiola Francisco, Michelle Rodriguez, and Rachel Blaufeld, when the recipe calls for one cup cluster and two parts fuck, I know I can always count on the four of you to keep it real—all day every day.

Christina, I freaking adore you! Thank you for making my book world life a little more organized and fun. Your friendship and support mean everything to me.

My Reader Group, ya'll know how to keep it #ClassyAF. Don't Change.

To My After Hours Book House #AHBH Bitches (Cary, Aubrey, Fabi, Jen, and Britt), I didn't choose the Tribe Life, the tribe life chose me. Thank you for all the support, snark, sass, and sarcasm. #MyTribe #Middlefinger #EggplantEmojis4Life

Huge thanks to Kylie, Jo, Jeananna, and the entire Give Me Books team for an amazing cover reveal and release.

Jennifer Norman Corzine, you are forever #GradysFirstLady

To all my author friends—you're always there when the going gets tough or someone uncorks the crazy sauce. From the bottom of my heart, thank you.

Each day, I am in awe of the incredible bloggers who work tirelessly to spread the word and love of our books to this community. Thank you for everything.

About the Author

Christy Pastore lives in the Midwest with her husband, two lovable dogs and their crazy cool cat. She has a Bachelor's Degree in Textiles, Apparel and Merchandising and Marketing. Writing has always been a part of her life. Her first writing gig was for a celebrity entertainment website. Later she went on to create her own blogazine and media company combining her love of writing with fashion and marketing.

When's she not writing flirty and dirty books or updating her celebrity fashion blog, she loves shopping online, binge watching her favorite shows and daydreaming.

She believes books, especially love stories are an escape from the real world.

A few of Christy's favorite things:
Bold Heroine's—Swoony Hero's with a Naughty Side—Guilty Pleasure Reads and TV Shows—Designer Handbags—Men In Suits—Black and White Photos—Sexy Accents—Snow—Pinterest—Twitter—Instagram—Wine—Champagne—Soy Latte's—Gummi Bears—Gourmet Grilled Cheese Sandwiches—Pickles—Popcorn—Sparkling Water—Eye Cream—Pedicures—Traveling—80's Music—Musicals—Movie Trailers—Celebrity Red Carpet Interviews—Award Shows—Making Lists.

Please connect with me on:

www.christypastore-author.com

Facebook: www.facebook.com/ChristyPastoreAuthor

Twitter: twitter.com/christypastore